Lock Down Publications and Ca$h
Presents

THE
LEVEL UP

Written By

Luxury King

First Edition 2024

Printed in the United States of America

This is a work of fiction. Names, characters, places, and incidents either are products of the author's imagination or are used fictitiously. Any similarity to actual events or locales or persons, living or dead, is entirely coincidental.

Lock Down Publications
P.O. Box 944
Stockbridge, GA 30281
www.lockdownpublications.com

Like our page on Facebook: Lock Down Publications
www.facebook.com/lockdownpublications.ldp

Stay Connected with Us!

Text **LOCKDOWN** to 22828 to stay up-to-date with new releases, sneak peaks, contests and more…

Like our page on Facebook:
Lock Down Publications

Join Lock Down Publications/The New Era Reading Group

Visit our website:
www.lockdownpublications.com

Follow us on Instagram:
Lock Down Publications

Email Us: We want to hear from you!

Dedications

This book is dedicated to the fallen. You guys have departed from this life way too soon. Gone but never forgotten: A.tek, Weezy, 3Jay, H. Money, Geo, Bwild, Qualeek, Mootha, Tank, Johnny, Fat Rah, Black, Kane, Nutso, Foot, and Vee. LONG LIVE THE KINGZ!

THIS ONE IS FOR THE HOOD!

Special Dedications

To my brother Sha-Meek "Ta Ta" Miller: The day you departed from this earth was really the worst day of my life. I still cry at times; I still feel weak at times, and I still get depressed when I think about you not being here. They say time heals all wounds, but it's been four years, and this hole in my heart is still fresh. They don't make men like you no more, bro. You were a real friend, a true friend, one who didn't have a hateful bone in ya body. Everybody who you came across loved you. That alone should speak to the type of person you were. They labeled you a gang leader because they didn't know you had a heart of gold, with the energy and spirit of a God. You were so many great things—my brother, a son, a brother, an uncle, a great godfather, and so much more. I'm just grateful I was able to call you my brother. We really been friends FOREVER! I remember when Master P was ya favorite rapper. (LOL!) We really came up together, bro, from babies to men. I just wish you were still here to see my growth and be a part of my success. Nothing I accomplish means anything without you here to share it with me. May you rest in peace, my brother!

LONG LIVE THE KING!
MISSING YA STYLE AND MISSING YA SMILE!

Acknowledgements

One thing I know for sure is that I'm so grateful for everyone who played a part in this project. It doesn't matter if you had the opportunity to read it before it dropped or I expressed my thoughts to you—you have my deepest gratitude. I am so grateful for my publisher, JV Publications. Thank you for having faith in my dreams, and don't worry, we are going to bless the streets with classics. I am honored to be the first author you signed. Thank you!

I am most grateful for my beautiful mother, Andrea Cooper. (R.I.P) THANK YOU FOR GIVING ME LIFE, QUEEN! I really wish you were here to see my growth. You departed from this life way too soon, but you live in my heart. To my beautiful grandmother, Ms. Arlene Cauley, thank you for all the sacrifices you made for me and my siblings. You are the strongest woman I know. Nothing you do goes unnoticed. You are truly a Queen! To Ms. Crystal, I love you like you were my mom! Ta Ta lives through us!

Crystal, my BFF, you are really a true friend. With all I've been through in life, you've never left my side. The love and loyalty that you give has gotten me through many tough times. I love you, sis!

Aisha, thank you for being such a true friend, as well. I love you more than you know!

Des, you are one of the realest women I've ever met. Thank you for always staying true. Ya love and loyalty has been proven. I love you always and forever.

My blood brothers, Trap and Coop, we got a classic y'all! The streets and the jails are gonna love this one. But on some G-shit, I love both of y'all. When I told y'all that I was writing a book, y'all were more excited about it than me. I can't ask for better sibilings. To my beautiful sisters, Love, Alicia, Tylesha, Emma, and Yolanda, we never really talk, but I love all of y'all unconditionally.

To my cousins, Lil Kevin, Sonia, Shay, Ranger, and Mel Staxx, I really love y'all.

Deidra, I'm so grateful that your love and loyalty to me hasn't changed one bit over the years. You are still a true friend, and your friendship means more to me than you know.

To my hood, Gravesend/B-rise, you made me the man I am today. I am who I am because of where I come from! REAL NIGGAS DON'T BEND OR BUDGE! #BIGFACTS My brothers who continue to stick by my side through these hard times: Fatboy, Ill Will, Killy, Barry B, Skrap, F.B and T-Money, I truly appreciate y'all for not leaving me for dead. Thanks for everything. I love y'all. NFO TIL WE GO #YKTV! The rest of my brothers who are currently confined behind these oppressive walls: Eazy, Chulo aka Lil Veto, Danny, BOOgz, Savage, Pop, Fresh, Mittens, Flizzle, Los, Slime, and Naj, they can't keep good men down. We will be back.

To the guys F.B, YOUNG WORLD, Quamel, Bode, Fat Kev, Murk, Breeze, Blizz (MMD), Kastro (MMD), Coke Da Don (BIG PAPER), Pash, Spuddy, Bra, Strips, Takeover, Wax (M.G), Killa Milla, Blast Mazi, Stizzy, MAC (SMOKEGANG), UNCLE SLICK, UNCLE HOV, MURDA, J-BLOCK & D-BLOCK, L-BODIO, RED ICE, NOVA.G. Love y'all, man.

To my captured comrades behind these oppressive walls: Dick Wolf, Santana, L-Smurf, Wopo, M.S(DOUBLE9), Bonifide (93g'z), Jada Hound, Ski, Bentley Buggz, Top EURO, Pistol Euro, Jah Mula (M.B), Kasper, L.R, Snype,

La-Brim, Light Hound, Y.B, Bam Bugatti, Mike Milly (D.O.D), Jacob, Toots (STACK PAPER), Ace Hound, Weezy B, Big Baby (ROCHESTER), Bugout, Chirp (Y.O), Charliee CEE, It's way too many niggas to name. If I forgot you, blame my mind and not my heart. #FREETHEREAL

To my Queen, you push me to be a better version of myself every day without even trying. It is you who motivates me way beyond my creative capacity. You make me feel like a superhero. You make me feel like you and I can take over the world together. You are my muse. I can never stop thanking you. I LOVE YOU SO MUCH! ☺

Chapter 1

"Inmate Moore, pack up!" the CO yelled down the line.

"I'm packed already. Pop my cell," Hitta yelled back.

Minutes later, his cell door slid open. As soon as Hitta crossed the threshold, he ran two cells back to say goodbye to his close friend Richard Royal aka Rolex Rich.

"This is it, old man," Hitta said, reaching his fist through the bars to give Rich a pound.

"Nah, young man, this is just the beginning," Rich replied. "Make sure you call the number that I gave you. My wife will be expecting your call. I should be going back to the Feds in a few weeks, so make sure you keep in touch, bro. I got big plans for you," he added, encouraging Hitta.

"Moore, let's go, or you'll be held until next count," the CO threatened, hurrying the men to finish their conversation.

"My word is all I have. Trust me; I'll be in touch. Loyalty isn't a slogan for me. It's my way of life," Hitta told Rich, then flashed his signature smile.

With that, Hitta reached for his things and ran toward the impatient CO. Although happy to be leaving prison, he was going to miss his talks with Rich. Because Rich had dropped so many jewels during the time they had known each other, Hitta felt well equipped to handle whatever would come his way.

An ex-kingpin, Rolex Rich had turned his multi-million-dollar drug enterprise into one of the biggest record labels in the industry, Royalty Records. Rich was the true definition of a self-made boss. The apples didn't fall too far from the tree as all three of his children were successful in their own right. Raymond Royal, his oldest son, was an NBA superstar. His second son, Richard Jr. aka Richie Rich, was a multi-platinum rap artist and Royalty Records' president. Last but not least, his oldest child and only daughter, Roxxy Royal, was a global supermodel who ripped the runway with the likes of GiGi Hadid, Kendall Jenner, and Karlie Kloss.

Rolex Rich had it all until state and federal charges caught up with him, landing him in prison. However, like any real boss, his power was limitless—even behind those cement walls. Meeting Rich would be life-changing for Hitta and those close to him. Hitta had touched some money, but it was nothing compared to the heights that working with Rolex Rich would take him.

Make no mistake, Hitta was no slouch. He had made quite a name for himself. He was what some would call a young street legend. He was once a member of the notorious "Murda Team" until he and his old friend, Matt Murda, founder of Murda Team, had a huge disagreement that ended in a shootout. Murda Team consisted of five members. They controlled the heroin flow out of Coney Island but were mainly known for robbing, kidnapping, and murder. Relo, the first member, was killed in a gunfight with a dirty cop. Gangsta LA was serving a three-to-nine sentence for manslaughter. Peso had been recently released after beating a bunch of charges, and as for Matt Murda, no one had seen or heard from him since Hitta shot him.

Hitta stepped out of Sing Sing Correctional Facility a free man in the eyes of the law, but he was a wanted man to his old friend and gang leader, Matt. Not only did Hitta shoot Matt, but to add insult to injury, Hitta and his right-hand man, Peso, went on to form a gang called the Untouchable Gorilla Family. There would definitely be some backlash behind all the moves Hitta and Peso had made. What Hitta couldn't predict was how fast his past would catch up to him.

A cocaine white Bentley GT pulled in front of Hitta, and the windows slowly lowered. Inside the car were two Hispanic dudes, neither of whom he recognized.

"Ayo! You Hitta, right?" the driver asked.

Hitta hesitated before responding, "Yeah, why? Wassup?"

"No need to have ya guard up, homie. You're in good hands. Rich sent us to scoop you."

The mention of Rich's name instantly calmed Hitta's racing heart. Without further thought, Hitta jumped into the backseat of the Bentley.

That old man is full of surprises, he mused as the car pulled off.

***

"Fuck!" the driver yelled while pulling the car over to the side of the road.

Hitta didn't realize he had fallen asleep so quickly. Both he and the driver exited the vehicle to see what they hit. Whatever it was, it had flattened one of the tires. The passenger, however, never moved from his seat in the front. Before Hitta had a chance to question his unresponsiveness to the situation, the trunk to the Bentley popped open, and Matt Murda jumped out with his gun aimed at Hitta, whose eyes widened with shock.

BOC! BOC!

Two shots plummeted into Hitta's body at point-blank range, sending his body to the pavement. Standing over Hitta's body, Matt Murda fired two more shots into him before calmly walking away.

A Few Weeks Later…

Hitta glanced around the room. Unfamiliar with the setting, he tried to make sense of where he could be and why. Hitta remembered being shot, but he wasn't in a hospital. His surroundings looked much like a bedroom. Seconds later, a woman who appeared to be in her fifties entered the room.

"Sweet Jesus, you're awake!"

"Who are you, and where am I?" Hitta asked, even more confused.

"I'm Ms. Betty, and you're at the Royal Estate. Young man, you were shot, and after you had surgery to remove the four bullets, Mrs. Royal requested to have you moved here for your safety," the woman explained.

It all started coming back to Hitta. He remembered clear as day what happened. Matt Murda had caught him slipping. What he didn't understand was how Matt Murda knew about his close relationship with Rich. Hitta's heart raced at the thought that he could have been killed.

"Can I have some water, please?" he asked, hoping it would calm him down.

"Sure, sweetie," she replied, then handed him a glass from the nearby nightstand. "I'll be right back. Let me go tell Mrs. Royal that you're awake."

While taking sips of the water, Hitta reflected on what happened and how he had allowed himself to be so vulnerable. Several minutes later, Mrs. Royal entered the room.

Damn, Hitta thought, reminding himself to breathe.

Katrina Royal was the definition of eye candy, her beauty breathtaking. At the age of forty-one, she didn't look a day over twenty-five. She reminded him of Lisa Raye facially, but that body was Serena Williams, hands down.

"I'm glad you're awake. Are you in any pain?" she asked, looking at him.

"No, not really, but I'm hungry as shit," he said, the hunger pangs rolling around his stomach.

"Of course, you are. I'll have Ms. Betty whip up something for you. By the way, I'm Katrina, but everyone calls me Kat," she informed him, extending her hand.

"I'm Amir. It's a pleasure to meet you. I wish it was under better circumstances," Hitta replied as he weakly shook her hand.

"You're alive, so that makes circumstances great. Now, I want you to make yourself at home. Oh, before I forget, my husband requested that I give you this."

Katrina handed Hitta a folded piece of paper before leaving the room. The minute he had some privacy, Hitta unfolded the paper and started reading:

Beloved Brother,

If you're reading this missive, it means you are alive and well. I'm glad you pulled through, young brother. I found out who was behind that attempt on your life. These young dudes talk like females. Matt Murda was behind the hit. Pete was on his payroll and feeding him info. You know I had him taken care of. The fuck boy left the yard on a stretcher. They moved me to the feds, so I'm now in MDC Brooklyn. Take as much time as you need to get better. Pardon me for having you moved from the hospital, but I couldn't take any chances. When you are well enough to move around, any car on my lot is yours. There are 100 stacks in a book bag under the bed – 50 for you and 50 for Peso. He's aware of the safety measures that I had to take, and so is your mom. When you're ready to eat, my wife has your first plate. You're free now, baby bro. Take advantage of your freedom. Be safe out there. Loyalty over love!

Your Captured Comrade,
Rolex Rich

Hitta folded the paper and gingerly rolled off the bed. The second his feet hit the floor, Ms. Betty walked in the room carrying a tray of food.

"Where do you think you're going?" she asked, placing the tray in front of him. "You need to rest so your body can heal."

"Thank you, Ms. Betty," he said, accepting the plate and instantly attacking the baked chicken and salad.

"I know you may have had another meal in mind, but you need to eat light for now. You don't need all that gas sitting in your stomach," she told him with a chuckle.

"Don't worry, Ms. Betty. This will do," he replied, his mouth full of food.

As she moved to exit the room, Hitta asked her, "Ms. Betty, can I have a towel and washcloth, please?"

"There's a setup in the bathroom waiting for you, sweetheart. The bathroom is the door on the left." She pointed, then headed out the door.

After eating, Hitta disappeared into the bathroom to wash up. When he came out, he noticed a brand-new Nike sweatsuit laid out on the bed, along with underclothes and a fresh pair of Jordan 3's. Once dressed, Hitta made his way around the huge mansion, looking for Katrina. When he finally found her, she was sitting in the home movie theater.

"Excuse me, Mrs. Royal."

"Boy, I told you to call me Kat," she commanded, smiling at him. "I see you're up and ready to move around, huh?"

"Time waits for no man," he replied.

"You're right about that," Katrina answered. She smiled again while looking at his messy ponytail. "Would you like me to braid ya hair before you go?"

"No, thank you. I'm kinda in a rush right now. When I come back, I'll be ready for my first job."

"You're not even fully healed, and you talking about the first job?" She shook her head and stood. "Follow me," she ordered him, leading the way out of the theater.

As they approached the driveway, Hitta glanced around in amazement at all of the cars. Rich had so many exotic cars that the driveway looked more like a dealership.

"Take your pick," Katrina told him, giving Hitta full access to the collection of vehicles.

Wanting to be low key, he chose a black-on-black Chevy Camero.

"The keys are already inside, and there's a Glock in the glovebox. I will bring you the bag Rich gave you along with a new phone. Rich is currently the only person with the number."

"I appreciate everything, Mrs. Royal—I mean, Kat. I will be in touch soon."

Hitta started the car and made his way down the driveway. Looking in the rearview mirror, he watched as Katrina walked back inside her mansion. He was happy to be home and knew it was only a matter of time before the bankrolls started rolling in.

Chapter 2

"Tyler, you hungry?" Mariah asked Peso, who was sitting on the edge of his daughter's bed.

"Nah, I'm cool, shawty," Peso said. "We both know you can't cook anyway," he joked.

"Boy, bye! You know I get busy in the kitchen," she replied, playfully hitting him with a pillow.

"Can you two keep it down? I'm trying to watch a movie," their 5-year-old daughter told them.

"Mya, don't get cute because your father is here. It's past your bedtime anyway. Now turn that TV off. You have school in the morning."

"But my favorite part is coming up," Mya whined.

"Mya, what did I say?"

"Relax, Mariah. The movie is about to go off," Peso commented, defending his daughter.

"Relax, my ass. That girl done seen that movie a thousand times," she replied, then turned off the TV. "Mya, say goodnight to your daddy."

"Can I have some ice cream before bed, Mommy? Pleeeease? Pretty please?"

"No! Now, lay down."

Mya turned to her father. "Daddy, please?"

Peso looked at his beautiful baby girl. He refused to deny her anything.

"Come on, princess. You can have some ice cream, but you have to eat it fast, baby girl, so you can get some sleep. Deal?"

"I can't eat it too fast, Daddy, because my brain will freeze." Being her dramatic self, Mya put her hands on her head.

The two of them shared a laugh before heading to the kitchen.

Although upset that he overrode what she had told their daughter, Mariah let them enjoy their daddy-daughter moment. Mariah knew there was nothing she could say to stop Peso from spoiling Mya.

Peso and Mariah shared more than a co-parenting relationship. They had a genuine friendship that nothing or no one could come between. Mariah was a strong-minded, drop-dead gorgeous woman who stood about 5'5" and had a honey brown complexion. She had Asian eyes, long black hair, and a body that most women would kill to have. She was four years older than Peso, but the young man truly had her heart.

A pretty boy, Peso had wavy hair, green eyes, a killer smile, and the perfect set of pearly white teeth. It wasn't only his looks that attracted Mariah to him. It was his swag and the way he carried himself. It was an added plus that he had never changed from the day she met him up until now. They were more like best friends than anything. Although their relationship's romantic side was over, their closeness made raising their daughter that much easier.

As Peso watched Mya finish the last of her ice cream, his cell phone rang. He looked at his iPhone. Peso didn't recognize the number, but he answered anyway.

"Hello?"

"What's the word?" the caller said.

"Man, I know this can't be my boy. Where the fuck you at?" Excited, Peso stood quickly to his feet. "I'll come get you right now, bro."

Before the caller could respond, the doorbell rang. Mariah looked through the peephole before snatching open the door. Hitta entered the apartment all smiles and carrying a book bag.

"Oh my gosh, Amir! You're alive!" Mariah exclaimed, reaching to hug him. She couldn't believe he was actually there.

"You know niggas like me don't die," he replied, flashing that smile everyone had come to love.

"Uncle Mir!" Mya yelled and jumped into his arms.

"Ahhh!" Hitta tried to pick Mya up but quickly put her down as he doubled over in pain.

"I'm sorry, Uncle Mir," Mya said, thinking she had done something to hurt him.

"It wasn't you, pretty girl. Uncle was already hurt."

He smothered her with hugs and kisses before walking over to Peso and greeting him with a tight embrace.

"Happy to have you back, brodie," Peso said, genuinely excited to be reunited with his best friend.

"Mya, say goodnight to ya daddy and uncle. It's time for you to get in the bed," Mariah told her.

Mya hugged her father and Hitta, then headed toward the bedroom with her mother.

"How you know I was here?" Peso asked Hitta.

"Come on, bro. I know you better than anybody. What's the word, though? How's shit looking out here?" Hitta asked, eager to be filled in.

"You know I make it happen. I got some decent dope and a few new runners, but shit ain't how it used to be."

"Well, that's about to change, my nigga. It's a hunnit stacks in the book bag—fifty for you and fifty for me. It's a gift from Rolex Rich."

"So, we really rockin' with this nigga, huh?"

"Bro, this is the move. Trust me, we about to level up for real. We've been waiting our entire lives for a break like this. The nigga is a millionaire, so you know the licks we gonna be going on is way more than worth it. We gonna be doing the same shit we been doing, just for a bigger price. So, you with me or not?" Hitta asked him.

"Nigga, you know I'm with you. We're brothers."

"Until death do us part," Hitta replied.

"Yo, Rich sent word that Matt Murda is the one who touched you," Peso said, shifting the conversation.

"Seen the nigga wit' my own two eyes. Boy caught me slipping, but when we meet again, he gonna pay for that. I got a headshot for him," Hitta responded with venom in his voice.

The two men sat and talked for hours as Peso filled Hitta in on the progress the Untouchable Gorilla Family had been making in his absence. Peso knew things would only go up from there.

Two Weeks Later...

Hitta and Peso were sitting in Hitta's Camero in Dobbs Ferry, New York. They were parked across the street from Zee's Pizza.

"Yo, bro, this shit is gonna be simple. The old man is opening up now. We got a twenty-minute window before the first regular customer shows up. The coke is stashed inside of a delivery van out back, and the safe is in the walk-in freezer," Hitta said, giving Peso the rundown. "You get the safe; I'll get the van. You ready to get this paper?"

"Nigga, I was born ready. Let's eat!" Peso responded.

Nothing more needed to be said. The two exited the car and made their way to the pizza shop.

"Welcome to Zee's Pizza. How can I help you, fellas?"

"You can help us by leading the way to that fucking safe," Hitta ordered, brandishing his Glock .45.

Peso jumped over the counter with his .9mm aimed at the old Italian man's head.

"There's no safe in here. Just take what's in the cash register and go," the man pleaded as Peso patted him down, making sure he wasn't carrying a weapon.

"Don't play dumb. We know everything. Now take us to the fuckin' safe," Hitta demanded. "We don't have all day."

Before another lie could cross the old man's lips, Peso yelled from the back, "I found the safe, bro!"

Hitta forced the man to the back of the shop, pushing him inside the walk-in freezer where the massive safe was located. Hitta nor Peso had never seen a safe of that size.

"Open the safe! And if you take too long, my brother here will go upstairs to ya house and kill that wife of yours," Hitta threatened.

The fact that they knew about his wife made the man open the safe without hesitation while shaking his head in defeat. Smiling, Hitta looked at Peso. The safe was filled with stacks of hundred-dollar bills wrapped in plastic. Peso walked away and returned with a bunch of black trash bags. He quickly began filling them with the money.

"Fuck you just standing around for? Help him fill those bags up," Hitta commanded, speaking to the man.

Once Peso secured the money in the bags, he pulled them out of the freezer.

"Now, where are the keys to the delivery van?" Hitta asked.

The man removed the keys from his pocket and handed them to him.

"Listen, I'm a very powerful man who can make both of you very rich. We can act like this never happened. Just tell me who sent you," the man pleaded.

"You may be a powerful man, but you're also a rat. And I don't like rats. Remember Rolex Rich?"

The sound of Rich's name caused the man's eyes to widen. Rich was good when it came to doing business. He was a true hustler and a loyal customer, but when the feds snatched up Zee and several other mob members, Zee couldn't give up his own. So, he rolled over on Rolex Rich, who was already legit and out of the game.

"Yeah, I figured you'd look surprised when I said his name. Rich wants you to know there are no hard feelings," Hitta said before raising his Glock.

BOC!

The bullet crashed into Zee's forehead, killing him instantly.

"Come on. Let's get these bags to the trunk. We're running out of time!" Hitta shouted, and the two men began dragging the bags to the van.

***

As Hitta drove up to the sprawling estate, Peso sat in the passenger seat beyond impressed. The beautiful, gated mansion nestled on top of the hill was amazing.

"This right here is motivation, bro," Peso commented, admiring the mansion.

"Facts! Soon enough, we gonna be living like this if we keep getting licks like the one we just caught," Hitta told him.

"How much money do you think is in the trunk?"

"It has to be more than two mill 'cause that's how much Rich is askin' for, and everything over two-mill, we keep. Drugs included."

"We'll fuck around and be millionaires after we done counting up, bro," Peso replied with a huge smile.

Katrina was standing out front talking on her cellphone when Hitta and Peso pulled up.

"You fellas can head to the dining area. I'll be inside in a few," she informed them, then continued her phone conversation.

As the two men entered the mansion, Peso's eyes took in the beautiful house and furnishings.

"This shit is fuckin' dope!" he commented.

"Watch that language, young man," Ms. Betty said, entering the dining area.

"I'm sorry, ma'am," Peso told her.

"How are you feeling today, Ms. Betty?" Hitta asked, greeting her.

"I'm fine," she responded, smiling. "I'm glad to see you're at a hundred percent. Looks like you've even gained a few pounds."

"Yeah, I'm feeling much better. Pardon me, this is my brother Ty. Ty, this is Ms. Betty," Hitta said, making the introduction as Ms. Betty and Peso shook hands.

"You are a very handsome man, and your eyes are so pretty," she said, complimenting Peso. "I bet you drive the young ladies crazy."

"The old ladies, too," he joked, and they all shared a laugh.

Minutes later, Katrina walked into the dining area carrying two money counting machines.

"Sorry I took so long. That was a very important call," she explained, then turned to Peso. "You must be Peso."

"Yeah, that's me," he replied with a smile.

"I've heard some great things about you. Oh my goodness, you have the most beautiful set of eyes. I'm Kat, by the way." She extended her hand, which Peso accepted.

"Thank you. It's a pleasure to finally meet you. I must admit you are more beautiful in person." His words caused her to blush.

"Thank you. Now let's get down to business. How was the job?" she asked.

"I think you should check the trunk of the car," Hitta replied, smiling broadly.

Katrina shot him a disapproving look.

"I know the two of y'all were not crazy enough to drive here with a dead body in the trunk."

"The only thing dead in that trunk is presidents."

"In that case, shall we count up?" Katrina asked, holding up one of the money machines.

Chapter 3

Rolex Rich was what you call legendary. Even in the federal prison system, he was treated like royalty. There was no such thing as being lowkey or flying under the radar for Rich. His face was known all over the world. Everyone knew about the former kingpin who beat the feds and turned his drug empire into a multi-million-dollar record label. But now the feds had him again, and this time, they had him by the balls. Game over. The judge handed Rich a fifty-year sentence. However, prison life for Rolex Rich was much different from what most men experienced. Nothing was out of reach for him. They placed him around wolves, and now he was leading the pack.

"Yo, Rich, we got a new body, and ya cell is the only one open. You wanna take this dude?" the CO asked.

Rich never looked up from the book he was reading.

"Send him in, but if he's a rat, he won't be stayin'."

"He's solid, Rich. You got my word on that. I'ma send him in," the CO replied and walked away.

Several minutes later, a short dude who was black as tar, sporting a bald head, and wearing a pair of Cartier frames entered the cell carrying his property. Rich removed a manila envelope from his locker and placed it on the top bunk.

"I'm Rolex Rich. In that envelope are my P.S.I. and sentencing minutes. I'm no rat, so I damn sure don't want one living in my hut. If you've ever worked with the feds in any way, this ain't the cell for you, fam," Rich said, staring the man in his eyes.

The man matched his stare as he replied, "For the record, I never told on a friend or enemy, but a bunch of niggas jumped on that stand and told on me. I just blew trial and got sentenced. My paperwork will be here any day. You the man around here, so I know you can have that big-shot lawyer you got look me up. Here, take this."

He handed Rich his inmate ID card. Rich reached, taking the card from his hand.

"I'ma look into you, homie. I'll be back in a few," Rich said before exiting the cell.

***

"Job well done, fellas. Rich asked for two million off the top, so every dollar over that belongs to y'all. Drugs included. Deal?" Katrina said after counting all the money.

"Hell yeah, we have a deal!" Hitta responded. "That leaves us with 1.2 mill to split, along with the ninety keys of coke. Not bad for a day's work, huh, Peso?"

Peso sat wearing a huge smile. He and Hitta had caught plenty of good licks, but this was by far the biggest lick to date.

"Not bad at all. It's time to put these streets back in a frenzy," Peso finally replied.

"I will have another job for you guys in a few weeks. In the meantime, both of you are invited to the family dinner I'm hosting here on Sunday. It's time y'all meet the family," Katrina told them.

"Sounds like a plan," Hitta replied. "Sunday it is."

***

After stashing the drugs and burning the van, Hitta and Peso drove around in the Camaro smoking sour diesel and drinking Henny.

"It's time we round up the troops and pass out some of this work. The faster we get rid of it, the better. I heard Breeze is doing his thing outta town. You think we should hit him off?" Hitta asked.

"The bro been on his job. I don't know why we shouldn't," Peso responded.

"Say less. I'ma call that nigga later and see when he can head this way. For now, call Heat and tell him to have all the bros in Kaiser Park by nine tonight. I'm 'bout to head to the borough and check Ashley. I know she's going crazy. You chillin' with me or nah?"

"Nah, I'ma let you get ya dick out the dirt, bro. Just let me out right here. I'll see you tonight, bro. Be safe," Peso said, giving Hitta a pound

"Yo!" Hitta called out as Peso got out of the car.

"Wassup, bro?"

"I love you, my nigga."

"I love you, too, bro. Drive safe."

Ten minutes later, Hitta pulled up to Malboro Houses on the borderline of Coney Island and Bensonhurst. Knowing that the dudes from Coney Island and Malboro didn't get along, Hitta checked his Glock .45 to make sure he had one in the head before exiting the car. When he finally made it to Ashley's building, a few dudes were standing out front. One of them looked familiar, but Hitta couldn't remember where he had seen him. While making his way inside the building, he laughed at the group of men who ice grilled him.

Hitta took the steps to the third floor and knocked on Ashley's door. Seconds later, the apartment door flew open, and Ashley stood in front of him wearing a long t-shirt and a pair of fuzzy slippers. Her hair was in a wrap. No make-up, no fake hair, no fake nails — her beauty was flawless.

"Wassup, baby girl?" Hitta greeted her with his trademark smile.

"Nigga, don't 'wassup baby girl' me! Yo ass been home how long, and I'm just hearing from you? Then, on top of that, you tell ya mother not to tell me where you were? Fuck you, Amir!"

"You gonna keep acting crazy, or are you gonna let me in so I can explain?"

Ashley stepped aside so he could enter and then locked the door behind him. The two weren't an item but had been holding each other down since they were kids. They never put a title on what they shared because they both felt doing so would only complicate things. Ashley was all about making Hitta happy. She had done a lot to prove her loyalty, even took trips upstate and smuggled drugs for him. She was indeed his ride-or-die chick. Not only was she a rider, but she was also a pretty redbone with a body most women paid for.

"You gonna sit there on the couch rolling ya weed or are you gonna tell me what took you so long to come check me?" she asked, refusing to loose the attitude.

"Come here, Ash," Hitta said in a soft tone.

Looking at her now, he couldn't wait to get his hands on her.

"Nope! Not until you tell me what took you so long to come check me. Keep it a hunnit, Amir. You got another bitch? Is that what took you so long? That bitch wasn't taking them long-ass bus rides up north with drugs in her pussy, nigga. I WAS! But you spend time with her before you come see me? I hope that bitch's pussy was worth it, 'cause I'm done with you. Take ya money and get the FUCK OUT, AMIR!" she screamed.

"Calm the fuck down and stop screaming like you fuckin' crazy," Hitta said as he calmly sparked his blunt. "Baby girl, you know me well enough to know I ain't been out here laying up wit' no bitch. I was in the hospital. I got shot."

Hitta stood up and lifted his shirt to show Ashley his scars.

"Oh my Gawd! I'm sorry, bae. I didn't know. Why didn't ya mom tell me?" Ashley's mood quickly shifted, realizing his silence was for a valid reason.

"It's a long story. What's important is that I'm here now. And for the record, you got some making up to do," Hitta said, licking his lips.

"Well, let me start now. I waited too long for this dick."

Ashley grabbed him by the hand and led him to the bedroom. Still holding the blunt, Hitta moved to sit on the edge of the bed, but she quickly stopped him.

"No outside clothes on my bed," she told him, and they shared a laugh. "Let me undress you, daddy. I missed you so much," Ashley said, becoming serious as she leaned down to kiss him on the lips.

It didn't take much to get his blood flowing, and Ashley took full advantage of it. Pulling his shaft from his boxer briefs, she began stroking him and then quickly swallowed him to the back of her throat, giving him the best head of his life. Still standing, Hitta leaned back against the armoire to keep his balance while running his fingers through her natural hair and gripping it tightly in his fist.

"Damn, I missed you, ma," Hitta moaned, looking down at her. "Did you miss daddy?"

She answered by sliding his dick in and out her mouth as her saliva dripped onto his balls. Not wanting to neglect them, she began massaging them with one hand while stroking his dick with the other. When Hitta couldn't take it any longer, he exploded in her mouth.

"Ugghhhh! FUCK!" he exclaimed.

Out of breath, he took a minute to regain himself. After Ashley stood to her feet, he pulled her into his embrace and stuck his tongue in her mouth, the two sharing a passionate kiss. As Hitta lifted her by her waist, she wrapped her legs around his midsection. He then walked over to the bed, where he laid her down gently on the queen-sized bed and positioned himself between her legs. Instead of rushing to enter her wetness, Hitta took the time to admire her beauty as she lifted her upper body slightly to remove her t-shirt. Her flat stomach and thick thighs were pleasing to his eyes. The black lace thong couldn't hide her fat, juicy middle, and it sent Hitta into savage mode.

"I couldn't wait to see you," he whispered in her ear. "Now, let me show you how much I missed you."

For the next two hours, they took turns pleasing each other. Afterward, Ashley slipped into a light slumber but was awakened a short while later by the movement of Hitta getting out of bed.

"Damn, so you just gonna fuck the shit outta me and then leave?"

"Don't start, baby girl," Hitta said while putting on his clothes. "You know I gotta get this money. A nigga got a lot of catchin' up to do, but I'll be back to spend some time with you," he promised, then kissed her on the forehead.

"I'ma hold it down this time 'cause I know you tryin' to get yo'self back situated, but next time you pull up, be prepared to spend the whole day with me," Ashley told him.

"I got you, mami. That's my word." Hitta stood up from the bed after putting on his sneakers. "Now come lock the door."

"Here, I made you copies," Ashley said, handing him a keychain that held a set of keys.

At the door, Hitta kissed Ashley on her lips and then made his way out of the apartment.

"Amir!" she called out to him.

"Wassup, ma?" He stopped in his tracks, turning to look back at her.

"You know I love you. Please be safe out there," she expressed sincerely.

"Love you, too," Hitta responded right before disappearing through the staircase door.

When Hitta exited the building, he bumped into Reem, an old high school friend. Reem was a Blood who Hitta met through Peso. The three of them used to commit robberies together. It had been a while since the two last saw each other.

"Oh shit! What's poppin', Hitta?" Reem said, greeting him with a one-arm embrace.

"Ain't shit, my guy. Long time, no see. Everything healthy?" Hitta replied.

"I'm livin', bro, but shit can always be better. I just touched down from a lil' parole violation. A nigga finally off them papers. Enough about me, though. Wassup with you and the bro Peso? I'm glad y'all beat them charges," Reem said sincerely.

As the two men spoke, Reem noticed two dudes with hoodies creeping up on Hitta. Aggressively pushing Hitta to the side, he pulled his .40 caliber and fired. A slug hit one of the hooded men, knocking him down instantly. The other dude returned fire, but Hitta spun around and let his .45 spit, taking down his target. When Hitta ran over to the man who was still breathing, he recognized him as one of the dudes who had been standing in front of the building earlier when he arrived. The man was now staring into the dark barrel of Hitta's gun.

BOC! BOC!

Hitta fired two shots into his face, silencing him forever before taking off toward the Camaro. Reem didn't stick around either. He got low as soon as Hitta let go the last shots.

***

Rolex Rich walked back into the cell where his new cellmate was unpacking his things.

"I did my homework on you, fam. You're solid. Pardon me if I offended you earlier. Anything you need while you're here, just let me know. It's not every day we come across men who still honor the code. Let's start over. I'm Rolex Rich," he said, extending his hand.

"I know who you are already. A nigga been studying ya format for years. You're a hustler's hope. They call me Jet Black."

The two men shook hands.

"You know where you going yet?" Rich asked.

"Hopefully, they send a nigga to Fort Dix. I heard that shit sweet. Plus, it's not too far from home, feel me?"

"I'm hoping I land there myself. You smoke?"

"Yeah, but I don't fuck wit' that K2 shit. I've seen niggas bug out off that deuce," Jet Black shared.

"This here ain't no deuce, my nigga. This a batch of that uptown's finest. Here, roll one up," Rich said, tossing him a Ziploc bag filled with weed.

The two men kicked back, smoked, and got familiar with each other. Rich was serious about not letting the wrong people get too close to him. Even though the chances of seeing the light of day were slim for Rich, he refused to let anyone jeopardize his reputation for being solid and would only surround himself with the real. He would make sure of that.

Chapter 4

It was 9P.M. sharp. The one hundred men who formed a circle on the Kaiser Park basketball court were all members of the Untouchable Gorilla family. Hitta and Peso stood in the middle of them.

"Caesar's home!" Hitta shouted.

"Call the national guard!" the crowd responded enthusiastically.

"For those of y'all who never met me, I'm Hitta. Me and my brother, Peso, built this family from the ground up, but it was y'all niggas who kept this shit alive in our absence. This family isn't nothing without all of you."

He paused to look around at the men before continuing.

"Loyalty ain't no slogan. It's a way of life—*our* way of life. In this family, it's loyalty over love, and disloyalty will not be tolerated. We all took an oath, so we must honor that shit. I ain't gonna talk y'all ears off, though. You niggas know wassup. I'ma let Peso get down to the purpose of this gathering," Hitta said, giving the floor to his best friend.

Smiling, Peso looked around. He was honestly proud of what he and Hitta had created. They had a team of hungry men who were willing to kill and die in the name of their family.

"Gorillas run the jungle!" Peso yelled, speaking the men's lingo.

"'Cause we untouchable gangstas!" the men shouted in response.

"I'm glad you brothers were able to make it on such short notice. For the fellas who couldn't make it, spread the word to them. Now, let's get down to business. No mouth goes unfed in this family. When one eats, we all eat. It's time we lock shit down in every way possible. All of us here are from one of the five boroughs. We may not be as deep as the other gangs, but that's only because we don't accept just anybody. There isn't always strength in numbers. I'd rather ten Gorillas over a hundred lambs."

Peso gave the men a minute to process his words.

"Starting now, we build a roundtable. The roundtable will consist of myself, Hitta, and two shot callers from each borough. The boroughs are now labeled as districts."

Peso went on to explain the breakdowns and who would head each borough.

"Is there anyone here who doesn't agree with our decision?" Peso asked, looking around at the men.

When no one said anything, he continued.

"I'm glad everyone approves. The level up is about to be crazy, fellas. We on now! Also, from now on, the shot callers will call the meetings amongst districts. Hitta and I will call roundtable meetings every ninety days to discuss our progress, any issues, and shit like that. Respect the chain of command. This will now conclude our meeting. Any issues, consult with your shot caller Heart of a Gorilla!"

"Spirit of a Hustler!" the group shouted in unison.

After the gathering, Hitta and Peso gave each district five kilos of coke on consignment and $25,000 apiece as a start to feed their districts. The shot callers would be responsible for bringing back the funds. One kilo was worth $36,000, so each district had more than enough room to eat.

"Yo, you don't think we should hit them with more work?" Peso asked after he and Hitta jumped in the Camaro to leave.

"Nah. I wanna see if they can handle what we just passed out. I ain't wanna give niggas the whole throw and they fuck up, feel me?" Hitta replied.

"Yeah, I feel you, bro," Peso responded as he picked up the blunt that Hitta had in the ashtray.

"I bumped into Reem when I went through Malboro earlier."

"What Reem? Our Reem?" Peso asked, surprised.

"Yeah, bro! The crazy shit is the nigga saved my life. Two niggas tried to bust a move, and Reem banged out for a nigga."

"Fuck you mean niggas tried to bust a move? Let's spin through there now," Peso said, feeling his waist to check for his piece.

"No need to, beloved. Both of them niggas are dead. The wicked shit about it is I seen one of them niggas before. I just can't remember where. Tomorrow we gonna spin through there and hit Reem off with something to get him right. You know bro just touched, too."

"Say less, but we gotta do some shopping first. I need a new whip. It's time we show niggas who got the streets."

"You think you the only one who gotta do some shopping? Nigga, you been home a month before me. I should be playing catch up," Hitta said, grinning.

"C'mon, Hitta. You know I couldn't ball out without my right-hand next to me. It just wouldn't feel right," Peso told him.

"So, in the A.M., we go see the jeweler, the dealer, and burn Fifth Avenue down."

"You ain't said nothing but a word. Let's show the streets we back, nigga," Peso said, giving Hitta a pound.

"That's a must."

***

Early the next morning, Hitta and Peso took a cab to a dealership in New Jersey. It had been years since the two of them had been to this lot and being there brought back a lot of memories for them. Hitta smiled to himself while thinking of the good ol' days before the Murda Team had their big falling out. All five members pulled off this same lot with BMWs in different flavors.

"Yo, brodie, you see that cocaine white beamer over there?" Peso asked, snapping Hitta out of his thoughts

"We did Beamers last time around. I'm finna really turn up. I got my eyes on that," Hitta replied, pointing to a royal blue Porsche 911.

"Holy shit!" a voice shouted from behind them. "If it isn't two of my favorite guys."

Hitta and Peso turned around at the same time. They both smiled when they saw the chubby white guy. Peso spoke first.

"Rick, wassup? Long time, no see."

Rick gave each a bear hug. "I'm glad you guys are back. I read about y'all in the paper when the incident first happened and was heartbroken. I see they really can't keep good men down. And by the size of those duffle bags, I know you two came to shop. What can I do for you guys?" Rick asked, flashing that smile salesmen often have when they see dollar signs.

Rick, the owner of Foreigner's Auto, had always been good to the men and their crew. There wasn't a car they wanted that Rick couldn't get his hands on. He made sure if he sold them something exotic, no one else in the area would have the same car. He understood the value of keeping them happy, so he always kept a good rapport with them.

"I got my eyes on that Porsche out there," Hitta told him.

"I see you still have great taste, my friend. It's a beauty. That right there is a Porche 911 Turbo S. I only have two of those on my lot — the royal blue one you have your eye on and that white one over there."

Rick pointed to the cocaine white Porsche. Peso instantly fell in love. White had always been his favorite color. So, the Porsche was definitely his speed.

"Both cars are new arrivals. Would you like to take a test drive?" Rick asked, seeing the mesmerized look in the men's eyes.

"When do we ever test drive, Rick? Just tell me what the tag is on it," Hitta responded.

"Other customers, a hundred and fifty thousand, but for you, my friend, a hundred and forty."

"I'll take the royal blue one," Hitta said, not batting an eye at the price.

"And give me the keys to that white one." Peso couldn't stop smiling.

Hitta turned to his best friend and said, "The level up starts now."

They gave each other a pound, and the three men made their way to Rick's office. Once inside, Hitta unzipped his duffle bag and started pulling out the hundred-dollar bills secured with rubber bands and neatly stacked them on Rick's desk. Peso followed suit.

"That's two-eighty large. You wanna count it?" Peso asked.

"Nah, you guys always been straight. Let me start the paperwork so I can get you guys out of here," Rick replied.

***

Meanwhile, in Upper Manhattan...

Matt Murda paced the floor of his condo in a complete rage while his mentor and connect, Jamie Estrada, and his brother-in-law, Rah-Rah, watched him.

"Fuck you mean that nigga ain't dead, Rah? I shot that nigga at point-blank range and left him on the highway to die. Fuck! I gotta find this nigga."

"Murda, I ain't no peacemaker, but maybe it's time you and Hitta bury all the bullshit. You got way too much to lose," Rah-Rah replied.

Murda laughed wickedly. "You sound like Timah right now, Rah. This shit is personal, and the only thing I'ma bury is Hitta's bitch ass."

"Bro, he shot you, and you shot him. This shit is played out. Nigga, you rich! Let's enjoy this paper and live our best lives. You are Matt Murda — a legend in the hood. You ain't got shit to prove. Let's keep getting this paper," Rah-Rah said, trying to speak some sense into his brother.

Jamie finally broke his silence. "Matt, Rah is making perfect sense."

"C'mon, Jay, don't start preaching to me, man. You of all people should know that once my mind is set, I'm going all the way."

"Murda, just hear me out," Rah-Rah pleaded. "Y'all niggas were like brothers. When Rico died, Hitta, Peso, L.A., and Relo, rest in peace, put in a lot of work in his name. You came home, and y'all niggas made history together, big bro. The Murda Team brought life back into the dope game. Y'all ran shit with an iron fist. I think you should reach out to ya comrade and dead all this bullshit."

Deep down, Matt Murda knew Rah-Rah was right, but he would never admit it. Murda was too stuck in his ways. When his older brother Rico died, The Murda Team was all he had. They were his brothers, but Hitta betrayed him when he stood in front of his gun for someone outside of The Murda Team.

"Yo, Rah, this shit won't be dead until me or Hitta is buried six feet deep. End of discussion. What I need you to do is let the squad know that every member of the U.G.F. gets smashed on sight. Let's show the Untouchable Gorillas that they can be touched," Murda instructed.

"Matt, if you need more manpower, let me know. I know this is a personal matter, but end this shit so we can get back to work," Jamie said.

"Call Veto and tell him I need his services," Matt Murda replied with a smile.

***

Peso cruised the Brooklyn streets in his brand-new Porsche 911 Turbo S. On his neck rested an 18-karat gold Cuban link. The chain didn't need a pendant because it weighed a kilo. He sported an 18-karat gold Rolex on his left wrist, the watch's face flooded with diamonds. He and Hitta both spent over three hundred thousand apiece on their shopping spree. They even splurged on Peso's daughter, Mya. One would have thought they had slowed down with that kind of spending, but they hadn't. The days they spent locked down only made them go harder.

As he cruised down Gates Avenue with his windows rolled down, bystanders admired his car and jewelry. Peso couldn't suppress his smile. He did it all for the people. He was what you would call motivation for the streets.

Peso turned up his music and rapped along with rapper Meek Mill as the hit single "I'ma Boss" spilled through the speakers.

I be riding through my old hood, but I'm in my new whip
Same old attitude, but I'm on that new shit
They say they gon' rob me, see me, never do shit
'Cause they know that's the reason they gon' end up on a news clip

Peso rapped along with the same passion as the recording artist. As he came to a stop at a red light, a black on black Range Rover pulled up beside him.

"I know that ain't my boy Peso," the driver of the Range Rover said as he and Peso locked eyes.

"Yeah, it's me in the flesh. What's shaking, Rome?" Peso replied, looking over at him.

Rome and Peso met on Riker's Island while Peso was fighting his case. They used to gamble against each other all day. The two would bet on anything. Rome talked big shit and had a big mouth. Since he would talk down on people who had less than him, Peso enjoyed taking his money even more.

"When you touch down?" Rome asked over the music.

"I touched down a couple months ago. Wassup, though?"

"Ain't shit, bro. You know me. Another day another dollar. What brings you to my side of town?"

"*Your* side of town? How's this *your* side of town when me and my nigga are running the city?" Peso arrogantly replied while eyeing Rome.

"Come on, Peso. You know I still let my money talk. You may be running C.I., but the Stuy is mine," Rome replied.

The two men were now holding up traffic as the light had already turned green.

"Lettin' your money talk?" Peso laughed. "I can't tell, nigga. You driving that old-ass Range Rover and rocking a bunch of 10-karat jewelry. Your money's talking real low right now, my nigga. I tell you what, Rome. You and your man pull up to my side of town; I got a job for y'all."

With that, Peso turned up his music and sped off, leaving Rome sitting at the light.

Some might call him arrogant. Some might even say he was cocky. But Peso was always willing to give you the raw truth. He could only hope Rome would receive his offer with open arms and not a jealous mind.

Chapter 5

As if Peso wasn't stirring up enough emotions in the Stuy, Hitta sat in his royal blue Porsche 911 dressed in his new Gucci attire. The huge Cuban link around his neck and the bust-down Rolex on his wrist only complemented his outfit and swagger.

Freedom is a blessing, he thought to himself before turning up the music and pulling off with MMG's song "Ambition" spilling from the speakers. Hitta rapped along with Wale and his favorite rapper, Meek Mill.

Well connected, well respected, and well protected
Ain't get accepted, was rejected and now they regret it
Ain't get my message, was no signal when I was texting
The niggas I was calling was fraud, and I learned my lesson
Now I move with aggression, use my mind as a weapon
'Cause chances are never given. They're taken like interceptions.

Turning up the volume more, Hitta bobbed his head to the beat. Seven minutes later, he pulled up in front of the liquor store across the street from Malboro Houses. Reem was standing there engaged in what looked like a heated conversation, which was cut short when one of the two dudes talking to Reem noticed Hitta's car. Hitta rolled down his tinted window, and Reem smiled when he saw him.

"Hop in, bro! Take a ride with me," Hitta said, matching Reem's smile.

Reem said a few more words to the dude before jumping in the passenger seat, and Hitta pulled off.

"This shit is sexy, bro," Reem said as he admired the inside of the luxury vehicle. "Damn, beloved, I see you out here on your bullshit. You pushing the latest Porsche; your neck and wrist are flooded. This is true motivation, my nigga!"

Reem couldn't hide his excitement. There was no envy in his eyes; his words were extremely sincere.

"Someone has to motivate the real. But on another note, I appreciate what you did for me, and here's a lil' something to show my appreciation," Hitta told him, pulling a stack of money from his pocket.

"On some g-shit, bro, I ain't do what I did that night for a reward. I did that shit from the heart. You're my brother. No matter how long we go without seeing each other, you never have to question my friendship or loyalty," Reem replied.

"Listen, I know what you did came from the heart. That's why I'm giving you this paper. It's coming from the heart, too. I know you just touched down, and shit may be a lil' hard for you at the moment. So, take the money, bro. It's time for you to bounce back. What type of friend would I be if I'm touching all this paper, and I got you out here on your dick? Now, let's discuss our future over a good meal. I'm hungry as fuck."

During the drive, they filled each other in on what was going on with each of them respectively. Although Peso and Hitta had always remained close, friendships and loyalty like this made Hitta believe in the real.

Hitta parked his car around the corner from Foot Steps, a well-known restaurant in Brooklyn. The two men entered the restaurant and took a table in the back. Hitta ordered the restaurant's famous Rasta Pasta dish with jerk chicken.

Reem also ordered Rasta Pasta, but he decided to add jerk shrimp to his instead.

"Them niggas who tried to bust a move on you that day was related to the nigga you parked behind that Rico shit," Reem informed him.

"Which one? Several niggas got parked behind what happened to Rico," Hitta replied with arrogance.

"They was related to that nigga Earn. They watched you walk in the building and lamped on you."

"Fuck it, they dead now. On to a lighter topic, I got some big shit in play, bro—some real big shit. I would love to have you on my team. Well, our team. Me and Peso built this together, and we're about to take the city over. I know you got a lot of status in that Blood shit, but we need you on our team, bro." Hitta said, trying his best to make his offer seem appealing.

"I'm already on your team, bro. You know that," Reem responded.

"You're with us now, but what if shit gets real and my movement ends up bumping heads with the Bloods? That leaves you having to pick a side. You're a natural-born leader; you lead your pack of wolves from the streets to the prison system. In a time of war, you're gonna ride with your family. It's your protocol. You took an oath, bro, so it's the right thing to do," Hitta said, looking Reem in the eyes.

Their conversation was interrupted by the waitress who arrived with their food. Reem waited until she walked away before he spoke.

"Hitta, you know I've been doing this Blood shit since I was thirteen. When my mother gave up on me, the Blood took me in and became my family. So, leaving them to begin another movement ain't an option. You know my heart bleeds Blood. Blood is my family. You and Peso are my family, too, and I'ma always ride for y'all. But when it comes to Blood, I can't go against that. This shit is something I hold sacred to my heart. I took an oath, which I'ma always honor," Reem expressed.

"I respect that, and honestly, I wouldn't expect anything less than that. I would just hate for our forces to bump heads," Hitta told him.

"We can form some type of alliance," Reem suggested. "In war, everyone needs an ally. Your movement has the least number of soldiers in the city. Having us in your corner can only help you."

"I appreciate the compromise, but you don't speak for every Blood in the city. You can only speak for your set."

"Nah, nigga I speak for my whole nation. I'm the youngest Godfather in this shit. If I stamp something, trust, mine will fall in line. They know I ain't gon' stamp no bullshit, bro," Reem assured him.

"I can feed you because you're family, but I can't feed your whole nation. If it wasn't for you, the Bloods would have been my first target because y'all are the strongest in the city," Hitta said, keeping it real with Reem.

"Don't worry about feeding mine, big homie. That's my job. I'ma make sure mine eat off of my plate."

***

M.D.C. Brooklyn…

Rolex Rich sat at the table engaged in a very intense chess game against Bobby Chu, an influential Korean man. The two men played at least three games of chess per day. On this particular day, they were tied one game apiece.

"I can't move until you do, Mr. Rich," Bobby Chu said.

Rolex Rich smiled and slid his rook down a few spaces.

"Checkmate, my friend," Rich said with confidence.

Bobby Chu shook his head in disbelief.

"I was hoping you didn't make that move. You're a very good chess player, my friend. Where did you learn the game?"

"My grandpa taught me a thing or two as a kid, and I've been playing ever since," Rich replied.

"The fact that you're a great thinker has made you a powerful man. The game of chess is very similar to war. It's all mental. From what I learned about you, Mr. Rich, I see you have beat all of your enemies by outsmarting them," Bobby said, sharing his observations.

"How you figure that?" Rich asked, almost defensively.

"Mr. Rich, I read all about your journey to success. You have made the Forbes list every year since you've been in prison. It takes a smart man to be able to accomplish such a task. The only opponent you didn't beat as of yet is the government, but if you start to think a little different, a little harder—if you start to think outside of the box, you will win this fight for your freedom."

Rolex Rich let his words sink in.

"I have to make a phone call," Bobby Chu finally said, breaking the silence. "I'll see you tomorrow for my rematch. You have a blessed day, Mr. Rich."

Rolex Rich remained at the table, stuck in his thoughts. Bobby Chu was a man of few words, but when he did speak, it was mostly in riddles. Rich stored Bobby Chu's comments in his mental notes and walked toward his cell. He needed to be alone, to sit in his thoughts. It was time to find a way to defeat his last and final opponent.

***

Hitta entered the Royal estate and made his way into the dining area. He had called Peso several times earlier but got no answer. The entire Royal family was in attendance. Well, everyone except Roxy, who's running late as usual.

"Hitta, I'm glad you could make it," Katrina said, greeting him with a hug. "Ray and Richie, this is Hitta, a very close friend of your father's. Hitta, these are my boys."

The three men shook hands.

"Yo, Hitta, where you know my pops from?" Richie inquired.

"We met while I was doing my bid," Hitta replied while taking a seat at the table.

"I'm going to get the food ready. You boys play nice," Katrina said, pointing at them, and then exited the dining area.

"So, Hitta, what do you do?" Richie asked, eyeing Hitta's jewelry.

"Wassup with all the questions? You writing a book?" Hitta responded sarcastically.

"Yo, lil' bro, chill. If Pop said he's family, then he's good, money," Ray told Richie.

"Ray, I ain't too heavy on sports, but you got busy that last game against Miami. Fifty-six points is kinda heavy going up against Bron and Wade," Hitta said, complimenting him.

"Don't forget the eleven assists, thirteen rebounds, and four steals," Ray replied with arrogance.

Outside, Peso pulled into the estate. A smoke grey Bentley GT pulled up beside him, and Roxy Royal got out of the driver's seat looking flawless.

Peso couldn't take his eyes off of her as he exited his Porsche. Roxy smiled when they made eye contact. She wondered who the handsome stranger was that was about to walk inside of her family's home.

"You lost or something?" she asked, flirting.

Peso was too busy admiring her beauty to answer her question.

Roxy Royal was a true supermodel. She stood at 5'9", and her hair framed her face in a bob. Her sun-kissed skin didn't have a scar or blemish, and her Asian eyes gave her an even more exotic look. She had an amazing body, a handful of breasts, a skinny waist, and the perfect apple-shaped ass.

"Excuse me. I asked you a question." She stepped in front of Peso, blocking his path.

"Pardon, love. I was kinda stuck for a second. What was your question?" Peso replied smoothly.

"I asked, are you lost?" she repeated, batting her eyes.

"Yeah, I'm lost without you."

He laughed, and so did Roxy.

"Boy, that was so corny! You need to quit."

"I made you smile, though. That's all that matters. But, nah, I'm not lost. I was invited for dinner. I'm Peso."

He extended his hand, and she gladly accepted.

"I'm Roxy," she replied, then the two made their way inside the mansion.

***

After a big dinner with the Royal family getting to know Hitta and Peso, Ray and Richie left, but Roxy stayed to spend time with Katrina.

"Roxy, give me a few minutes to speak with the fellas," Katrina said.

"Okay, Ma. I'll be in the theatre if you need me," she replied, eyeing Peso as she exited the living room.

"Now we can get down to business. Would you fellas like another drink?"

"Yeah, some Henny would be great," Peso answered.

"I'll have the same," Hitta said.

Katrina walked away, then quickly returned with a bottle of Hennessy, a bowl of ice, and three glasses.

"You guys did a great job on the first lick. Now it's time to turn up the tempo. Or would you guys like one job at a time?"

"We can handle whatever you throw at us. Just fill in the blanks on these new jobs," Hitta responded.

"Well, job number one is simple, but these guys are dangerous. So, I need the two of you to be on point."

"Who's the largest?" Peso asked.

"The Mexicans are making a drop. Two hundred kilos of coke and six million in cash is the score. All you guys have to do is intercept the play. The drop will be made in a FedEx truck in New Jersey. The address and routes they're taking are written down on a piece of paper inside the envelope that I'm going to hand over before you leave."

"What's the split?" Peso asked.

"You guys will bring back five mill. That will leave y'all with a million in cash and the drugs," Katrina replied.

Peso quickly did the math in his head. If he and Hitta sold each brick for thirty grand apiece, they would both walk away with three million.

"A mill up front and six mill for us to split after we have the work ain't bad." Hitta turned his attention to Peso. "You with it?"

"You know that shit, bro," Peso replied with a smile.

"I'm glad you both agree. Now job number two is a little different. It's more of a kidnapping. There's a jeweler who owes Rich some money. Five mill, to be exact. Rich only wants what's owed to him, so every dollar over that belongs to the two of you. In three days, you'll hit the Mexicans. Once that is done, y'all can fly out to Miami and take care of the jeweler. Deal?"

"Deal," both men replied in unison.

Back in Brooklyn...

Reem sat at the kitchen table in his aunt's apartment, staring at the two kilos of coke that Hitta gave him on consignment. Hitta wanted thirty thousand dollars back off of each kilo, which would give Reem more than enough room to eat. Reem was good at stretching cocaine, so he planned to do just that.

"Nephew!" his aunt Libby called out as she entered the kitchen.

"Wassup, Auntie? Talk to me."

"You got some good coke on your hands. To be honest, that was the best shit I've had in years. That shit is way too potent. I can tell it's pure and has never been stepped on. If you wanna make some real money, bring the volume down on it a lil' bit so the sniffers can enjoy their high."

"You just telling me it's fire 'cause you want more," Reem joked.

"Boy, I don't want none of that until you cut it. I ain't tryna die off that shit." She laughed. "But I do need twenty dollars real quick so I can pay my cab."

Reem peeled off a hundred-dollar bill from the stack of money Hitta gave him and handed it to her.

The minute she walked out, Reem got straight to business cutting and packaging the kilo. The sound of his phone ringing interrupted his work.

"Yo!" he answered.

"What's poppin', Blood?" the caller yelled from the other end.

"That five poppin'. You know that shit. Where you at? I'ma pull up on you."

"Me and Dame at the spot."

"I'll be over in a minute," Reem said, then ended the call.

Chapter 6

In a hooptie they purchased solely for the occasion, Hitta and Peso sat parked a block away from the address where the drop would happen.

"Yo, Hitta, that's the FedEx truck coming now," Peso informed him.

"I'ma pull out when they get a lil' closer. When they hit the car, get out and act a fool. I got it from there."

"Kopy!"

As the FedEx truck approached, Hitta quickly pulled out of the parking space, which resulted in the truck rear-ending them. Peso jumped out at the same time the two Latino men exited the truck.

"What the fuck! You didn't see the signal?" Peso yelled.

"I'm sorry, sir. It was a mistake," the FedEx driver pleaded.

Hitta jumped out next.

"This is my mom's car. Somebody's paying for this, or I'm gonna sue the shit out of ya company," Peso threatened.

"We have money to pay you. We'll give you two thousand dollars to fix the dent in the car," the driver offered. "Just please don't call the police,"

Two shots rang out, hitting the driver in his head and neck, killing him instantly. The passenger reached for his gun, but Peso beat him to the draw and let off a single shot from his P89, taking out his target. Hitta hopped in the FedEx truck while Peso quickly jumped behind the wheel of the hooptie. Both men fled the scene in a hurry.

An hour later, they were on a dead-end street in Coney Island unloading the contents of the truck. There were four boxes filled with cocaine and three filled to the top with hundred-dollar bills. After putting everything in the trunk of the hooptie, they wiped down the FedEx truck and left the scene.

Meanwhile...

Back at his aunt's place, Reem sat at the kitchen table. The only difference this time was he didn't have any coke sitting in front of him. Instead, he was staring at a total of $120,000 in cash. After he paid Hitta the $60,000 for the two kilos, that would leave him with $60,000 in cash for himself. One thing about Reem, he knew how to hustle. He turned the two kilos that Hitta gave him into three and then sold two of them wholesale at $40,000 apiece. He broke down the leftover kilo and hit some of his homies on consignment. The work sold so fast that it felt unreal.

After counting the money for the third time, Reem reached for his iPhone and placed a call to Hitta. The call went to voicemail, so he called the number a second time. This time, Hitta picked up on the first ring.

"Wassup, my boy?" Hitta greeted from the other end.

"Ain't shit. What's poppin', beloved? I'm ready for you. When can you pull up?"

"Damn, that was fast. I just seen you like three days ago," Hitta said, surprised by Reem's response.

"C'mon, man, you know how I do," Reem bragged.

"That's what I'm talking about, but check it, I'm a lil' tied up at the moment. So, you gonna have to pull up on me. I'll make it worth your while, though."

"Say less. Where you want me to pull up?" Reem asked.

"Meet me in front of my mom's building. You remember where that is, right?"

"Nigga, how can I forget? I'm calling a cab now," Reem replied.

"Just hit me when you're in front of the building."

"Bet. See you in a few," Reem said before ending the call.

Back in Coney Island...
Hitta and Peso sat running bills through the money counters.

"That was Reem. I passed him two bricks three days ago, and he's done already."

"That's a good look," Peso replied, looking up at Hitta and then back at the money. "Knowing him, he prolly danced all on the work."

"As long as that shit moving, I wouldn't care if he breakdanced on that shit."

They both laughed.

"Just like I said, P, all three boxes got two mill in each of them," Hitta said after pulling the last stack of bills out of the money counter. "We can take Kat her cut in the morning. Right now, we gotta figure out where to stash all this work. We just came up two hundred joints, and we still got fifty-three left from the last lick."

"I'ma take one hundred and put them downstairs in Quana's crib. You gotta find somewhere to put the rest. Then all we gotta do is pass out whatever we have left," Peso told him.

"That'll work. Since Reem moved them two I passed him so quick, I'ma smash him with ten when he pulls up. Deal?" Hitta said, consulting with his partner.

"I'm cool with that. Bro just moved the two you gave him in three days. He prolly gonna flush ten joints in a week and some change. That boy knows how to hustle."

The sound of Hitta's phone ringing cut their conversation short. He picked up, and after saying a few words, he ended the call.

"Yo, that was Reem. We gonna meet him on the third floor. He gonna be on the balcony," Hitta informed Peso while packing ten kilos in a book bag.

***

Reem stood on the balcony with a book bag on his shoulder, smoking a blunt. He smiled when his two longtime friends emerged from the staircase. It had been years since the three of them were in the same place at the same time.

"My nigga Reem." Peso flashed a huge grin while greeting him warmly.

"Long time no see, my brother. How's the lil' one?"

"She's great, bro. Just spoiled as shit," Peso commented.

"As she should be," Reem responded, then turned his attention to Hitta. "What's the word, bro?"

"Ain't shit. I'm glad to see you're back where you need to be."

"Thanks to y'all. The money train came, and a nigga didn't miss it. I turned the two you gave into three, and I don't have one gram left," Reem informed them, his chest puffed out with pride.

"I told you this nigga was the cut master," Peso said, and the three men shared a laugh.

"So you moved three birds in three days?" Hitta asked, still not believing it was possible.

"Yeah, bro, every single gram sold. I got a line that will never die and a team of wolves who trap hard. But, check it. I got the sixty racks I owe y'all plus another sixty for two more," Reem said, handing Hitta the book bag.

Hitta unzipped the bag and looked inside.

"Each stack is ten grand?" he asked.

"Facts," Reem replied.

Hitta took out six of the stacks, tossed three of them to Peso, and put the other three stacks in the pocket of his hoodie. He then handed the bag back to Reem with the remaining sixty thousand dollars inside.

"Keep that, bro. We wanna see you win. You don't gotta pass no money upfront. We gonna toss you ten on the arm," Hitta said, handing Reem the bag containing ten kilos.

***

Once they finished their business, Peso dropped Reem off and hit the highway. It was early on a Thursday night, so he headed across town to meet up with one of his comrades. He pushed his Porsche sixty miles per hour while inhaling the grade A Sour Diesel, making it to the East New York section of Brooklyn in no time. He pulled up in front of Building 350 in "Bamma's". The weather was pretty nice for March, and several people were standing in front of the building.

When Peso got out of his car, all eyes were on him. He was sporting an all-white G-star sweatsuit and a pair of all-white Balenciaga sneakers. The Cuban link on his neck and the Rolex on his wrist complemented his attire. Peso pulled out his iPhone and placed a call. Minutes later, a chubby light-skinned dude walked out of the building.

"Stacks, what's shaking, bro?" Peso said, greeting him with a pound of his fist.

"Ain't shit, my guy. A nigga tryin' get like you. This your whip right here?" he asked, admiring the Porsche.

"Yeah, I treated myself to this pretty lil' bitch. I'll fuck around and cop a Lambo next. It's time to show niggas who got the streets. On another note, though, I pulled up because I told your brother that I would pass you some shit for him."

Stacks' older brother, Tye-Murda, was one of the U.G.F. leaders.

"Yeah, I know. He already put me on. I'm leaving tomorrow night to go see him," Stacks replied.

"Say no more. Grab that footlocker bag that's sitting on the passenger seat. It's an ounce of dope and a few packs of that K2 shit." Peso pulled a stack of money from his pocket, peeled off ten one-hundred-dollar bills, and handed them to Stacks. "Send that to him, as well. Yo, who these two joints?" Peso asked, eyeing the two people who were approaching them.

Looking to his right, Stacks saw his lady, who was seven months pregnant, and her sister.

"Oh, that's my baby mama and her sister," Stacks replied.

"Wassup, bae?" Stacks greeted his girl with a kiss.

Both young women were attractive, but the sister was what Peso pictured in his head as his dream girl. She favored the model/video vixen Cat Washington. Not only was she pretty, but her body was amazing.

"This is Peso. Peso, this is my lady, Imani, and her sister Princess," Stacks said, introducing them.

"Wassup, ladies?" he said, greeting them smoothly.

"Hey!" both ladies replied.

"Wassup, Princess," Peso said, giving her all of his attention. "You gotta let me make you my queen," he openly flirted.

"Oh no, he didn't! Check ya boy out, bae." Imani laughed. "I'm going upstairs. Peso, it was nice meeting you," she said before leaving the two to finish talking.

"Likewise. You have a goodnight," Peso replied, then shifted his attention back to Princess once again. "You still didn't answer my question."

"Boy, you better stop. I don't even know you," Princess told him, finally speaking up.

"How about you get to know me over a bite to eat? Let me take you out. I'll be the perfect gentleman. I promise."

"I don't know about that. You look a bit too young for me. How old are you?"

"I'm twenty-one," Peso stated confidently.

"Boy, you're a baby. Goodnight, Mr. Peso," Princess responded, walking off.

Peso gently grabbed her hand before she got away.

"I'm not your average young boy, love. Just one date. If you're not feeling the energy, we can act like it never happened."

She looked at the handsome young man and smiled. Everything in her wanted to walk away, but it was something about him. She was curious to find out what it was. She looked over at Stacks for reassurance.

"Sis, the bro is valid. Go enjoy yourself. You're in great hands. Peso, I'ma make sure Murda gets this. Y'all be safe and have a good time," Stacks said while giving Peso some dap and heading towards the building. "Yo, hit me up soon as you get back from seeing ya bro. I got something I need you to be a part of."

"Right. Say less."

When Stacks entered the building, Peso turned to Princess.

"You coming, baby girl?"

"Yeah, I'ma come," she replied.

Soon as the words left her mouth, Peso reached to open the car door for her.

"Let me find out."

"Told you I'll be the perfect gentleman," he said, then winked at her before closing the door and rushing to jump into the driver's seat.

***

"Fuck me, daddy! Yesssss, right there. I'm coming!" Ashley screamed as Hitta hit it from the back.

"Whose pussy is this?" he growled, slapping her ass twice.

Ashley yelped in delight as Hitta delivered powerful strokes, making Ashley's ass bounce and jiggle with every hit.

"It's yours, daddy. All of it. Come inside me. I wanna have your baby," she moaned, her body beginning to shake uncontrollably as the orgasm took over her body.

Hitta felt his release building. Seconds later, he exploded inside of her before collapsing on the bed. Ashley laid down next to him, pulling him close and putting her head on his chest.

"You really are my everything, Amir," she said, breaking the silence.

"As I should be," he replied, smiling with arrogance. "On some real shit, though, you're my everything, too. I know I've been on the move since I've been home, but don't feel like I don't appreciate everything you did for a nigga while I was locked up, 'cause I do. I haven't committed myself to you one hundred because I don't wanna have you and end up breaking ya heart. Just understand, even without a title, my heart belongs to you," he expressed sincerely.

"I know that, Amir. The bond we share is different. Our connection is next level. I know you love me, but I also know you love the streets. Them streets got a hold on you. I feel like you love the streets more than you love me," Ashley responded.

"That's not true, Ash."

"Maybe it is, maybe it isn't. Just go hard, get ya money, and get the hell out of the streets. Don't let the game claim you, Amir. You claim the game."

And with that, she kissed him on the cheek before pushing off the bed and going into the bathroom.

Meanwhile, in Harlem…

Matt Murda slowly walked through the Lincoln Houses projects where a lot of U.G.F members lived. As he approached one of the buildings, he saw three dudes standing out front. They were drinking Hennessy and passing blunts back and forth between them.

"Aye, one of you niggas got some loud?" Matt Murda asked.

"Yeah, wassup?" the overweight one responded. "What you looking for?"

"Let me get a seven," Matt Murda requested to the unsuspecting crew.

"Kopy. That's eighty cash. I'll be right back."

Matt Murda pulled out his .9mm, and the fat kid froze in fear before he could take two steps.

Boc! Boc!

Both shots hit the young man in the head, instantly killing him. One of the other dudes rushed Matt Murda and tried to grab the gun. The last of the three saw an opportunity to escape and ran inside the building.

Boc! Boc! Boc!

Matt Murda let off three more rounds, and the kid fell to the ground while holding his stomach. Standing over him, Matt Murda put one more bullet in him, silencing the kid forever.

"Police! Freeze! Put the gun down!" an off-duty cop yelled from behind him.

Matt Murda quickly spun around, firing a single shot and hitting the cop before fleeing the scene.

Chapter 7

Peso woke up to the sound of his phone ringing. He looked at the screen, and after seeing Eazy's name, he accepted the call.

"Yo, this shit better be important, bro. It's seven in the fucking morning."

"Shit nasty! Somebody came through last night and shot two of the bros!" Eazy shouted through the phone.

"What?! What the fuck happened?! Who got hit?!"

"I don't know. Just got the call telling me B-Rilla and Chubbs got hit. Neither of them made it, bro. They both gone."

"I'm about to head ya way now. Listen out for ya phone," Peso replied, ending the call.

After hanging up with Eazy, he called Hitta, who answered on the first ring.

"Talk about it," Hitta said from the other end.

"Where you at, bro?" Peso asked.

"I'm on my way to take Kat these boxes. Why? Wassup? You gucci?"

"Yeah, I'm straight, but we lost apes last night in harlem. Eazy just called me. I'm 'bout to head that way. Just hit me after you come from Kat's."

"Kopy, bro. Be safe."

"Always, bro. You, too."

Peso looked over at the shapely frame next to him, staring at Princess as she slept. The two had gone out for drinks and shared a great night. Since both were too tipsy to drive, they ended up at the Marriot. They talked most of the night until Princess fell asleep. She didn't give up the box, but Peso took it like a champ and remained a gentleman.

"Yo, baby girl, wake up," he whispered, gently shaking her body.

"What time is it?" she asked, wiping the sleep from her eyes.

"It's early, but I gotta get going."

"Hmmm, lemme guess. We leavin' early 'cause I ain't give you none, right?" she said with a slight attitude. "Typical nigga," she added before Peso had a chance to respond.

"Shawdy, you got me fucked up. I ain't thirsty for sex. I could have jacked off to catch a nut. As much as I would love to lay in this bed with ya pretty ass, I can't. I just got a very important phone call, but I'ma come scoop you up as soon as I finish taking care of business. You got my word on that."

***

Forty-five minutes later, Peso was sitting in his Porsche outside the Foster Houses in Harlem. Eazy got in the car with a huge shopping bag. The look on his face let Peso know he was hurting behind the loss of their commander.

"Gorillas run the jungle!" Peso saluted.

"'Cause we untouchable gangsters," Eazy replied.

"That's a buck twenty-five in the bag. I know we just took a lost, but business don't stop."

"That's a fact, but what the hell happened?" Peso asked.

"I don't know, but whoever hit the bros also hit an off-duty undercover cop. Ray was out there with them, but he got low. I'ma link up with him when he comes from seeing his P.O. His head is prolly all fucked up. You know Chubbs was his lil' brother."

"Yeah, I know. Just get some answers and get back to me. Find out if Ray saw that nigga's face. Also, let him know me and Hitta will take care of the funeral expenses. I gotta breeze. I'll spin through later and drop some more work off," Peso informed him.

"Say no more. I'll be ready."

"Before I forget. I got some good news and bad news. Which one you want first?"

"I'll take the bad first," Eazy responded.

"The bad news is the price is going up to thirty a joint, but the good news is y'all will be getting twenty on the arm instead of five. Just make sure you feed the bros. Everyone must eat."

"That goes without saying," Eazy told him. "I'ma hit the streets and get some answers. Hit me when you on ya way back."

"Say no more, beloved," Peso replied. "Safe it up."

***

After dropping off the money to Katrina, Hitta ripped the highway back to Brooklyn. He called Peso twice but didn't get an answer. He parked his car and called the hood's weedman, who was also one of his good friends. Before going to link up with Illy to get some bud, Hitta walked to the store to grab some Fonto leaf tobacco and papers.

"I know that ain't my young boi Hitta!" he heard someone yell from behind him.

When Hitta turned around, he was greeted by Pretty Tony, who was a legend in Coney Island and the brother of Hitta's fallen comrade T.K.

"Oh shit! Wassup, big homie? Long time no see." Hitta greeted him with a slap of the hand and a one-armed hug.

"Ain't shit, lil' bro. You know a nigga still gettin' this paper. I see you back at it like you never left—all jeweled up and shit. That Cuban looks like it weighs more than you," Pretty Tony joked.

"I see you still got jokes," he replied, both of them laughing.

"On the real, Hitta, T.K. would be proud of you. All he ever wanted was to see you win."

Hearing Pretty Tony mention his brother's name crushed Hitta. T.K. was the one who schooled Hitta to the game. He was also the person who gave him the name Hitta. When he was murdered, Hitta's heart turned ice cold.

"I know he would be proud. That nigga taught me damn near everything I know. I just wish he was here to enjoy all this shit with me. How's Mama Luv doing?"

"She's okay, bro. I just sent her on vacation. I'ma let her know ya ass is back on the streets. She gonna be happy as hell. You know she loves you and Peso like her own kids. Speaking of Peso, wassup with bro? You need to get his ass back in the studio. I was just listening to some of his old tracks. Bro is definitely what the game needs," Pretty Tony expressed.

"That nigga be acting like he can't rap no more. I'ma get him back in the booth, though. But, yo, do you know anybody who be copping weight off the soft?" Hitta asked.

"How much weight you talking?"

"I got whatever niggas need," Hitta told him. "But I'm really only tryin' to move whole thangs, though."

"You know my lane is the dog food, but niggas out of town be payin' high for the coke," Pretty Tony informed him. "What's the number on a birdy? If the price is right, I might take them off ya hands."

"For you, twenty-five a joint."

"Not bad. If I need ten right now, can you fill my order?" Pretty Tony asked.

"Nigga, if you need *twenty* right now, I can fill your order. I'm plugged in, big homie," Hitta responded, his tone dripping with arrogance.

"Let me get twenty then. I'ma go snatch the bread. Put ya number in my phone."

Pretty Tony passed Hitta his iPhone. Hitta stored his number, then handed it back.

"Bet! I'ma hit you in like thirty minutes. Listen out for ya phone," Pretty Tony said.

"Say less. Just hit my line," Hitta replied, and the two men parted ways.

When Hitta made it to his building, Illy was standing out front waiting on him.

"Wassup, bro?" Hitta asked, pounding fists with him.

"Ain't shit. My guy about to go pick up the lil' ones real quick," Illy answered while quickly handing Hitta a Ziploc filled with sour diesel.

Hitta smelled the plastic bag and smiled.

"This that gas right here, bro. How much you charging ya boy?"

"Two-twenty for you."

"Heard you," Hitta replied, pulling a stack of hundred-dollar bills from his pocket. He peeled off three bills and handed them to Illy.

"Keep the change, bro."

"Good looking out, my nigga. Be safe out here. I'ma hit ya line a lil' later so we can smoke something," Illy said as he walked off.

"Say dat, bro. Just hit me."

Seconds after Hitta entered the lobby, Peso pulled up and exited his Porsche carrying a large duffle bag. He met Hitta in the lobby, and the two men headed up to Hitta's mother's apartment. They entered the apartment to find Ms. Sharon smoking a Newport while sitting on the couch. Ms. Sharon was like a mother to Peso. She was 5'7", light-skinned, and had beautiful, long silver hair. It was a wonder people hadn't nicknamed her Storm because that's the vibe her hair gave off. Ms. Sharon loved to have children around her, so it was no surprise that she and Peso's daughter, Mya, had built a strong bond.

"Ma, put that out. You don't need to be smoking," Hitta scolded.

"Boy, I'm grown! You better get out my face with all that noise," Ms. Sharon responded and then turned her attention to Peso, who greeted her with a tight hug.

"Hey, Mommy, how are you?"

"I'm fine, baby. Where my pretty little grandbaby?"

"She's with her mom. I'll bring her over to see you tomorrow."

"You better. How is ya mom?"

"She's well. Just stressing me out."

"Boy, you're probably the one stressing her out. You sound just like Amir." Ms. Sharon laughed as Peso followed Hitta upstairs to his bedroom, locking the door behind him after he entered.

"Yo, I picked up that bread from the bro Eazy. He couldn't tell me much about what happened last night. All I know is B-Rilla and Chubbs are both gone. Ray was with them, but he managed to slip away. I told Eazy to link with him and get more details," Peso informed Hitta, then added, "That shit fucked up a good night."

"A good night? You must've slid up in some new pussy," Hitta said, laughing.

"Actually, shawdy ain't let me hit, but I'm jocking her, though. I'm digging her vibe. It's something different about her."

"Shawdy must be a fucking nun. I don't know a female that could resist Pretty Boy Peso," Hitta joked.

Peso smiled humbly. "I see you got hella jokes, my nigga."

"Jokes? Nah, nigga, I'm deadass," Hitta said, laughing even harder.

Peso shook his head and had no choice but to laugh with him.

"But, on a more serious note, Breeze just hit me and said he's coming down here to snatch three joints," Peso told him, bringing them back to business.

"That's a good look. I just seen Pretty Tony. He asked about you. That nigga about to come cop twenty bricks. If we front Breeze twenty and top off the three he already ordered, that leaves us at two hunnit even," Hitta said before lighting a blunt he had sitting in the ashtray.

"What you think about adding to what we are already fronting the apes?"

"Don't matter to me. How much you talking?"

"I was thinking we front each district twenty bricks so that we're not just holding a bunch of work. Once we pass that out, we down to a hunnit joints."

"Let's make it happen," Hitta said, passing Peso the blunt.

"When we leaving for that outta town lick?" Peso asked as he took a pull from the blunt.

"The party is on Sunday, so we gonna slide out on Friday. Things are finally about to be how we planned. It's fucked up that it's just you and me instead of the whole team, though," Hitta commented.

***

Reem watched the traffic going in and out of the building, and all he could do was smile. Thanks to Hitta and Peso, he was back on his game. The coke they gave him on consignment put him and his team back on the map. He looked down from the rooftop of the building in amazement. There hadn't been this much drug traffic in years. Today, he had two of his goons with him, Bricks and Dame. Bricks was stocky, dark-skinned, and ruthless. He had been around putting in work since he was a kid. Pretty Boy Dame hustled harder than most of the homies on the set, but he was far from the gangster type.

"Ayo, y'all see all this money walking thru here? I gave these projects life again, and I'm feeding the family in the process. Shit will only get better," Reem said, wearing a wide grin. "Look at this shit! We got a view of the entire area. Nothing is outta sight. That's why I'm always up here."

Bricks and Dame looked around in amazement. They hadn't seen so many crackheads in years.

"I come up here every day just to watch the money flow. I swear to God this shit gives me a rush. But I also see things that make me sick to my stomach. Especially when I'm smoking my morning blunt and see niggas exiting cop cars and shit. One thing I hate is a fucking snitch," Reem said, reaching for his .357.

Both men became nervous from the sight of the gun.

"How do you feel about rats, Bricks? Do you think they deserve to live?"

"You know the old saying—snitches get stitches," Brick replied.

Reem turned to Dame. "What about you, blood? How you feel about rats?"

Dame was extremely nervous, but he refused to show his fear.

Looking Reem in his eyes, he said, "All rats must die."

Reem simply laughed and aimed his .357 at Dame's head.

"What's this about, big homie?" Dame calmly asked, although he knew he was knee-deep in shit.

"You know what the fuck this is about, nigga. For the last three nights, you've been meeting up with the police. The first time I saw you, I thought I was bugging. Then I saw the Crown Vic drop you off two more times, and I knew ya bitch ass was working with the cops."

"On the set, big homie, I don't be fucking with the boys. You got the wrong nigga. That wasn't me," Dame lied with a straight face.

"So this ain't you?" Reem asked, handing over his iPhone. "Press play, nigga. Bricks, watch that shit."

Dame's heart sank as he watched the footage of himself exiting the Crown Vic. Bricks looked at Dame in disgust.

A few months prior, Dame got caught with a gun charge and turned informant. He already had two gun convictions on his record and knew the third one would finish him. So, instead of taking his chances in court, he decided to save himself.

"Blood, I swear it ain't what it looks like," he pleaded, but his pleading fell on deaf ears.

"Explain that shit to God, pussy!"

BOC!

The shell from the .357 hit Dame, transitioning him to the other side in an instant. Bricks was disappointed in his right-hand man, but he knew there was nothing he could've or would've done to save him. Hopefully, with Dame dead, it would stop any damage he was trying to cause.

Chapter 8

Outside Greene Correctional Facility, Peso sat in a black BMW waiting for the prison to release his little brother Shoota, who just finished serving a two-year bid for gun possession. Peso and Shoota had it hard while growing up, with their pops not being around and their mom being hooked on drugs most of their childhood. So, the streets were the inevitable choice for them both.

At exactly 9:15 A.M., Shoota strolled out of prison. Peso smiled. His little brother no longer looked like a baby boy. With facial hair covering his handsome face and his now muscular body covered in tattoos, Shoota looked like a grown man.

"Baby girl, that's my lil' brother right there," Peso said to Princess before exiting the car. He watched as Shoota looked around for a few seconds.

"Over here, lil' nigga," Peso called out, getting his brother's attention.

Shoota smiled as he ran over to Peso. Dropping the bag he was carrying, Shoota grabbed Peso up in a bear hug. Peso hugged him back tightly.

"Welcome home, baby boy. I'm glad to see you, man," Peso said with his arms still around Shoota.

"Glad to see you, too. Better believe I'm happy to be back. Damn, bro, this beamer is mean," Shoota said, admiring the car.

"I'm glad you like, 'cause this shit ain't my style no more. I done leveled up," Peso commented with a smirk.

"So what you sayin', bro?" Shoota asked, smiling like a kid in a toy store.

"I'm sayin' this shit is all you, nigga," Peso replied.

Shoota started running around the car like it was Christmas morning, and Peso couldn't help but laugh at his antics.

Princess got out with the keys in her hand and extended them to Shoota.

"Hold up, big bro. Does this lovely lady come with the car?"

Peso laughed. "Hell no, baby bro. This lovely lady came with me. Shoota, this my lady friend, Princess. Princess, this my brother, Shoota," he said, introducing them.

"Princess, please tell me you got a sister that looks as good as you."

"I do, but she's taken, sweetie," Princess replied with a smile.

"All the good ones are always taken," he responded with a chuckle, then hopped in the driver's seat.

Two and a half hours later, they pulled up on Park Place in the Crown Heights section of Brooklyn. The three of them entered the building and walked upstairs to a second-floor apartment. When Peso rang the doorbell, a woman in her early forties, with the prettiest set of hazel eyes, answered the door. Peso was the spitting image of his mother. The only difference between the two was his eyes were green instead of hazel. Peso looked at his mother and couldn't help but smile. Even after years of drug abuse, she was still beautiful, but her eyes told a dark story. Shoota was hiding around the corner in the hallway when the door opened, so she only saw Peso and Princess.

"My baby!" she yelled, jumping in Peso's arms.

"Hey, Momma, look who I found," Peso said.

Shoota came out from hiding. He couldn't wait to wrap her in his arms. She showered her youngest son with kisses all over his face.

"Oh, my Lord! Welcome home, baby! I missed you so much."

"I missed you more, my queen. How are you?"

"I'm great now that my boys are here. And who is this beautiful young lady standing in my living room?" she asked, taking in Princess's beauty.

"Mommy, this is my lady friend, Princess. Princess, this is my lovely mother, Mary," Peso said, making the introduction.

"Hello, Ms. Mary. It's nice to meet you," Princess said, stepping up to extend her hand.

"What you reaching that hand out for? We hug in this family," she responded, opening her arms to Princess and hugging her tightly.

"Tyler, you said this is ya friend? You better move up before someone snatches her up, and it's too late. This young lady is gorgeous."

"Thank you," Princess replied, blushing.

"Ma, stop it." Peso laughed.

"Stop nothing. You brought her to meet me, which means you like her a lot. Anyway, y'all hungry?"

"Ma, I been away from your cooking for two years. You know I'm hungry," Shoota responded while grinning and rubbing his hand together.

Ms. Mary looked at her son and smiled. "Look at my baby. You put on all that muscle. I can't believe how big you got, Tymel," she said, referring to Shoota by his government name.

"What do you want me to make, baby?"

"I've been dying for some of your lamb chops, spicy garlic potatoes, and sweet corn. Oh, wait! If it's not too much to ask, I would like some of your homemade lemonade."

"Coming right up, baby boy," Ms. Mary told him, then started making her way toward the kitchen.

"Ms. Mary, can I help you with anything?" Princess asked.

"Sure, sweetie, come on. Let's do some woman things while the boys catch up."

Princess cheerfully joined Ms. Mary, leaving Peso to enjoy some time with his brother.

***

Rolex Rich sat at the table with Bobby Chu. This time, the two men weren't playing chess. Instead, they were engaged in a deep conversation. Rich found the Korean to be very interesting.

"Bobby, I've been thinking about what you said to me the last time we played chess, and I still don't understand the message. I'm just hoping you weren't suggesting that I compromise my integrity," Rich said.

Bobby Chu chuckled lightly before speaking.

"I would never suggest a man turn snitch, my friend. I said to think outside the box, and working for the government doesn't take much thinking."

Bobby Chu chuckled again.

"Let me tell you a little story," he continued. "I once knew a poor Korean boy who came to this country with nothing at all. Yet, he found a way to become a very wealthy man. During his journey to the top, he came across a bump in the road when his closest friend, turned federal informant, took down his whole organization. The man spent top dollar on the best legal defense team money could buy and still ended up with fifty years, but he never gave up on the battle. He used the best weapon known to man—his brain. He used his brain to strategize, thinking outside the box."

Rich stared at the man, trying to read between the lines of his story.

"Mr. Rich, the Korean understood that everyone has a price tag, even the most powerful government in the world. So, he paid his way, but the payments were made indirectly. He had someone else make a deal with the feds for his freedom. He placed five hundred million dollars, thousands of machine guns, bombs, ammunition, and tons of pure heroin in a warehouse. The government seized it, and no one got arrested for it. The man lost a lot of money and merchandise, but he kept his integrity and regained his freedom."

Rich wore a look of intrigue on his face as Bobby Chu continued.

"The funny thing is, the government only reported three hundred million, which means they pocketed the other two hundred million dollars for their troubles. I have to call my wife. Will you be up for a chess game later?" Bobby Chu asked, abruptly ending the conversation.

"Yeah, man, most definitely," Rolex Rich replied before Bobby Chu walked off to use the phone.

***

"Yo, Hitta!"

Hitta heard someone call out his name as he came out of the corner store. He turned around to see his little cousin, Heat, running towards him with a swollen eye and blood on his clothes.

"What happened?" Hitta asked with a concerned look.

"I need some shells for my .380. I ran out. These niggas on 23rd Street jumped me," Heat explained.

"Go clean yaself up and meet me in the parking lot. Hurry the fuck up!"

Hitta was furious as he walked to his car. Seeing Heat all fucked up made his blood boil. One thing for sure and two things for certain, somebody would pay for what they did to his cousin.

Five minutes later, Heat came strolling through the parking lot wearing a black hoodie. Hitta was leaning against his Porsche, talking to one of his young boys. When Heat approached, the dude walked away.

"You got those shells for me?"

"Nah. I got a grip for you, though. Are you sure you ready for this? 'Cause once you get in this car, ain't no turning back. You can just tell me who jumped you, and I'll handle it," Hitta offered, but Heat looked at him like he was crazy.

"Nigga, this ain't my first drill. I ain't no lil' nigga no more. All you gotta do is pass that grip, and I'ma put in my own work," Heat responded angrily.

Hitta couldn't help but smile.

Hitta got in the driver's seat of his car and hit the locks for Heat to get in the passenger's seat. Hitta then handed him a .357 python and pulled off. They were at the corner of 23rd Street and Mermaid Avenue. Several people were standing in front of the chicken spot on the opposite side of the street.

"There go two of them niggas right there," Heat said, exiting the car.

Hitta got ready to get behind him, but Heat wasn't with that.

"Nah, cuzzo, this is personal. Just keep the car running."

Hitta wasn't used to not getting his hands dirty, but he respected his cousin's wishes to handle his own business. Hitta made a U-turn and drove a few feet up so that he was on the same side of the street as Heat. Since the police precinct was on the corner, he didn't want to drive in that direction. He watched Heat's every move through the rearview mirror. Heat approached the crowd of men with the .357 aimed at them.

BOOM! BOOM!

Two shots dropped his first target, and everyone took off running. Heat began chasing his second target, who was running toward Hitta. Hitta was tempted to get out of his car, but he let Heat handle his business.

BOOM!
Another shot knocked the victim off of his feet. Heat ran up to his target, and while standing over him, he fired another shot, silencing him forever. Hitta smiled like a proud dad whose only son had just graduated from high school.

"This nigga is definitely my family," he said to himself.

***

Princess was in the kitchen washing the dishes. Shoota was taking a shower. And Peso and his mother were in her bedroom having a deep conversation.

"Ma, you ready to leave Brooklyn?" Peso asked.

"And go where, Tyler?"

"Anywhere you want, Ma. You can start house shopping now. I'll pay for everything. You know I got you," Peso reassured her.

"Baby boy, I love you to death, but I know you get your money illegally. I refuse to let you spend your money on a house for me, then somewhere down the line, the feds come and take it from me," she said seriously.

"I don't agree with how you live your life, but you are a grown man and make your own decisions," she continued. "I haven't always been the best mother, so my choices forced you to become a man at an early age. If I could start over, I would never choose drugs over my family," she expressed with tears in her eyes.

Peso wiped them away while hugging her.

"Don't cry, Momma. I wouldn't trade you for anyone else on this earth. We all make choices, Ma—some good, some bad. But we learn from our bad decisions. Don't blame yourself for the way I'm living, 'cause honestly, I probably would still be doing the same thing I'm doing now. Let me tell you this, though. I'ma make some moves to cover my tracks. So, when I buy your dream house for you, the feds won't be able to take it. Deal?"

"Deal," she responded. "Now, let's change the subject and talk about that gorgeous young lady who's in my kitchen. I like her."

"Ma, Princess is just my friend."

"Well, you need to make her more than your friend. My intuition tells me she's special, Ty. Just by talking to her, I can tell she's the one for you. You know Momma knows best," Ms. Mary told her son.

"I'm glad you like her, but one more person has to approve."

"And who might that be?" she asked, curious as to why her opinion wasn't enough.

"Mya. If Mya likes her, then we can move forward. But I have to get going, Ma. Me and Amir are heading to Miami for a few days. I love you, Ma." He kissed her cheek.

"I love you, too, baby boy. You be safe out there, and I would like to see my grandbaby this weekend."

"I'll have Mariah drop her off," he said, walking toward the bedroom door.

"Tyler!" his mother called out.

"Yes, Momma?"

"When you gonna leave them streets alone and focus on your music? That's your gift from God. I think you should take advantage of your talent."

Peso smiled at his mother. Besides Hitta, she had always been his biggest fan when it came to his music.

"Soon, Momma, soon," he responded, then left out the room.

Chapter 9

Anticipating the task before them, Hitta and Peso were all smiles after their plane landed at Miami International Airport. Both men had a feeling that what they were up against would change their lives forever. They came to Miami to kidnap one of the most prominent jewelers in the United States, partying while doing it. The lick was simple. Kat got them on the guest list at a big party the jeweler would be attending, and the two of them would take it from there.

As Peso and Hitta walked out of the airport, Hitta spotted a gentleman standing next to a black stretch limousine and holding a sign with his government name on it.

"Oh, we doing it like that now?" Peso asked, wearing a huge grin.

"We might as well get used to this, 'cause this is how we doing it from now on," Hitta told him, acknowledging the driver as they approached him.

Once inside the limo, they were driven to the Ritz Carlton Hotel, where a thirty-five-hundred-dollar-a-night suite had been reserved for them for the next five days, courtesy of Kat.

"I can get used to this, brodie," Peso said as he stood making himself a drink at the in-suite bar.

"Me, too. This is living right here, bro. What's the word, though?" Hitta inquired. "We both been on the move these past few days. We got some catching up to do."

"I just been spending time with the family," Peso replied. "You know Shoota finally home, so I been getting him situated. Other than that, shawdy that I been telling you about…we been vibing. I'm digging her style. She got a good head on her shoulders. Plus, Momma loves her. So, I might keep her around."

"You keeping a chick around don't even sound like you, nigga. Yo' ass still ain't smash that yet, huh? You said Mommy like her, which means you introduced her. Boy, you open, nigga. I gotta meet this one."

"I ain't hit it yet, but I ain't been pressing her for the box. A nigga really just be enjoying her company. She's a good one, bro. Twenty-six years old, no kids, works, goes to school, and she's bad as fuck. Body is amazing; feet are pretty. She likes rap music AND basketball! Shawdy's my type of lady," Peso said, speaking highly of Princess. "Fuck all that, though. Wassup with you? Fuck you been up to?" Peso asked, taking the attention off himself.

"You know me, bro. Just tryin' win," Hitta replied, pausing to take a swig of the Hennessy that Peso had prepared for him. "Heat got jumped on 23rd Street. So, we spint the block, and he put in some work. Lil' nigga laid two down. He on his bully right now. I know for a fact we got the same blood flowing through our veins. Now that he got Shoota back on the streets with him, shit gonna be outta control," Hitta said excitedly.

"Can't forget about that lil' crazy motherfucker, Caine. You know he's their road dawg, too."

The sound of Peso's phone ringing interrupted their conversation.

"Hold up, bro. This is Mariah calling."

***

Reem and Bricks sat waiting for B-Gunnz in the visiting area of Wende Correctional Facility. Reem knew he would have a hell of a time trying to explain to his comrade why his brother was dead by his hands. He prayed B-Gunnz would see his actions as business and not personal. Rules were rules, and no one was immune to them.

Reem and B-Gunnz came from the same projects in Brooklyn. B-Gunnz was several years older, but he always had a tremendous amount of respect for Reem. Reem terrorized the streets the same way B-Gunnz did when he was young and putting in work for the New York chapter of the Bloods. Every big homie on the east coast knew him, and when B-Gunnz got his own set, he chose Reem as his co-Godfather.

B-Gunnz walked into the visiting room dressed in a white Gucci collar shirt, state-issued green pants, and a pair of white Gucci loafers. He approached the table and greeted his comrade with a one-armed hug.

"Peace, blood," he saluted in a solid tone.

"Peace, Almighty," both men replied.

B-Gunnz took a seat and locked eyes with Reem.

"What happened to my brother, scrap?" he asked, his eyes displaying sadness.

"I'ma give it to you straight, bro. Dame turned informant, so he had to be touched."

"Fuck you mean turned informant?" B-Gunnz asked, clearly in disbelief.

"I mailed you the proof, bro. You should be getting it any day now."

"So you made a call to have my brother touched without speaking to me? You think you're bigger than the hood now, scrap?"

"I didn't have him touched. *I* touched him. As for checking in with you, why would I do that when you gave me the streets? I did what had to be DONE! We all took an oath. It's death before dishonor. I ain't bending the rules for nobody, 'cause that wouldn't be leading by example," Reem stated, standing firmly in his position.

"Dame was my brother, Reem…my only brother."

"So I'm supposed to act like the rules don't exist because that rat was family? You made me give T-Time the same fate when he snitched, and he was my family. I ain't gonna be biased, homie. A rat is a rat," Reem replied with conviction.

B-Gunnz was heated, but he knew Reem was speaking the truth.

"You right, Blood. I'm just a lil' fucked up about it. Let's change the topic, though. I'm hungry as shit."

"I'm hungry, too," Reem said. "I'ma go to the vending machine. What you tryin' eat?"

"You know I love those hot wings. Get a few packs of those, some chips, and a Pepsi."

Reem got up to go to the vending machine. Once he was out of earshot, B-Gunnz looked Bricks in the eyes.

"When y'all get back to the hood, slump that nigga, and you'll get his spot. The streets will be yours."

"Kopy, big homie. Say no more," Bricks replied, the prospect of power dancing in his eyes.

***

"Excuse me. I want to rent a car for three days," Hitta told the concierge at the hotel.

"I can help with that, sir. What type of car will you be needing?" the concierge asked.

"I need something that will have heads turning. I want all eyes on me when I pull up. Price isn't an issue."

"I think I have the perfect automobile for you. Please give me a few minutes," the concierge replied.

Several minutes later, the concierge returned wearing a huge grin and handed Hitta a set of keys.

"Here you go, sir. I picked out a showstopper."

"Thank you," Hitta responded, taking the keys from his hand.

"Your automobile will be waiting for you in front of the hotel."

"Thanks for the help." Hitta pulled three crisp hundred-dollar bills from his small stack of money and handed them to the concierge.

"Just doing my job, sir," the concierge replied, gladly accepting the tip as Hitta walked off.

When Hitta saw a white Rolls Royce Phantom Drophead waiting for him, he couldn't help but smile.

"Peso is gonna love this shit," he said to himself.

***

The night of the party had finally arrived, and Hitta and Peso were super excited. Peso stepped out in an all-white, tailor-made Tom Ford suit with a pair of matching loafers. His fresh haircut had his 360° waves swimming. The only piece of jewelry he wore was his Rolex. Tonight, Peso was strictly on his grown man shit.

Not to be outdone, Hitta was dressed in a tailored, sky-blue Salvatore Ferragamo suit with matching Ferragamo shoes. His straight hair was pulled back into a slick ponytail complemented by a fresh shapeup. Just like Peso, Hitta wasn't too flashy. His only accessories for the evening were a Rolex and a pair of diamond earrings. Dressed to impress, both men would fit in perfectly with the rest of the attendees.

When the men arrived at their destination, they were shocked by the sight of the large structure. The mansion was beautiful and much bigger than either of them expected. It made the Royal family estate look like an apartment building. Tonight, they were running with the big dawgs.

Peso noticed some heavyweights in the entertainment industry were in attendance—A-list actors, rappers, singers, athletes, and supermodels alike.

"Everybody who is somebody is here, bro! This is some next-level shit," Peso expressed with excitement.

"You ain't never lied, bro. If we weren't here on business, I would definitely be humping on someone's favorite actress," Hitta responded with a chuckle.

Both men took a seat at one of the many bars located on the mansion's first floor. Hitta soaked in everything mentally as his eyes roamed all over the mansion. Just like Peso, he was wondering how they could pull off the task. Despite being nervous, both men were ready.

A quarter after midnight, Nick Lafrenz finally made his grand appearance. He was wearing an off-white Givenchy suit and a pair of loafers. With all eyes on him, he stole the show. It's like the room paused. Peso and Hitta kept their eyes on him as he mingled with a few people and had a few drinks. When Nick took a very beautiful lady's hand and headed towards the staircase with her, Hitta pushed to his feet without hesitating, cautiously following Nick. Peso was right behind him. Both men kept a safe distance from their target. Nick and his lady friend walked up to the second floor of the mansion. Hitta knew this stunt would be a dangerous one, but he lived for the thrill. Not sure which room Nick and the lady went in, Hitta and Peso placed their ears against several different doors, trying to listen for them.

"I think it's this one, bro," Peso whispered to Hitta, waving him over.

Peso slowly turned the doorknob, and to his surprise, the door was unlocked. Both men crept slowly into the room. Nick lay on the bed with the girl's head in his lap. They were so caught up in the moment that neither of them heard the door open.

"Hate to fuck up ya lil' session, Mr. Lafrenz, but we have some business to discuss."

The sound of Peso's voice caused the girl to yelp. She quickly put her hand to her mouth to silence herself.

"Who the fuck are you two?" Nick asked, angry that they were fucking up the best head he ever had.

"We ain't nobody special. A friend sent us to speak on his behalf. He couldn't make it tonight. Hey, beautiful," Peso said, addressing the young lady, "do you mind giving us a few minutes of privacy?"

Giving an awkward smile, she made a hasty retreat, not waiting around to be asked twice.

"Now, where were we, Nick?"

"You were saying something about speaking on a friend's behalf," Nick answered, still confused as to why they were there and who was the friend that had sent them.

Hitta was there to answer all his questions, though.

"Nick, you fucked over a good man, and we are here to collect a debt you owe. Now, this can go one of two ways: you can leave with us and continue to live, or you can die right here. Doesn't matter to me. So, what's it going to be?"

"I have one question. Who is this friend that sent you?" Nick inquired.

"You remember Rolex Rich, right?" Hitta asked.

The sound of Rich's name made Nick visibly nervous. Richard Royal was a very dangerous man; Nick knew that much about him.

"Listen, fellas, I have the money I owe him, and I'll even give you guys something extra for your trouble. Please don't kill me," Nick pleaded.

"Deal! Come on, let's go. And if you try something funny, we'll kill you in front of everybody. Get ya'self together," Hitta ordered. "Yo, bro, go get the car ready," he told Peso, who exited the room.

By the time Hitta and Nick made it to the mansion's entrance, Peso was in the car waiting for them. Nick lived in a waterfront estate in a gated community called Cooper City. When they entered the estate, Peso and Hitta went straight to work.

"I don't keep much cash here. I'm a jeweler. My money is in accounts," Nick explained.

"Nick, we didn't come here to play. We will tear this house apart, find the money, then kill you," Hitta threatened, pointing his gun at Nick.

"Yo, bro, bring that nigga upstairs!" Peso yelled out.

"You heard him. Get yo' ass up them steps," Hitta ordered.

When they got upstairs, Hitta started grinning upon seeing the two safes that Peso found hidden behind some artwork on the wall.

"I see you been holding out on us, Nick. I thought you didn't keep much money here? What's tucked away in the safes?"

"There's nothing in there," Nick lied.

Peso smacked him across the face with his pistol, leaving a cut under his eye. Nick's hand went quickly to his face, wincing from the pain.

"Don't insult my fucking intelligence, nigga. Open the safe!" Peso shouted.

The look in Peso's eyes told Nick that he meant business, so he followed the order given. Nick opened both safes—one filled with bricks of gold and the other containing neat stacks of hundred-dollar bills. While clearing the second safe of the money, Peso noticed a black cloth in the back of the safe. He couldn't believe his eyes when he unwrapped it.

"Yo, bro, look," Peso said to Hitta.

Nick shook his head in defeat.

"Fellas, those diamonds belong to some very important people. Please don't take them," Nick begged, his request falling on deaf ears. "I have an account with thirty million in it. Every penny of it is yours, but please don't take the diamonds."

"Thirty million for the diamonds?" Peso asked.

"Yes! All you have to do is give me an account number, and I will wire the money right now."

Hitta pulled out his phone and called Katrina, who picked up on the second ring.

"Mrs. Royal, I have a jeweler who loves your company so much that he wants to donate thirty million dollars to your label's next project," Hitta informed her, speaking in code in case one of their phones was tapped.

"Thirty million? That's quite a donation," she replied, sounding intrigued.

"Well, Mr. Nick Lafrenz sees the potential growth in your company. Just text me the account info, and I will have the money sent over. We'll talk more when I get back to New York," Hitta told her.

"No problem. I'm texting it now, and please tell Mr. Lafrenz how much I appreciate this gesture. You gentlemen have a blessed night."

"You, too, ma'am," Hitta replied, ending the call. "Where is ya laptop?"

"It's in my bedroom," Nick responded, praying the transaction would save his life.

"Well, lead the way."

When they reached the bedroom, Peso hit the light, and just like Nick said, the laptop was on the nightstand. Hitta watched Nick's every move to ensure he didn't alert anyone of their presence.

A huge smile appeared on Peso's face when he stumbled upon Nick's immaculate watch collection. He had over two hundred watches from Rolexes to Audemars, Cartier, Franck Mullers, and other designer watches he never heard of and could hardly pronounce. Peso continued to search around the house while Hitta kept all of his attention on Nick. Minutes later, Peso entered the room with a large Gucci suitcase. When Nick looked up and saw him loading the suitcase with his watch collection, it damn near brought him to tears.

"Come on, man. Don't take my watches. I'm handing you guys thirty million dollars."

"Check this out, Nick. We're the niggas with the guns. I could clip you and still leave with the watches and everything else you got in here. Besides, you're a jeweler.

This shit is probably insured anyway." Peso then turned his attention to Hitta. "Aye, bro, I'ma take all this shit to the car while you handle our lil' friend here," he said and exited the bedroom.

Hitta stood over Nick and watched the transaction go through. Once he saw the money deducted from Nick's account, he called Katrina to make sure things were straight on her end.

"Good job, Nick. She told me that the money made it to the account," Hitta informed him.

On the inside, Nick was jumping for joy, but he wouldn't show it.

"Can I have the diamonds back now, please?" Nick begged.

"Nah, those diamonds are coming with me. You should have never crossed Rich. You're lucky he's letting you live. Take the L, homie. And if you involve any police, my next visit will be with the sole intent to kill you and everyone you love. Be cool," Hitta said, leaving Nick in his room looking like he wanted to die.

Back in Brooklyn…

Reem drove around, making drops to his homies. Life for him had been great since getting back in the loop with his old friends. Hitta and Peso put him back on top of his game. Pulling up to his projects, he parked his BMW 7 Series. Seconds later, his phone rang, and Bricks' name popped up on the screen. Reem answered immediately.

"What's poppin', fool?"

"We poppin', B-dawg. That five poppin'. I'm ready for you," Bricks replied, referring to the money he had for Reem.

"Kopy, scrap. Say no more. I'll be over to you in like twenty minutes."

"Hit me when you on ya way up," Bricks said, ending the call.

As soon as Reem's feet hit the pavement, an all-black Impala pulled up in front of him. He knew it was the police before they rolled the window down. Reem didn't have any drugs on him, but he did have a duffle bag full of dirty money and a .357 in his possession.

"Well, if it isn't the big homie, Reem. What's poppin', slim?" the detective asked, trying to be down.

"Ain't shit poppin'. Is there a problem? Why y'all stop me?"

"Because there's been a lot going on around here lat—"

"I'm barely around, so why does that concern me?" Reem interjected.

"C'mon, Reem, don't play dumb. You run these piece-of-shit projects. Everything that goes on, you play a part in it." The detective paused and looked at Reem's hand. "What's in the bag?"

Boom! Boom! Boom!

The Impala quickly pulled off at the sound of the loud gunshots, the detectives hoping to catch the shooter.

"Saved by the gun," Reem said to himself, then quickly crossed the street toward the projects.

Reem headed straight for the closet after entering his stash spot and removed three kilos, placing them in a sneaker box. Then he put the box in a plastic Footlocker bag. After his little encounter with the detectives, he decided to leave his gun behind along with the duffle bag containing the money. He never kept his money in the same spot as his drugs, but he didn't see anything wrong with it since he was only going to the next building. Before leaving, he called Bricks and let him know that he was on his way.

Five minutes later, Reem was standing in the lobby of Bricks' building. He called and told him to come downstairs. Two minutes later, Bricks stepped off the elevator.

"What's poppin', big homie?" Bricks said, greeting him with the Blood handshake. "Same ol' shit. Just tryna get this money. Here, that's three birds. Break them down and feed the homies," Reem said, handing him the duffle bag.

"Where that money from the last flip?"

"Nigga, you think I'ma come down here with a bag full of dirty money. The bread is at the crib. Stop acting Hollywood and pull up. Come on, smoke with the homie," Bricks told him.

Both men entered the elevator, and as soon as the door closed, Bricks pulled his .40 cal. Reem quickly reached for his gun.

BOC! BOC!

Both shots hit him in the chest, knocking him back against the elevator wall. Reem wore a look of shock, coughing up blood. The elevator door slid open.

"B-Gunnz said ya number has been called. Flatline, homie."

BOC!

Bricks fired one last shot into Reem before taking off.

Chapter 10

"Daddy!" Mya screamed, running to Peso and jumping in his arms. "I missed you so much," she said, planting kisses all over his face.

"Where's Granny?" Peso asked while hugging her tightly.

"She's laying down. Granny doesn't feel too good," Mya explained.

"Come on, Princess. Let's go check on her." He carried Mya into his mother's bedroom.

"Hey, Momma Bear. You okay?"

"Yes, baby boy. I'm fine. This lil' cold I got is kicking my butt, though." She coughed. "Come give Momma some love."

She opened her arms for a hug. As soon as Peso wrapped his arms around her, Mya jumped in, too.

"Group hug!" she yelled, and the three of them shared a hug while laughing.

The three spent the remainder of their day eating ice cream and watching movies. After Mya and Ms. Mary fell asleep, Peso went into the living room and rolled a blunt. The minute he sparked it up, the doorbell rang. He walked to the door and looked through the peephole to see Mariah standing there looking like a diva. When Peso opened the door, she grabbed him up in a hug so tight that he almost dropped his blunt.

"Oh my Gawd, baby daddy! You're back!"

"Sounds like you missed me," Peso jokingly flirted.

"Maybe I did, maybe I didn't," Mariah replied as she walked past him to enter the apartment.

"Where's my baby?"

"She's in the bed sleep with my mom. They look so peaceful. Please don't wake her. I'll bring her home in the morning."

"I gotta work early tomorrow, Tyler. So, you're gonna have to bring her when I get off instead. I bet they look so adorable. I'ma go take a picture of them."

"Do it for the 'Gram," Peso laughed, mocking her.

The second Mariah disappeared into the back of the apartment, his phone alerted him of a Facetime call from Princess. He quickly answered and smiled when he saw her face.

"Wassup? How you feeling?"

"Hey, stranger. I'm fine. I see you don't know me anymore."

"How can I forget you? I've missed you like crazy."

"It don't seem like it," she retorted.

"Don't be like that, bae. I just got back from outta town this afternoon. I spent the day with my mom and daughter. Now, I'm about to spend the night with my lady if she's not busy."

He flashed that smile that always left her weak.

"So now I'm ya lady? Check you out," she responded, blushing.

"So wassup? You busy or nah?"

"Never too busy for you," Princess told him. "What time are you coming?"

"I'ma leave my mom's crib in five minutes."

"Okay, bae. I'll see you when you get here."

When Peso ended the call, he looked up from his phone to see Mariah staring at him.

"What?" he asked, feeling like he got caught doing something he shouldn't have been doing.

"You're such a man whore. You need to change your ways, Tyler. You have a daughter, for crying out loud."

"I really like shawty, Riah. She may be the one who gets me to change my ways," he replied, then walked to his mother's bedroom to kiss his sleeping daughter on the forehead before he and Mariah left the apartment.

***

Hitta walked inside the Royal Estate and hugged Katrina, who was sitting at the dining room table drinking a glass of wine.

"Mission complete," he told her while taking a seat.

"Good job. I see things went well. Nick Lafrenz was a great score. I really hate it had to be him. He was like family until he crossed Rich," Katrina reflected. "Nick and Rich have known each other since they were teenagers. Rich saw his vision and gave him a five-million-dollar loan to start his business. Nick took off and became one of the biggest jewelers around. The deal was for Nick to pay Rich back when he got on his feet, but when the feds grabbed Rich, Nick felt like he no longer had to pay his debt," she explained.

"They say money is the root of all evil. I'm just glad the sucker got what was coming to him."

"You and me both. Are you hungry? Would you like something to drink?" Katrina offered.

"I'm cool on the food. I'll take some Henny, though. Can I smoke in here?" he asked, pulling out some weed and a package of Backwoods.

"You sure can. Let me get that Henny for you."

She pushed out the chair, walked over to the bar area, and reached for a glass to prepare the drink. Hitta wasn't immune to the swing in her ass. He shook his head, shaking the spell that Katrina was putting him in. He was aware that she was off limits, period. But Hitta couldn't stop thinking what it would be like to suckle those delicious breasts that were damn near spilling out of her blouse.

Katrina came back to the table and took her seat. She noticed the look on his face. He was fighting it, his craving for her. At this point, Katrina knew all she had to do was bid her time, and she would be fucking the shit out of Hitta in no time. She had to be careful, though, because that thing called *loyalty* might get in her way. She had to remind herself that Hitta and her husband were men of honor.

"Damn, you rolled that shit quick." She laughed as she watched Hitta light the blunt and take a puff.

"Kat, there is something I wanna discuss," Hitta said while internally fighting himself to keep from staring at her big titties.

"Speak your mind, handsome," Katrina replied, openly flirting with him.

Ignoring her comment, Hitta tried to keep it strictly business.

"I need a way to clean the money you have sitting in that account for Peso and me. So, I was thinking you could give us a label deal. The good thing is you don't have to come out of pocket. You're just giving us money that's already ours."

He looked Katrina directly in her eyes.

"I gotta secure this bread," he continued. "So when I buy shit for my mom, the feds can't fuck with her. You give us an imprint under Royalty Records; we sign for the twenty-five mil you have to give us. We'll then give you three albums. You distribute it through your company and take twenty percent. My only request is that we keep all masters and full control of our music, album releases, and shit like that," Hitta said, laying his cards out on the table.

"That doesn't sound like a bad idea, and I know Rich wouldn't deny you anything. So, I guess you got yourself a deal. Do y'all have an artist?"

"We're gonna focus on Peso first. My brother is a musical god."

"Sounds good to me. Here is what I need you to do. You and Peso have to go to the bank and open up a business account for the label."

"Say no more. That will get done ASAP."

"Well, in that case, welcome to Royalty Records!" Katrina said as she raised her glass.

***

"Bae, I passed the exam! I'm officially a registered nurse at Lutheran Medical Center! I start tomorrow!" Princess exclaimed, unable to control her excitement.

She and Peso were sitting inside of Peter Luger's Steakhouse in Brooklyn having dinner.

"Congrats, love. I'm happy for you." Peso reached for her hand to squeeze. "Excuse me," he said, stopping the waitress who was passing by their table. "Bring me your finest bottle of champagne."

"Coming right up, sir," the waitress replied, then walked off to fulfill his request.

"You didn't have to do that, bae," Princess said, thinking his gesture wasn't necessary.

"I know I didn't have to, but I wanted to. We're celebrating. Don't worry, though. Soon you won't have to work. You can stay home all day and be my sexy lil' housewife." He smiled.

"I'll pass on that one, bae. Momma gotta get her own coins. One day, I'ma have a chain of hair salons and a bunch of properties for sale." My hair and eyelash line are doing well, so at the end of the quarter I'm going to invest my profit into my first property.

Peso smiled again. He loved the fact that she was so passionate about her dreams.

The two of them ate, sipped champagne, and talked for a while before heading out of the restaurant. It was eleven o'clock by the time they got back to East New York. After pulling in front of her building, Peso put the car in park.

"Thank you, baby. I really enjoyed myself tonight. And I'm a lil' tipsy." She leaned over to kiss Peso on the lips.

"You don't have to thank me for doing what I'm supposed to do. I really hate that the night has to end so early," he added.

"It doesn't if you don't want it to," she replied seductively.

"What you trying to say, shawdy?" he asked.

"I'm tryna say that I'm tipsy, horny, and I want you."

With that, she winked, grabbed her purse, and attempted to exit the car. Before she could exit the vehicle, Peso was standing at the passenger side door to help her out. Princess placed one last kiss on his cheek and then made her way toward the building. Peso just stood there watching her. When she reached the door to the building, Princess turned around.

"You coming or what?"

"Hell yeah, I'm coming," he responded with a smile.

Once they got inside, Princess went on the attack. She was all over Peso, pulling at his pants. Finding his zipper, she pushed it down and inserted her hand through the opening.

"I want you so bad, Tyler." Princess moaned while gently stroking his manhood. "You have to be gentle with me, baby. It's been a while," she confessed.

"Don't worry, ma. I got you," he replied softly.

Peso worked until he had stripped her of all her clothing, then he stood taking in her beautiful body. She was the epitome of perfection. Peso couldn't wait to get his hands on her. Laying her on her back, he began at her feet, suckling her toes one at a time and causing her to whimper. He kissed her thighs, moving to the apex of her body. He planned to make her beg for him. He teased the bend of her body with his tongue, sucking and biting her nipples. Teasing her with his fingers, he played with the center of her body. Peso grew even more aroused by her wetness. Princess reached for him, wanting to show him what she had made him wait for was worth it, but Peso gently pushed her hand away. This was about satisfying her. He moved lower and kissed her mound, which made her jump from the contact.

"Please don't tease me, baby," Princess moaned, moving her body against his mouth.

Ignoring her, Peso placed her legs over his shoulders, leaned in, and softly licked her clitoris. Princess responded by putting her hands on his head as she arched her back and moaned his name. Once he found her center, he didn't let her go. Princess wrapped her legs around his head and tightened every muscle in her body. Peso continued his attack until she shook, screaming his name.

"Ahhh, baby! Please stop! I can't take it anymore," Princess begged with her eyes squeezed shut, but her pleading only gave him fuel to keep going.

He brought her to a second stunning climax. Still, that didn't stop him from feasting.

"Don't run, baby. Daddy got you," Peso said, raising his head slightly to see her face as he licked her into a frenzy.

"Oh my Gawd! I'm coming again, babe!"

Focused on bringing her to her third orgasm, Peso licked and sucked on her until she exploded, leaving Princess in a sexual daze of pure pleasure. Then he climbed on top of her. She was soaking wet. Her pussy spoke to him as he slowly entered her. Peso felt every inch of her love box. He began stroking her slowly, wanting her to feel every inch of him and trying to maintain control himself.

"Oh my Gawd, Ty. What are you doing to me? I'm about to come again!" she screamed as her body shook uncontrollably. "I can't take it like this no more, daddy. I wanna ride. Please let me ride it," she begged.

"Don't tap out on me, baby. I'm just getting started," Peso told her before swiftly flipping positions, giving his lady what she requested.

He loved staring into her eyes as she slid down on his rod. He couldn't imagine, nor did he want to be anywhere else except for inside of her. They continued to go at it until they were both exhausted. Afterwards, Princess fell asleep in his arms.

***

Hitta left the Royal Estate feeling great. Things were coming together perfectly for him and Peso, and he was proud of himself for not giving in to the urge to fuck the boss' wife. Katrina didn't make it easy, dressing and looking like she did. However, Hitta wouldn't fool himself to believe if he fucked her once, it would be enough for him. He knew that was impossible. Katrina *looked* like she had some good pussy, and that was the problem.

Hitta shook the thoughts from his head. Things were going well, but the devil never sleeps. He was always ready to knock on the door, upsetting everything. Sure enough, the bastard made an appearance.

Hitta got a call from some chick telling him that Reem was laid up in the hospital all shot up. He called Peso several times but didn't get an answer. Knowing this couldn't wait, he drove twenty miles over the specd limit to get to the hospital.

When Hitta arrived at Lutheran Medical Center, he saw Reem's aunt, sister, and some female he hadn't seen before standing around in the waiting area. All three women were in tears. Kamilla, Reem's older sister, walked over to Hitta and hugged him. Her eyes were bloodshot red, and she looked as if she hadn't slept in days. Hitta consoled her and wiped her tears away with his fingertips.

"How is he?"

"We don't know yet. He's still in surgery. They say he was shot three times—twice in his chest and once in the face."

"Kamilla, you know me, and you have my word that whoever did this is gonna pay. Where did this happen?"

"They found him in an elevator in Malboro," she responded.

Hitta shook his head in disgust because he knew it was some foul play involved. The pair walked over to Reem's aunt, who embraced Hitta warmly. Next, Kamilla introduced him to the female unknown to him. Her name was Sonia, and she was Reem's lady. Hitta hugged her and then took a seat next to both ladies. He pulled out his phone and called Peso, but once again, he got his voicemail. So, he decided to send him a text to let him know what happened to Reem.

After waiting for what felt like hours, a doctor approached them, removing his surgical cap. Everyone waited with bated breath for the doctor to speak. He directed his attention to Reem's aunt.

"Excuse me, are you the mother of Kareem Daniels?"

"No, I'm his aunt," she replied somberly.

"Okay, well, I have to be completely honest with you. Kareem's body has been through a lot, so I can't make any promises that he will make a full recovery. He's in a medically induced coma, and the machines are keeping him alive for the moment. We are trying to give his body a chance to rest and recover. If there is any hope for recovery, this is the best way to start. I don't know how long we will keep him this way, but it's his best chance. One of the bullets missed his heart by a half-inch," the doctor shared with them.

"Can we please see him? He needs to know his family is here. He's a fighter. It will give him strength," Kamilla explained, her eyes filled with tears.

"Yes, you can see him, but I ask that there only be two of you in the room at a time. He will be able to hear you, and I don't need him getting too excited. The more rest his body can get now, the better. Follow me," the doctor said, leading the way to ICU.

When the family entered Reem's room, their hearts broke at the sight of him hooked up to the many different machines with tubes running from all over his body. Hitta hated to see his comrade like this. Not too long ago, Hitta was laid up the same way, minus the broken jaw.

"I can't stand to see him like this. I'ma let you ladies spend time with him. I'll come back," Hitta said.

Kamilla could see the pain in his eyes.

"I will keep you posted on his condition. You be safe out there, Amir," she told him.

"I will," he said before exiting the room.

Hitta's mind was racing one hundred miles per hour. He just hit the biggest lick of his life and couldn't even enjoy it because his comrade was laid up in a hospital bed fighting for his life. He could only pray that Reem pulled through.

When he got in his car, he checked his phone. He had three missed calls from Ashley and a few text messages from Katrina. He lit up a blunt before opening the first message from Katrina:

Kat: Hitta, the contracts are ready to be signed. You can come pick up the checks for you and Peso. Luxury Records will officially be an imprint under Royalty Records once you've signed on the dotted line.

The next two messages took him by surprise. They were pictures of Kat standing in the mirror naked. He stared at them, going over her body with his eyes. *Gotdamn!* Hitta had to admit Katrina looked good, and from the way she was posing in the pictures, *she* knew she looked good, too. Her breasts were firm, and her ass was taut. Feeling his erection stirring in his pants, Hitta rubbed his hand across the hard bulge. He shook his head. Hitta was glad Katrina hadn't shown herself like this in his presence. Without a doubt, he knew he would have fucked the shit out of her. But then he reminded himself that this was his mentor's wife. Royal Rich trusted him, and he would not give him a reason not to. Hitta was well aware of the consequences of such a breach. No pussy was worth dying for, but that didn't stop him from going over her pictures once more before sending a reply to her first message.

Hitta: *Thank you, Kat. I'm happy to be a part of something so special. Peso and I will be there to sign on the dotted line tomorrow. By the way, I believe you texted those pics to the wrong person. I don't think they were for my eyes.*

The last part of the text was Hitta's poor attempt at fighting back. Seconds later, he received another message.

Kat: *They were for your eyes. Did you like them?*

He chose not to respond, leaving her to her own conclusions. Next, he pulled up the messages from Ashley and called her back. She picked up after the second ring,

"Hey, baby, I've been calling you all day. Did you hear about Reem?" she asked.

"Yeah, I'm just leaving the hospital. But check it, pack your shit. You're moving out of them funky-ass projects today. It's about to get real ugly over there." Hitta said.

"Okay, but are you good, though? How's Reem?" Ashley asked, worried about Hitta's mental state as much as Reem's physical state.

"I'm okay under the circumstances. Just worried about bro. He's in a coma, and the doctors aren't sure what's going to happen next. But, anyway, I'm about to head your way. I'm hungry. Did you cook?"

"No, but I can if you want, though."

"Nah, just be dressed. We gonna go grab something to eat. I'll be there in twenty minutes."

Chapter 11

Seven days later, Reem slowly opened his eyes. His vision was so blurry he could barely see. His mouth was dry, and his jaw wired shut. His body ached so bad that he felt too weak to move. Beyond all of the cons, Reem was grateful when he realized all that pain meant he was still alive. After being in a coma for a week, he woke up with murder on his mind. He remembered what happened to him clear as day. While in the coma, all he saw was Bricks' face, and he kept hearing Bricks' last words: *B-Gunnz said ya number has been called. Flatline, homie.*

Reem tried to move but felt a sharp pain in his chest. So, he kept his body still. Once the pain passed, he tried to move again. Turning to his right, he saw Hitta and Peso in the corner of the room sleeping. He mustered a smile, realizing even more how Hitta and Peso felt about him. Reem pushed his body to sit up. The pain showed up again, but this time, he ignored it. The sound of Reem moving in the bed woke Peso.

"Oh shit!" Peso moved quickly to stop Reem from hurting himself. "Relax, bro. I'ma get the doctor. Hitta, get up. Reem is awake," he said before leaving the room.

Peso returned shortly with the doctor, who ordered them to leave so they could run some tests on Reem.

The following day, Reem was moved out of the intensive care unit to a room on the second floor. When Hitta walked into the room, Sonia, Reem's lady, was sitting on the side of

Reem's hospital bed. Hitta greeted her, then approached his comrade.

"You a'ight, beloved?" Hitta asked.

Reem shook his head slowly, letting Hitta know he was good. With his jaw wired shut, he could not speak. Reem pointed to a folded piece of paper on the nightstand next to the bed. Hitta picked it up, and after reading the names on the paper, he looked at Reem with a confused expression.

"Bricks did this to you, bro?" Hitta asked in disbelief.

Reem nodded.

"Say less. I'll be back later. Get ya rest, bro."

As Peso walked through the hospital's entrance with Princess, Hitta was leaving.

"I was just about to call you, bro," Hitta said as the two men exchanged a one-armed hug.

"You don't gotta call me now. I'm already here. Wassup? Talk to me."

"We gonna talk in the car," Hitta responded, then turned to Princess. "You must be the lovely lady who has my brother open," he joked. "I'm Hitta."

"Hi. I'm Princess," she replied before turning her attention to Peso. "You open, huh?" she asked, blushing the entire time.

"I've heard so much about you that it feels like I know you already. He's a good man. Keep him happy, sis. He deserves it," Hitta told her.

"Trust me, I will. He better keep me happy, too. You know it's a two-way street." She smiled, then addressed Peso. "Babe, let me get to work. Are you picking me up later?"

"I don't know, ma. Today might be hectic. Just take my car. I'll have bro drop me off at ya crib later."

Peso handed his car keys to her before kissing her goodbye. Hitta and Peso then exited the hospital, hopped in Hitta's Porsche, and pulled off.

"Yo, bro, what did you need to holla at me about?" Peso asked.

"Bricks is the one who shot Reem."

"Which Bricks? Blood Bricks?" Peso asked, confused and not believing what he was hearing.

"Yeah, Blood Bricks. The sucka-ass nigga who's supposed to be his man. Reem can't talk because his shit is still all wired up, but he wrote son's name on a piece of paper."

"So, fuck it. Let's go make them projects look like the Fourth of July," Peso snarled.

"You know we gonna do that."

The minute those words left Hitta's mouth, a black Ford Taurus signaled for them to pull over.

"You dirty, bro?" Hitta quickly asked Peso.

"Yeah, I got this lil' pocket rocket on me," Peso answered. "It's in my briefs, though. Pull over. We good."

"You sure?"

"Yeah, I'm Gucci," Peso replied.

Once Hitta pulled the car over, two plainclothes detectives hopped out the Taurus and approached the vehicle—one cop on each side.

"What seems to be the problem, officer?" Hitta asked after rolling down his window.

"Oh shit! When the fuck they let you out?"

Hitta's blood began to boil as soon as he locked eyes with the cop. It had been years since the two men had a run-in. Detective Brown was a dirty cop who had it out for the Murda Team years back when they first took over Coney Island's dope trade. Every case he put on a member of the group ended up getting dismissed because his star witness always turned up dead or disappeared right before trial. Detective Brown made it to the top of the Murda Team's hit list when he murdered their comrade, Relo, in cold blood.

"I ain't tryin' to kick it with you, Brown. Why you pull me over?" Hitta asked, becoming agitated.

"Come on, I know you niggas ain't still salty over what happened to Relo. The past is the past. Wassup, Peso?"

"Fuck you, pig!" Peso replied.

"What did you pull me over for, Brown?" Hitta asked again.

"I heard you were back and wanted to personally let you know I'm on ya ass. You niggas have a good day," he replied, then both detectives walked back to their vehicle.

"One day I'ma kill that nigga," Hitta said as he pulled off.

"Nah, *we* gonna kill that nigga," Peso replied.

Ten minutes later, they pulled up in front of Hitta's mother's building. As they were entering the lobby, Breeze was stepping out of the elevator.

"Oh shit, my guys!" He greeted them with the U.G.F. handshake.

"Heart of a Gorilla." Peso saluted.

"Spirit of a hustler. You know that shit," Breeze replied.

"Where you headed, bro?" Hitta asked.

"Nigga, I came down low to check y'all niggas. I just left ya mom's crib looking for y'all."

"You came just in time. You drove?" Hitta inquired.

"Yeah, I got a lil' renty. What's the word?"

"One of the bros got hit in Malboro. We about to go spin that way. You riding with us?" Hitta asked him.

"What type of dumb-ass question is that? C'mon, we out," Breeze replied with no hesitation.

"Hold on. We gonna go change up, then we out," Hitta told him.

The three of them entered the elevator and rode it to the 7th floor. Hitta's mother was leaving out of her apartment just as they got off the elevator.

"I see you found them, Sha," Ms. Sharon said, referring to Breeze.

"Yeah. When I was leaving, they were coming in the building," he replied.

"Hey, Ma." Peso gave her a hug.

"Hey, baby. How's the little momma?"

"Spoiled!" Peso replied.

"Well, you're the one who spoils her. Amir, I'm going to get your sister. I'll be back."

"A'ight, Ma. Drive safe."

Together, the three men went into the apartment. Peso and Breeze took a seat on the couch while Hitta ran up to his bedroom. Minutes later, he returned to the living room with two shoe boxes and placed them on the table.

"Y'all niggas just sitting there. One of y'all roll something up. I'm tryin' get high before we dip," Hitta told them and disappeared back in his room.

When he returned, he was dressed in an all-black Nike sweatsuit. He tossed a sweatsuit to Peso and handed Breeze a hoodie.

"Peso, that's the sweatsuit you left here, and Breeze, you a big nigga, so you can't fit none of my sweats. But that hoodie should do the job," Hitta said as the two men started changing clothes.

When Hitta opened the shoeboxes, he grabbed his Glock .45, Peso reached for a .40 cal, and Breeze took a blue steel .357. Peso lit the blunt he rolled, and the three smoked before leaving out. Ten minutes later, they pulled up to Malboro Houses in the rental.

"Yo, y'all see them niggas standing in front of the liquor store?" Hitta asked from the front seat while cocking his Glock .45.

"Yeah, but I don't see that nigga, Bricks," Peso responded.

"Me either, but I see Skeeno and a bunch of other niggas that be with Bricks every day. So, them niggas are guilty by association," Breeze added.

"Touch one of ours, we touch ten of theirs," Peso said, exiting the back seat of the rented Chevy Impala. Hitta was right behind him.

The six dudes standing in front of the liquor store were so caught up in their conversation that none of them noticed the two hooded men approaching with guns drawn until the first shot was fired. Peso hit the first dude, his body collapsing to the ground. Hitta followed suit, taking out his target. The rest of the dudes took off running across the street towards the projects, but they couldn't outrun the bullets aimed at them. The two dudes that did make it across the street were cut short by the shells from Breeze's .357. After the mission was complete, they made a clean getaway.

Two Weeks Later...

Hitta walked inside his New York City highrise condo that he now shared with Ashley. After kicking off his sneakers, he headed straight to the minibar to pour himself a drink. Caught up in his thoughts, he didn't hear Ashley creep up behind him.

"You okay, bae?" She wrapped her arms around his waist and rested her head on his back.

"Yeah, I'm cool," he replied, hoping she wouldn't pick up on his sullen mood.

"You never were good at lying to me. What's wrong, Amir? Talk to me. You look like you have the weight of the world on your shoulders."

Hitta sighed before throwing back his head and downing his shot of Hennessy. He immediately poured another one. He knew Ashley wasn't going to let up until he shared what was bothering him. So, he began to vent.

"It's like as soon as shit is going good, the devil knocks on my door. Peso and I just signed a huge label deal with Royalty Records. But this is Peso's dream, not mine. I'm not a rapper. This is a good way to clean my money, though. Plus, I wanna see Peso live his dream so he doesn't have to do this street shit for the rest of his life. We should be celebrating our newfound success, but instead, we are the frontline in all this madness. I need a break, baby girl. That's all."

"Amir, I love you so much, and the thought of losing you really scares me. Get out while you can. These streets don't love you, and you have nothing to prove. You're a legend at a young age. Look at all the shit you've lived through. Look at all you've accomplished. These niggas would die to have the hand you have. Maybe it's time you fall back from the streets. The only things promised is death or a life sentence. I'm riding 'til the wheels fall off, but I ain't tryin' love you from no prison cell. I need you here with me," Ashley confessed.

"Leavin' this shit alone ain't easy."

"Why the hell not, Amir? You ain't doing this shit to survive, because ya money is super long. You're doing this shit for the action, for the thrill."

A knock at the door interrupted their conversation.

"That's Peso, baby girl. Get that for me, please."

"We're gonna finish this convo," she said, cutting her eyes at him before walking to the door.

Peso walked in with a smile like always.

"Hey, sis." He hugged Ashley.

"Wassup, brother? How you been?"

"I'm great."

"Did Mariah move into her place yet?"

"Yeah, they moved in today," Peso responded.

"That's wassup! Lemme call my bitch and congratulate her," Ashley said, leaving the room.

"Wassup, bro?" Peso greeted his best friend.

"More money, more problems. Big said it best, nigga," Hitta replied, giving Peso a pound. "You want a drink, bro?"

"Is a pig's pussy pork? Hell yeah, I want a drink, nigga!"

They both laughed.

"Tell me you got some rollup. I left my Woods in the car," Peso said.

Without responding, Hitta tossed him a pack of Backwoods before walking over to the minibar to grab the bottle of Hennessy and another glass.

"Kat called me earlier and said in two months, Royalty Records is gonna throw a big-ass party to welcome us to the label. You finally got ya shot, bro. You ready?"

"Born ready. I was made for this. All the paperwork for Luxury Records is complete. I had the name copywritten since I was up north."

"We just gotta go to the bank and open up a business account and personal accounts for ourselves," Hitta told him. "We can go handle that in the A.M."

"Nigga, I believe we can do that shit online. On another note, I can focus on music until we settle the score with Murda and that nigga Brick."

"Let me focus on this street shit," Hitta countered. "You just get ya ass in the booth and make some fucking hits."

"Nah, we in this together," Peso said. "Never forget that. I gave Breeze the rest of the work I had in shawdy's spot. We gotta get a plug for when this shit runs out."

"I know, bro. I'm on it. We're gonna keep the bros flooded with work. Oh, I forgot to tell you. I spoke to a realtor like an hour ago. She said she has two properties right next to each other out in Plainfield, New Jersey. We should go check them out. It's time to move our mothers out the hood."

"Let's make a toast, bro," Peso said, holding up his glass. "To more success!"

"To more success!" Hitta repeated as they touched glasses.

Chapter 12

Peso sat at Rico's gravesite in Pine Lawns Cemetery drinking a bottle of Remy Martin Grand Cru and smoking a fat blunt of sour diesel—two of Rico's favorites.

"Damn, big homie, I miss you so much. A nigga wish you and Relo was here to see how far a nigga done come. We rich, bro. I'm talking millions. Niggas done leveled up for real, but none of this money means shit without y'all niggas. Shit is bittersweet. Ya brother and Hitta out here tryin' to kill each other."

Peso vented to his fallen comrade, letting his tears fall freely. So caught up in his pain, he never noticed someone creeping up behind him until he heard the click of the gun.

"Turn around, nigga! You know shooting someone in the back ain't my style, and you better not reach for nothing," the voice threatened.

Damn, I'm slipping, Peso thought to himself.

***

Hitta sat in the Royal Estate's dining room smoking a blunt and waiting for Katrina to finish up what seemed to be an important phone call. After a few minutes, she finally strutted into the room.

"Hey, handsome. Sorry for keeping you waiting," she said with a smile.

"I was starting to think you forgot I was sitting here," Hitta joked. "But let's get down to the reason you called me here."

"I have a job. This isn't a robbery, though. It's a hit." She paused and looked Hitta in the eye. "The job pays five million. You will get two up front and the rest when the job is done. Both checks will be through the label, so the money will be clean."

"Who's the lucky guy?"

"Jay Kelly," Katrina responded.

"Why does that name sound so familiar?"

"He's the police commissioner."

"How did *he* end up on the hitlist?" Hitta inquired.

"Some very important people want him dead, and they're paying top dollar. This may also help Rich get home. You wit' it or nah?" Katrina pressed.

"Hell yeah, I'm down. But this won't be easy. He has more security than the president."

"Everybody has a weakness, Hitta, and we know his. Let's just say Mr. Kelly has a thing for young black hookers. Just be at this location next Monday at ten P.M. sharp." She slid him a piece of paper. "The two million will be wired to you by the end of the night. It will go to your label's account."

"Say no more," Hitta said, then stood to leave.

When he made it to the door, Katrina called to him, closing the distance between them.

"Yeah, wassup?" he asked, thinking he had almost escaped.

Katrina didn't say anything as she stood in front of him. Deciding she would seize the opportunity, she wound her arms around Hitta's broad shoulders, pulled his head down to her face, and kissed him softly on his lips.

"What are you doing?" Hitta asked, attempting to pull her arms from him. "We can't do this, ma."

"Yes, we can. I want you so fucking bad, and I think you want me, too," she replied breathlessly.

"Nah, I ain't doing this. That nigga will kill us," Hitta responded, still trying to remove her arms from his body.

"That nigga ain't here. If you don't tell, I won't," she said with a sly grin.

With her breasts pressed against his chest, his eyes fell upon them for a split second. Hitta quickly redirected his gaze, but it was too late. Katrina had seen him.

"You want to suck and kiss them, don't you?" she asked, pulling the material back to reveal her left breast.

Oh my God, Hitta thought to himself.

"No!" he damn near yelled.

"Baby, there are not many men who say no to me, and you are *not* going to be the first," Katrina informed him while running her hand over his dick as she kissed and suckled his neck.

Hitta groaned from the pleasurable feeling.

"How about this time I send you away with food for thought," Katrina said, smiling.

Hitta didn't know what she meant until she dropped to her knees in front of him and unzipped his pants. At this point, Hitta was helpless. It was like watching a movie, and he was the headliner.

"I knew you wouldn't disappoint," Katrina mused, looking at the size of his dick.

As she proceeded to lick the mushroom head, Hitta gave in to what she was doing. Katrina took all of him inside her mouth. Her goal was to suck his dick so good that he would be back begging her for it. Hitta's mouth fell open, struggling to get air into his lungs. Any thoughts of his loyalty to Rolex Rich went out the window. He told himself this would be one and done. What could be the harm in this?

Katrina went on the attack until Hitta exploded in her mouth. She didn't stop until she sucked him dry. When it was over, Hitta's pants were down around his knees. He quickly reached for them, pulling his pants up and zipping them.

"That dick was good, baby," Katrina said, complimenting him while wearing that same sly grin. "I can't wait until we fuck," she added.

"I don't know what you're used to, but I'ma act like this shit never happened, Kat. You have a good day," he said before leaving, thinking his statement would help him regain control of what their relationship was going to be.

"Whatever you say, baby," Kat responded, having heard it all before.

After hopping in the Porsche, Hitta banged on the steering wheel with his fist as he sped away from the estate.

You fuckin' stupid, he chided himself.

Rolex Rich would have him killed instantly if he found out about what went down. However, Hitta had to concede that Katrina gave the best head he ever had.

Looking at the time, he saw that it was still early. Since he was already in Long Island, he decided to stop by the cemetery to visit Rico. It was where he went when he needed to clear his head.

***

Peso slowly turned around to see who the voice belonged to behind him.

"Long time no see," Peso said calmly.

"Yeah, 'cause you chose sides, nigga," Matt Murda spat.

"Right is right, homie! We told you that T.K. was off-limits, and you still tried to put the press on him. But none of that shit matters now. Bust ya gun, nigga."

"My issue ain't with you, pretty boy. Call that nigga Hitta and tell him to meet you here, and you better act normal. Do any funny shit, and I'ma rock you," Murda ordered.

Peso laughed. "If you got an issue with my brother, you got an issue with me, homie. You better off bustin' ya gun. You know I ain't gonna make that call."

Soon as those words left Peso's mouth, Hitta approached with his gun aimed at Matt Murda.

"You might wanna lower that strap, homie," Hitta instructed Matt Murda.

"You might wanna lower ya strap, also," a female voice behind Hitta advised, but he remained unfazed.

"Amir, put the gun down," the female repeated.

The voice belonged to Timah, Matt Murda's longtime girlfriend.

"Timah, you know me better than that. I ain't lowering my strap until Murda lowers his."

"Matt, lower ya gun. Are you guys crazy? Rico must be turning in his grave right now," Timah said, scolding the men. "Y'all are family."

"Nah, we used to be family," Murda told her while lowering his gun.

Once he put his gun away, Hitta did the same. Timah followed suit.

"Out of respect for Rico, y'all not going to do this here," Timah said, looking around at all of them, meaning what she said.

"I ain't gonna bring the drama to you right here, but next time you aim ya strap, you better use it. Because the day you're on the opposite end of my strap, I'ma kill you," Peso said firmly while locking eyes with Murda.

"You know death don't scare me, homie! We can take this to a different location."

"Anytime, anyplace," Hitta said, sizing him up.

Peso pulled Hitta back.

"C'mon, bro, we not gonna disrespect Rico. We gonna get our chance to dance. Believe that!"

Those were the last words exchanged before Peso and Hitta walked away, leaving Matt Murda and Timah behind.

***

"Royal, you have a visit!" the C.O. yelled over the loudspeaker.

Rolex Rich got himself together, then headed off to the C.O.'s bubble.

"I'm ready," Rich told him.

The C.O. got up to unlock the iron bars.

"Enjoy ya visit, Royal."

"Good lookin'," Rich replied, stepping in the corridor with the other inmates who were headed to their visits.

They all praised Rich like he was a god, but he remained humble even with his celebrity status.

When Rich stepped on the visit floor, he couldn't hold back his big Kool-Aid smile when he saw Hitta sitting at the table dressed in designer gear and dripping in jewelry. Rich approached the table, and they greeted each other warmly.

"What's the word, big homie?" Hitta asked, glad to see him. He fought to put the image of Katrina sucking his dick out of his head.

"Glad to see you, baby boy! Look at all that drip around ya neck. I see you shining. I told you that I'd make you rich in no time. You really doing major work."

"I try, I try," Hitta replied humbly.

"To try is to fail, young nigga. You doing it," Rich said, and the two men nodded in agreement.

"I ain't know what you wanted, so I got you a lil' bit of everything."

Hitta was referring to the food and snacks he purchased from the vending machine. Rich opened a bag of M&M peanuts and threw a few in his mouth.

"Hitta, I appreciate all that you and Peso have been doing. You kept ya word, and I've kept mine. That shows we're both honorable men. That being said, I have something that needs to be done. This is a lil' more serious, though."

"I spoke to your wife already," Hitta told him. "Consider it done. We not even gonna waste time speaking on that. What's already understood doesn't need to be explained. I never let you down before, so I damn sure ain't 'bout to start letting you down now."

Although Hitta was speaking genuinely, he felt like a fraud and vowed at that moment there would never be anything between him and Katrina ever again.

Rich just smiled at his response.

"Well then, let me change the subject. Welcome to Royalty Records. Luxury Records is the first imprint under my label."

"Thanks for putting together such a great contract. Peso is gonna shut the industry down, bro. That nigga got some heat. I don't think the game is ready for my nigga. We about to take shit over, believe that."

"And y'all gonna make a lot of money while doing it. I wanna see you win, Hitta, for real," Rich said sincerely.

The two of them sat for another hour or so until the C.O. announced the visit was over.

***

With his mother in the passenger seat, Peso pulled into the driveway of a large structure located in North Plainfield, New Jersey. The area was quiet and filled with beautiful homes.

"Tyler, whose house is this?" Ms. Mary asked, looking around. "This shit is huge."

"Come on, Ma. We'll talk inside," Peso replied, smiling.

"I'm not going anywhere until you tell me whose house is this."

Peso and Ms. Mary went back and forth until Shoota pulled up in his BMW.

"Wassup, big bro?" He greeted Peso with a pound.

"Ain't shit. Tryin' get Mommy out of the car, but she ain't moving until I tell her whose crib this is," Peso responded with a chuckle.

Shoota laughed, knowing what obstacle Peso was up against.

"Mommy is bugging, but this shit is beautiful, bro," he commented.

"Momma, come on, please. I have somewhere to be in less than two hours," Peso pleaded with her.

"Tell me who this house belongs to," Ms. Mary inquired for the umpteenth time, refusing to budge.

"Ma, it's yours! I didn't buy this with dirty money either, so you can accept it."

"So how the hell did you pay for this if yo' ass don't have a job?"

"I took your advice and followed my dream. I signed a label deal with Royalty Records. Me and Amir have our own record label, Ma."

Ms. Mary couldn't hide her excitement.

"I'm so proud of you, baby boy," she said with tears in her eyes.

She finally got out of the car, wrapping her arms around her son. Shoota stood there taking pictures of his mother and brother to put on his Instagram page.

Peso led the way, and Ms. Mary almost fainted when she stepped inside. She instantly fell in love with the six-bedroom, seven-bathroom, six thousand square foot custom-built home.

"And guess what, Momma? You won't be lonely because Amir bought Ms. Sharon that beautiful house across the street," Peso said with a smile.

The joy he felt being able to buy his mother a home was unexplainable. It was a dream come true for both of them.

Chapter 13

A week later, Malboro Projects was crowded. The beautiful spring weather had people out enjoying the sun. The block was alive with activity, and several young men stood in front of the buildings. The sun had just set, but the kids were still running around playing tag and manhunt. Bricks stood at the lobby door kicking it with a bunch of his homies, drinking Hennessy, and watching his workers serve the fiends.

Since Reem wasn't around, Bricks was like a hood celebrity. He had his side of the project in a frenzy. He was jeweled up, the gold reflecting his success on the street. The soldiers around him were all ears as he talked his shit.

"Niggas ain't putting that pain in like us, blood," Bricks declared. "Y'all think Reem had shit poppin' out here? I'ma show niggas what's really good, and anybody who ain't with us is straight food."

Bricks stopped talking shit when he noticed a light-skinned hunny walking into the building. As she passed the group of goons and entered the lobby, they all admired her petite figure.

"I'll be back. I'm on her body," Bricks said, quickly following her into the elevator.

Little did he know, his thirst for the female saved him.

Two dirt bikes could be heard riding through the projects. The riders were both dressed in all black. Shoota and Heat heard about what happened to Reem and decided to take matters into their own hands. As soon as they heard that Hitta and Peso pushed the button on the Bloods, they were the first to put in some work. Even though Reem wasn't a member of the U.G.F., he was still family. The young boys had murder on their minds and big guns in their waistbands.

A Blood named Moe was the first to notice the two dirt bikes.

"Who the fuck is these niggas?" he asked Dino, the homie that took the floor when Bricks walked off.

Dino dropped his cup of Hennessy when he saw the matching .9mm.

"It's a hit!" Dino shouted, diving to the ground.

Shoota was the first to pull the trigger, then Heat followed up.

"Gorilla Gang, muthafuckers!" they yelled out.

The whole project seemed to stop moving at the sound of the rapid gunfire, the smell of gunpowder filling the air. Moe and Dino both took headshots. Their comrades tried to make a great escape, but shells from both guns chopped them down quickly.

***

It was 10P.M. sharp. Police Commissioner Jay Kelly exited the small Queens townhouse, making his way to his Escalade where his driver awaited him. As Mr. Kelly moved closer to the truck, Hitta slipped from behind the brushes, his gun aimed at his head. The poor guy didn't even get a chance to turn around.

BOOM!

The bullet hit him in the back of the head, sending his body to the pavement. The driver heard the shot and attempted to exit the truck, but Peso pulled up beside him in a rental car and fired twice, each bullet hitting their target. Hitta jumped in the passenger seat, and they took off.

An hour later, they were back in Coney Island inside one of their spots.

"Mission complete, bro." Peso gave Hitta some dap.

"And we're both two and a half million dollars richer," Hitta responded with a smile.

"Kat's gonna wire the rest of that paper in the morning. But, yo, you never came and took ya half of the jewels from that last lick."

"'Cause I know that shit is in good hands. Ain't like we doing anything with them diamonds and bricks of gold. All that shit is for a rainy day. But just know I'm coming for my half of that watch collection. You ain't low, nigga," Peso said, grinning.

"Nigga, you know where them shits at. Whenever you ready, they're at the crib for you," Hitta replied, passing Peso the blunt and then standing. "Let me slide up outta here. I need to go shower and relax."

"Yeah, I gotta pick Princess up from work. So, I'ma slide, too," Peso said, giving Hitta a pound. "Give me that strap, bro. I'ma get rid of these joints. We can't be moving around with these hot-ass guns."

Hitta handed over the gun to Peso.

"I love you, bro. Be careful with them joints, for real."

"I love you more, bro. Don't worry. I'ma get rid of these shits as soon as I leave here," Peso replied as Hitta walked out the door.

***

Stepping inside of his condo, Hitta saw that all the lights were on. He shook his head because he hoped Ashley would be sleeping. All he wanted to do was wash the gunpowder off and slide in the bed without her asking a bunch of questions.

When he walked into the bedroom, Ashley was sitting on the bed with rollers in her hair, smoking a blunt, and watching *Love & Hip-Hop*. He greeted her with a kiss on the lips.

"Sup, baby girl?"

"Hey, babe. Ya plate is in the microwave."

"A'ight, thank you. I'ma jump in the shower first, though," he said while removing his clothes, then headed to the bathroom.

"Everything okay, Amir?" Ashley asked. Her woman's intuition was kicking in.

"Yeah, everything is healthy," he replied dryly.

The thing with Katrina was replaying in his mind yet again.

"There you go lying again," she shot back with an attitude.

Ashley could be relentless when she wanted to know something.

"Fuck I gotta lie for? I just told you everything is healthy," he said, raising his voice.

"Don't fuckin' get loud with me, Amir. I can't help but worry about you. When you out in them streets doing God knows what, I'm here praying you make it home. Am I wrong for that? Am I wrong for loving you?"

Hitta didn't respond.

"You walk in our home smelling like gunpowder. I'm just afraid one day I'ma lose you." She started crying.

Hitta hated seeing her so upset. It crushed him. He was so used to her being strong that sometimes he forgot about her emotions. This was the reason he kept things to himself.

"Baby girl, I ain't going nowhere," he reassured her.

"You sound so sure about that, Amir, but you don't know when God is going to call ya number. Everybody has an expiration date," Ashley responded, trying to get him to understand.

"Yeah, but I ain't gonna expire no time soon."

"Do you realize what you do for a living? You may not tell me shit, but I know you have blood on ya hands. Ever since Reem got shot, every day when I turn on the news, it's more bodies dropping in those projects. Looking over your shoulder every day is no way to live. God has a bigger plan for you, bae."

"Ash, you preaching to me ain't gonna change shit! So, miss me with that 'God's plan' shit, please. Where the fuck was God when I needed him, huh? Where was God when niggas killed Rico? Where was God when them crooked-ass cops killed Relo? Where was He when niggas killed T.K.? Where was God when you had that miscarriage? Where is God when these babies who never had a chance to sin get diagnosed with these diseases and shit? You sitting here telling me about God's plan. I'm living His plan, Ashley. This shit is my reality," Hitta ranted without taking a single breath.

Ashley stood up from the bed.

"Instead of cursing God, you should be thanking Him. God is the reason you woke up from that coma. So, whatever beef you have with God, you better patch it up."

"Nah, baby girl, my will to live and my thirst for revenge got me out that coma."

Ashley cut her eyes at him.

"Listen, ma, it's been a long day. I wanna shower, eat, smoke a blunt, and hold you for the rest of the night. Can I do that, please?"

Ashley sat back down on the bed and stared at the TV. No response was good enough for him, so Hitta turned and headed to the shower.

***

Peso pulled up at Lutheran Medical Center and parked his Porsche. He arrived a few minutes before Princess got off work, so he decided to grab a juice out of the vending machine. When he entered the hospital, Princess was standing around talking to a few of her co-workers. The biggest smile appeared on her face when she saw Peso. His smile matched hers. Even without makeup and with her medical scrubs on, her beauty was flawless. Princess walked over to Peso, wrapping him in her arms.

"Hey, baby," she greeted, planting a kiss on his lips.

"Wassup, ma? You ready?"

"You're a little early, but I'm good to go. Let me go get my things."

"Cool. I'ma snatch a juice out this vending machine. You want something?"

"No, thank you, but I am hungry. Can we go to IHOP?"

"We can go wherever you want, my love. I'ma pull the car up in the front."

As usual, the IHOP on Church Avenue was crowded with diners. Customers filled the booths and tables, while others waited in the lobby for an open table. The hostess told the couple that the wait would be approximately thirty minutes, but when Princess's cousin saw them, they got a booth after only waiting five minutes.

"I missed you, Ty. How was your day today?" Princess asked after they placed their order.

"I missed you way more, ma. My day was light. Can't complain about nothing. How was ya day? How was work? Hope they ain't working you too hard."

"Bae, they was slaving me. I been on my feet all day." She pouted.

"Don't worry; I'll rub them for you. Kick ya shoes off," Peso replied, willing to rub his lady's feet in the restaurant.

"I'ma wait till we get to the crib 'cause I might get horny," Princess replied with a wink.

"Oh yeah?" Peso smiled. "On another note, I got an invite to a party that Royalty Records is having, and I need something nice on my arm. You tryna be my date or what?" he asked.

Wanting to surprise her, he left out the details that the party was to welcome him to the label.

"Does a bear shit in the woods?" she joked. "Hell yeah, I'll be ya date! You gotta get me something nice to wear, though."

As soon as the words left her mouth, her energy instantly evaporated. Peso peeped her mood swing.

"What's wrong, ma?"

"My annoying-ass ex just walked in. Let's get our food to go, please. I don't wanna eat here anymore," Princess said, attempting to grab her purse and cell phone from off the booth's seat.

"That nigga ain't running us outta here. We gonna continue to enjoy our night. Fuck that nigga," Peso told her.

"Tyler, he's crazy. Can we just please go? I don't want any drama. Oh my God, he's walking over here."

Princess dropped her face in her hands, which was pointless since he had already spotted her. Peso sized up the stocky dude who was approaching their booth wearing a neck full of jewelry.

"Wassup, Princess? This nigga the reason you ducking my calls?" he asked as if Peso couldn't hear him.

"Shawn, I haven't been answering ya calls 'cause we don't have shit to talk about. We were over a long time ago. Get that through your head."

"Let me talk to you in private."

The dude reached for Princess's arm, but Princess slapped his hand away. Peso stood quickly.

"Dude, don't touch my lady. You doing too much. I ain't gonna tolerate the disrespect. She not checking for you. So, spin!"

"Mind ya business, homie 'fore you get yourself fucked up in here," the dude threatened, then turned his attention back to Princess. "Like I was saying, let me holla at you in private."

He reached for her a second time, but Peso quickly threw a right hook that connected, sending him crashing to the floor.

"Nigga, are you crazy? I told ya bitch ass to step!"

All eyes were on Peso, but he didn't notice because he was in a trance. His temper got the best of him, and he swiftly reached for his .380 and put it to the dude's head.

"You don't even know who you playing with! I will rock you right here, nigga."

"Ty, please, he's not worth you going to jail. Let's just go," Princess begged with tears in her eyes.

The sound of Princess's voice snapped Peso out of his trance, and he put his gun away while looking around. The people looking on were recording the incident on their cell phones. Pulling out a stack of money from his pocket, Peso dropped it on the table before exiting the restaurant with his woman.

***

Hitta stood on his balcony watching the sunrise while smoking a fat blunt of sour diesel. His thick hair was pulled back in a ponytail. Wearing only a pair of Ralph Lauren boxer briefs, his tattooed upper body was on full display. Hitta looked down at the people below—some jogging, some walking their dogs, and others heading to work. The Columbus Circle neighborhood was quiet as usual, making it easy for him to meditate while inhaling the potent weed.

After finishing his blunt, Hitta stepped off of the balcony into his bedroom. The room was dark, but the sun coming up over the horizon helped to illuminate it. He looked at Ashley, who was sleeping peacefully, and planted a kiss on her forehead before leaving the bedroom.

Sleep didn't come easy for Hitta the night before. He had a lot on his mind—Matt Murda being one of them. He wanted to kill his ass yesterday. Katrina was another thing. Hitta couldn't understand what he had been thinking. He loved Rolex Rich and would never have thought of disrespecting him by getting with his lady.

With nothing else to do and needing to clear his head, Hitta began his morning calisthenics. He started with pushups, then pull-ups on the portable pull-up bar he had attached to the wall. Once Hitta finished working out, he took a shower and then went to the kitchen to prepare breakfast for him and his woman. The meal consisted of cheese eggs, French toast, and turkey bacon. He knew Ashley didn't always feel appreciated. So, he tried his best to do the little things to let her know she still meant the world to him even after all this time.

***

Just like Hitta, Peso hadn't gotten much sleep either but for different reasons. After a long-heated argument with Princess, he dropped her off and headed to Mariah's condo. After taking a hot shower, he climbed into the bed with his daughter. He slept on and off for a couple of hours, then watched Mya as she slept peacefully. By 6A.M., Peso was fully dressed and ready to walk out of the door. He called Lee, his engineer, and informed him that he was on his way to the studio. Lee looked at the time and told Peso to stop by a little later, but Peso insisted. Giving in to one of his favorite artist to work with, Lee rolled out of his bed and headed to his studio.

Lee was a white boy who loved hip-hop. He owned a building on Canal Street that he turned into a music studio. Peso was the first artist to ever record in his studio, and the two men had great chemistry. Peso's lyrics and Lee's production behind the machine was a match made in heaven. When Lee first met Peso years ago, he saw a hunger in the young man's eyes that he had never seen before in anyone. Creating music came naturally to Peso. Sometimes he doesn't even use a pen. He broke many nights making hits in Lee's studio.

When Peso walked inside the studio, he was in a zone, determination written all over his face.

"Lee! Wassup, my brother? It's been a while."

Peso greeted him with a pound and a one-armed hug.

"Yeah, it's been a minute, my brother. Since you made me get out of my bed, you better be ready to lay down some legendary shit," Lee responded with a smile.

Peso handed Lee a CD and told him to go to the third track. Then he stepped into the booth. When Lee played the beat, he noticed it was a track he made for Peso years ago. Lee smiled because he knew Peso had a trick up his sleeve.

Inside the booth, Peso held the headphones to his ear, listening to the beat play out. After listening to the entire beat for the fourth consecutive time, he instructed Lee to play it back from the top and let his words ride the beat. Lee sat on the other side of the glass, grinning from ear to ear while bobbing his head to the music.

Three hours later, Peso had laid down four tracks, and Lee loved every one of them. Peso came out of the booth after recording his final track.

"That shit was D-O-P-E," Lee said, complimenting Peso. "What you gonna name this one?"

"*The Real is Back*," Peso responded, then pulled out his iPhone to place a quick call.

***

Hitta was getting dressed when his phone rang. Looking at the screen of his iPhone, he saw Peso's name.

"Top of the morning, bro."

"Top of the top. Where you at?" Peso asked.

"I'm about to leave the crib."

"Kopy. I'm at the studio. Come scoop me."

"I'll be there in twenty minutes. You at Lee's shit, right?"

"Yeah, but check it. Bring some bands with you. We going car shopping," Peso said before ending the call.

Hitta just shook his head and smiled. Peso was back in the studio doing what he did best, and Hitta couldn't wait to hear the tracks he had laid down. Once he put on his sneakers, he kissed Ashley and headed out the door.

True to his word, Hitta pulled up in front of the studio twenty minutes later. Peso slid in the passenger seat of the Porsche and slapped hands with his best friend.

"What's the word, bro?"

"Ain't shit. Had a long-ass night. I think I fucked shit up with Princess," Peso replied honestly.

"What the hell happened?" Hitta asked. "Y'all was just on some lovey-dovey shit."

"I knocked her ex out in IHOP yesterday. And before you chew my head off, just listen. Me and shawdy was enjoying ourselves, and dude walked up to the table. She dismissed him, but this nigga started tryna grab her up and shit. I told dude to step, and he got on some fake gangsta shit. So, I knocked his ass out, then put the strap to him. If Princess didn't remind me where we were, I prolly would have did him in front of everybody. I ain't mean to embarrass her. I just lost my cool."

"She gonna get over that, my nigga. That's a small thing. You prolly just scared her a little bit. Give shawdy some time. You gotta understand, you showed her a side of you that she hasn't seen before, feel me?"

"Yeah, I feel you, bro. But fuck the small talk. Let me plug my phone up so you can hear these tracks I just put together."

Peso hooked up his phone to the aux wire and pressed play. He sat quietly as Hitta listened to all four tracks. Once the final track ended, Hitta looked over to his right-hand man and gave him a pound.

"The industry ain't ready for you, bro. You the best rapper alive, nigga. Play them joints back, and let's go fuck up the car lot," Hitta said, pulling away from the curb.

Chapter 14

The day finally came for Reem to be discharged from the hospital. Despite his jaw still wired shut and being in a lot of pain, the only thing on his mind was revenge. B-Gunnz pushed the button and had Bricks try to take him out, but he survived and would make both men pay for their actions.

Reem paced the floor of his apartment in deep thought. He had to think of a plan fast. B-Gunnz blackballed him and had every Blood in New York City on the hunt for him. Reem was labeled "food," which meant the Bloods would shoot on sight.

Unlocking his iPhone, he sent a text message to his most loyal comrade, Sho-Tyme.

Reem: Peace Blood!
Seconds later, Sho-Tyme replied...
Sho-Tyme: Peace Almighty! What the fuck is going on, Blood?
Reem: You tell me, skrap. I'm hearing B-Gunnz gave y'all niggas the green light on me.
Sho-tyme: Bro, do you think I give a fuck about what B-Gunnz chatting about? Strong or wrong, I'm riding with you 100 percent. I'm under your banner. My loyalty is to you. How you feeling, though, big homie?
Reem: I'm glad to know you're still in my corner. I'm feeling okay. In a little bit of pain, but ain't nothing I can't handle. They gonna need a banana clip to kill me.

Sho-Tyme: LOL! Talk ya shit, big bro.

Reem: But on a more serious note, what's been going on out there since I got hit?

Sho-Tyme: A lot of bloodshed. Niggas coming through, dropping shit left and right. The block is super hot right now. They got police in front of damn near every building. Besides that, the homies been worried about you, bro. Niggas ain't really feeling Bricks. You got a lot of homies that love you, bro. We just waiting on ya call.

Reem: Listen, Blood, y'all keep doing what y'all doing. When the time is right, I will tell you when to move. Until then, I need you to be my eyes and ears. Don't tell nobody that you spoke to me. Niggas will feel my wrath real soon. Just stay safe and buster-free, Blood.

Sho-Tyme: I got you, Blood. Just take the time you need to heal up. I will keep you updated on all that's being said and done on this end. I love you, big homie. Blood up!

Reem sat his phone down and smiled on the inside. Not only because a few homies were still in his corner, but mainly, Hitta and Peso were putting in a lot of work on his behalf. Now it was time for him to even the score.

***

When Peso and Hitta walked into the dealership with the large duffle bags, Rick was all smiles. He knew the two men were there to spend big money.

"My two good friends, what can I do for you guys today?" Rick asked as he shook their hands.

"We're looking for something exotic—two Lambos maybe," Peso replied.

"My friend, New York is no place for a Lamborghini. The roads here are too bad, way too many potholes. I have something better for you. Follow me."

Rick led the way to the showroom floor, approaching two of the most beautiful automobiles Peso had ever seen.

"This right here, my friend, is a Ferrari 458 Spider, fully loaded, Nero Daytona exterior and cuoio interior. You will be the first one with this. No actor, rapper, or athlete has this yet."

"I can't lie, Rick. I love this shit, but I need this in another color," Peso said.

Being the salesman that he was, Rick pulled out his phone and showed Peso a picture of the same car in a different color. Peso handed the phone to Hitta.

"That's it, bro. You better get it before I do," Hitta told him with a smile as he handed Rick back his phone.

"What I just showed you is the same automobile, just in a different flavor. The exterior is white, and the interior is cream. What do you say? Does that color fit you better?"

"I want that one, Rick. When can you have it for me? And what's the tag on it?"

"I can have it here for you in two days, and the tag on it is four hundred large."

"Cool. I'll pay you today. Yo, Hitta, what you got your eyes on?"

"You said this one right here ain't your color, right? Well, I think it's perfect for me," Hitta replied with his trademark smile.

Thirty minutes later, they left the dealer after dropping eight hundred thousand dollars on matched whips yet again.

***

"Holy shit! Matt, my friend, how are you? It's crazy that you showed up today. Your friends just left. Those guys spent close to a million dollars just now," Rick said when Matt Murda walked in his office.

"My two friends?" Matt Murda asked, confused.

"Yeah, Hitta and Peso. They bought two beautiful Ferraris, fully loaded. One of them will be back in a couple days because the color he ordered wasn't in."

Matt Murda just smiled. "I'll be right back. Hold that thought," he said, leaving the office.

Several minutes later, Matt Murda re-entered Rick's office with a small black device and placed it on Rick's desk.

"Rick, do you know what this is?" Murda asked, referring to the device he placed on the desk.

"It looks like a tracking device to me," Rick replied.

"You're a very smart man. That's exactly what it is. I need you to do something for me, Rick."

"Matt, I can't involve myself in your illegal activities."

"Rick, you been involved in illegal shit since I met you. When you had that lil' problem with the Asians, who took care of that? When them gangbangers didn't wanna pay their debt, who collected that paper for you?"

"You did," Rick answered with his head down.

"Do you know why? Because I consider you a friend. Do you consider me a friend, Rick?"

"You know you're my friend, Matt. I just don't wanna be involved in this, man."

"Friends take care of friends, Rick. I need you to come through for me how I always come through for you. Just place the tracking device on the car, and I'll give you fifty thousand for your troubles. Deal?"

Rick wasn't about to turn down a free fifty grand.

"You have a deal, but don't let this come back to me, Matt. I'm begging you."

Matt never gave the confirmation Rick was requesting. He simply turned and walked out of Rick's office.

Good looking out, big homie, he said, looking up to the sky.

***

Peso and his daughter, Mya, were leaving the playground when a group of young boys from his projects stopped him.

"Peso, what's good, big bro?" Isiah, the young boy leading the pack, greeted him.

"Ain't nothing. Wassup with y'all?"

"We would like to make you an offer."

Peso laughed. "What type of offer?"

"We want you to coach us in the Starbury Summer League. I know you a busy man and stuff, but don't nobody wanna give us a chance because we from back here. We rather be playing ball this summer than run around getting into trouble," Isiah stated.

"I'll tell you what. Meet me on the basketball court Sunday morning with y'all squad, and we'll take it from there."

"What time in the morning?"

"Ten on the dot. Don't be late," Peso replied.

He looked at the five young men standing in front of him and knew he couldn't let them down. He wanted to give them a chance that he nor his comrades were never given.

"Ayo, big bro, can we get a few dollars to get us something to snack on?"

Peso pulled out a stack of money and handed the boy a hundred-dollar bill.

"Y'all split that up evenly. I'll see you guys on Sunday," Peso said while picking up Mya, putting her on his shoulders, and heading to his car.

When they made it to Peso's Porsche, he buckled Mya in the passenger seat and then hopped in the driver's seat. He laughed to himself because he knew his mother would have a fit if she saw Mya sitting anywhere other than the backseat.

"Daddy, can we go get some ice cream?" Mya asked.

"We can go anywhere you wanna go, baby girl," Peso replied.

"Anywhere?" she asked, smiling.

"Yes, anywhere."

"Okay, so can we go buy some toys, too? Because I saw this new Barbie house on TV."

"Yes, we can. I know just the place," he told her, then pulled off.

When they got to the highway, Peso's cell phone rang. He looked at the screen and saw it was Princess, so he answered the call.

"Hey you," Princess softly said from the other end of the phone.

"Wassup, shawdy? I'm glad you finally remember me."

"I never forgot you, Ty. I was just upset and needed time to think," she responded honestly.

"Think about what?"

"How about you come get me. We can talk in person."

Peso looked over at Mya, who was smiling while staring at him.

"I have someone I want you to meet. Are you in the mood for ice cream?"

"Sure. It's been a while since I had some cookie dough."

"Cool. Be downstairs in twenty minutes," Peso said, ending the call.

"Baby girl, I want you to meet somebody, and if you don't like this person, you let me know. Okay?"

"Okay, Daddy."

Twenty minutes later, they pulled up in front of Princess's building. She was standing out front dressed in a Nike sweatsuit and a fresh pair of white 270s. Her hair was pulled back into a perfect ponytail, and she wasn't wearing any makeup. Princess was an all-natural beauty; that's one thing Peso loved about her.

Peso got out of the car to greet Princess, kissing her cheek. Then he moved Mya to the backseat. After Princess took the front seat, Peso rounded the car and got in.

"Who is this beautiful young lady?" Princess asked, smiling as she turned to look at Mya, who blushed at the compliment.

"Princess, this is my daughter, Mya. Mya, this is my friend, Princess," Peso said, introducing them.

"Is Princess your real name?" Mya asked.

"Yes, Princess is my real name."

"That's a pretty name, and you're a pretty lady."

"Thank you so much. You have a pretty name, also. Oh my gosh, I love your hair."

"Thank you," Mya said, still smiling."

***

Hitta got back into his Ferrari after making a stop. Ashley was riding shotgun, looking beautiful as ever. Her thick, wavy hair hung down her back, and she was sporting a white Fendi button-up shirt, some soft-white denim Fendi pants, a yellow Fendi belt, and a pair of white and yellow low-top Fendi sneakers with a purse and shades to match.

"Baby, my mom just texted me. Everyone is at Jade's house. Her brother just came home," Ashley told him. "Let's stop over there real fast."

Jade and her brother, Jamel, were Ashley's first cousins. Jamel had been away for five years, so it was only right that Ashley showed her face at his "Welcome Home" gathering.

"They still live in the Stuy on Madison?" Hitta asked.

"Yeah, bae," she responded.

Thirty-five minutes later, they pulled up to Madison Street in the Bed-Stuy section of Brooklyn. A lot of Ashley's family members were out in the front yard when they arrived. Ashley led the way, with Hitta walking behind her. Everyone greeted the two as they made their way inside the house. Along the way, Ashley exchanged hugs with her cousins, aunts, and uncles.

"Where's my mom?" Ashley asked Judy, her aunt.

"She's in the backyard smoking that stink-ass reefer. Who is this handsome young fella here?" Aunt Judy asked, looking Hitta up and down.

"This is Amir. Amir, this is my aunt, Judy," Ashley said, introducing them.

Hitta reached to shake her hand, but she hugged him instead.

"If Ashley brought you over here, that means you're family, 'cause she don't bring nobody around us."

Hitta smiled. "It's nice to meet you, Ms. Judy."

"Boy, call me Aunt Judy," she replied, then turned to go to the backyard. Ashley and Hitta followed.

The backyard was full of family members who were enjoying the beautiful spring weather. Ms. Juanita, Ashley's mother, was the life of the party. When she saw Ashley and Hitta, she couldn't help but smile.

"Amir, come give me some love." She greeted Hitta with open arms.

After engaging in a brief conversation with Ms. Juanita, Hitta walked over to Jamel, who went by the name Melly on the streets.

"Melly, what's the word, boy? Welcome home." Hitta greeted him with a hug.

"Hitta, what's good, my guy. I see you ain't waste no time getting back to the money. You looking good, bro, real talk," Melly replied.

"You know time don't wait for no man. I told you when we were up north that once I touched down, the streets was gonna be mine. You been gone for a while, bro. Shit done changed. These young boys out here wildin' for respect. You an official dude, though. Don't force ya way back out here, and don't try to bully the young off the block. A lot of dudes we were locked up with came home and got picked off because they didn't respect the up-and-coming. Don't go against them. Take them under ya wing, teach them, and feed them."

Hitta spoke sincerely, and Melly soaked up the knowledge.

"What's ya plans now that you're back on the pavement?"

"I just wanna get money, my nigga," Melly replied.

"You my nigga and my lady's favorite cousin, so check this out. I got my hands on some fire coke. The shit is A1. You can step on it, and it's still gonna be ten times better than that bullshit niggas got out here. I'ma front you a brick, but if you fuck up, you will be cut off. I don't do second chances," Hitta told him.

Hitta then dug in his pocket and pulled out five grand. Next, he took the 18-karat gold Rolex off his wrist and handed both the money and the watch to Melly.

"Welcome home, and welcome to the Untouchable Gorilla Family. I'll have that brick dropped off to you by the A.M. Just bring me twenty-eight racks back. Enjoy life and enjoy ya freedom, my nigga. I gotta bust a few moves. I'll spin back to check on you in a few days."

***

After getting ice cream at Cold Stone Creamery, Peso and Princess took Mya to Toy-R-Us to buy her some toys. The three of them had a great time together. Mya and Princess got along wonderfully, and Peso couldn't be happier. Little did Princess know, that was the second test, and she passed it. The first test was her meeting his mother. If his mother and daughter didn't like her, there was no way he would keep her around.

On the ride home, Mya fell asleep in the backseat. Peso took this time to address the elephant in the room between him and Princess.

"Babe, you still mad at me?" he asked.

"After a wonderful day like this, how can I be? On the real, Tyler, I was never mad. I was more disappointed than anything. The way you handled that incident in IHOP scared me."

"I'm sorry, babe. My temper got the best of me. At the same time, though, I wasn't gonna allow ol' boy to disrespect you or me."

"Well, hear me out," Princess began. "I don't want a street dude in my life. I tried that already, and it got me nowhere. I want a good man. I deserve a good man. Seeing you pull out that gun in front of all those people showed me a different side of you. I did my homework on you and found out you're a cold-blooded gangster. That's something I don't need."

Those words hurt coming from her.

"I was ready to walk away," she continued, "but seeing you interact with that beautiful little girl in the backseat showed me that you are a man—a very good man. There is nothing more attractive to me than a man who respects his mother and worships his daughter. You do both. I wanna build with you, Ty. Just keep the street shit far away from us. Think like a gangster, because with a past like yours, you can't afford to slip up. But be a man because you have people who need you around. And please don't respond to what I just said, babe. Just let my words sink in."

For the rest of the ride, Peso remained silent, lost in his thoughts.

Mariah was getting out her Mercedes Benz when Peso pulled up. The dark-tinted windows of his Porsche prevented Mariah from seeing inside. Peso double-parked and got out of the car.

"Hey, baby daddy. How are you?" Mariah greeted with a hug.

"I'm taking it easy. I'm glad I caught you before you went in the house. You can help with these bags. Your daughter sure knows how to spend money, just like her mother." Peso chuckled.

"You spoil her too damn much," Mariah told him.

"I spoil ya ass, too. That is a new Benz you're pushing," Peso said, reminding her that she benefited from his spoiling, as well.

"It sure is," Mariah shot back with a Kool-Aid smile as she began walking towards his vehicle.

"I have someone in the car I want you to meet," Peso said.

Mariah shot him a look but continued to the car. Peso opened the back door and slowly lifted Mya out, being careful not to wake her.

"Babe, pop the truck so we can get the bags out," he told Princess.

She did as she was asked and then hopped out to help Mariah with the bags.

"Riah, this is Princess. Princess, this is my daughter's mother, Mariah."

Princess extended her hand, which Mariah gladly accepted.

"So you're the lovely lady who has my baby daddy open, huh?" Mariah asked while shaking her hand.

Princess blushed.

"It's a pleasure to finally meet you, Princess. I knew you were special when he let you meet his mother. Girl, if you could only see this man's face when you call his phone."

"Oh really?" Princess responded, wearing a wide grin and cutting her eyes at Peso.

The ladies shared a laugh as they removed the bags from the car.

"Mariah, shut up! Ya ass always talking too much," Peso joked.

After entering the condo, the two women continued walking to the kitchen while talking. Peso attempted to lay Mya on the sofa, but she woke up before her head hit the cushion.

"Daddy, are you leaving?" Mya asked.

"Yes, baby girl, but I will be back tomorrow to take you for a ride in my new car," Peso promised.

"Can I say goodbye to Ms. Princess?"

"Of course you can. She's in the kitchen with ya mommy."

Mya quickly jumped up from off the couch and ran out of the room toward the kitchen. She surprised Princess by giving her a tight hug.

"Goodbye, Ms. Princess, and thank you. I had fun with you today," Maya said, looking up at her.

"You're welcome, sweetie. You can see me whenever you like, as long as it's okay with your mother," Princess responded, hugging Mya back.

After they all exchanged goodbyes, Peso and Princess left the condo.

Chapter 15

Reem was feeling much better physically, besides the fact that his jaw was still wired shut. Sho-Tyme kept him abreast of everything going on in the streets. Bricks was running around crazy, letting the power he obtained go to his head. Based on what Sho-Tyme told him, eighty percent of the Bloods under the banner sided with B-Gunnz and Bricks. What hurt Reem most was that even some of his day one homies he came from the dirt with sided with the enemy. Bricks was just the puppet. It was really B-Gunnz who was pulling strings and calling the shots. Reem had an idea of what would hurt B-Gunnz deeply. No one was off limits. B-Gunnz didn't play fair, so Reem wasn't going to play fair either.

It was ten o'clock on a Saturday night, and Reem was sitting in a Chevy Malibu parked a half block away from a Brooklyn brownstone. He exited the car, walked down to his destination, and rang the doorbell. An older guy in his early 50s answered the door wearing one of the biggest Cuban links Reem had ever seen. The pendant on the chain was a playing card—the King of Diamonds, to be exact. A huge 24-karat gold bracelet covered his right wrist, and an 18-karat gold bracelet Presidential Rolex adorned his left.

"Oh shit, Reem. Haven't seen you in a minute. What brings you this way? Let me guess; my son sent you to me for some work," the old head said as he stepped back to let

Reem in the house. "I was just about to slide out. You want a drink?"

"Nah, I'm straight," Reem mumbled through the wires in his mouth.

"What the hell happened, Reem?"

"B-Gunnz!" he grunted.

The old man looked at him with confusion on his face. Reem pulled a piece of paper from his pocket, handing it to the old head. He unfolded the paper to read what it said and shook his head.

"C'mon, man, you here to rob me? After all that you and my son done been through?"

Reem didn't answer him. Instead, he pulled his gun quickly, aiming it at the old head.

"You're a snake, man. If B-Gunnz was home, you wouldn't be doing this. It's niggas like you who fuck the game up. NO LOYALTY!" the old head shouted.

"Lead the way to your bedroom," Reem mumbled, remembering that the old head had two floor safes under his bed.

The old head followed orders, leading the way to his bedroom. When Reem pointed to the bed, the old man shook his head, not believing this was happening.

"You don't forget shit, do you? I showed you these safes when you were still pissing in the bed," he said while moving the bed.

Reem smiled to himself when the old head opened the two safes. One contained ten kilos of dope, and the other was nearly stacked to the top with hundred-dollar bills.

"Wrap everything up in that blanket," Reem mumbled.

Once all the money and drugs were tied up in the blanket, Reem stripped the old head of his jewelry and then shot him twice before making his escape.

***

Peso pulled up to Kaiser Park in his brand-new Ferrari. As he walked to the basketball court, he couldn't help but smile when he saw Isiah on the court with his ten-man squad. Isiah ran over to him.

"I'm glad you made it, Coach."

"Well, I'm a man of my word. I couldn't let you down. I told Hitta to meet us here," Peso replied, stepping in the middle of the court. "For those of you who don't know me, I'm Peso, and I will be coaching you guys this summer in the Starbury League. The age range is fourteen to fifteen years old. Everybody here is one of those ages, right?"

The young men shook their heads. Peso then made them stand in the line and introduce themselves.

"Now that we're all familiar with one another, let me get some laps around the court."

"How many we gotta run, Coach?" one of the kids asked.

"Until I say stop," Peso replied, then pulled out his phone and texted Hitta to tell him to bring a case of Gatorade.

Fifteen minutes into practice, Hitta showed up with Ashley on one arm and a case of Gatorade in the other. Peso slapped him five and hugged Ashley.

"Alright, everybody bring it in," Peso said to the team, and they formed a circle around him and Hitta. "I want you guys to meet the other coach. This is my brother, Hitta."

After they all introduced themselves to Hitta, Peso had them run a few more laps before running through a few drills. Two hours later, practice came to an end. Before the boys left, Peso had them write down their names, contact info, and shoe sizes.

"Yo, bro, them lil' niggas gonna be a problem when the tournament starts," Hitta said.

"That's a fact," Peso agreed. "Them young boys can hoop. What you getting into for the rest of the day?"

"I'ma drop Ashley off, then head to LI to holla at Kat. I need to pick up the tickets for the party. I know that shit gonna be lit! You ready for ya introduction to the industry?" Hitta asked his best friend.

"Been waiting on this moment since I was a young'un. I'm about to slide to the studio now. When you done, meet me there, bro," Peso said as the three of them headed in the direction of the parking lot.

"Say less. I'll be there after, bro," Hitta replied, and they slapped each other five.

"Ashley, I'll see you later, sis," Peso said, hugging her.

"Okay, bro. You be safe out here," she replied.

***

Rich sat back on his bunk reading through a *DuPont Registry* magazine. Looking at all of the exotic automobiles gave him flashbacks of the good ol' days.

"You want some of this?"

Jet-Black offered him the blunt, interrupting his thoughts. Rich reached his hand out and took it.

"Wassup, bro? You haven't been ya'self lately. Everything straight?"

"Yeah, Black, everything is everything," Rich replied. "I just kinda been in my feelings lately. You know how this shit goes. Some days are better than others."

"Trust, bro, I know the feeling."

After the two men finished smoking the blunt, Rich left the cell, hoping to get in a chess game with Bobby Chu.

However, before he could locate Bobby Chu, he heard the C.O. yell over the PA system, "Royal, step to the officer's station."

Chapter 16

When Gangsta L.A. got called for a visit, he was confused because nobody told him they were coming to visit. He figured it was his lady attempting to catch him slipping— trying to see if another female had been there to see him. Cautiously, he stepped into the visiting room and searched for her face, but to his surprise, his lady was nowhere to be found. Seconds later, he heard a familiar voice call out his name.

"Yo, L.A.!"

Gangsta L.A. would recognize the voice anywhere. He turned around in complete shock as he locked eyes with one of his closest comrades.

"Don't just stand there looking stupid! Come show a nigga some love!" Peso shouted with a smile.

L.A. stepped closer, reaching to give Peso a big bear hug.

"I see you got ya weight up." Peso stepped back, taking a look at his long-time friend.

"I'm trying, bro. I'm trying," L.A. replied as he took a seat.

Peso sat across from him.

"What's the word, bro? How's everything?"

"You know me; don't nothing change. Just taking shit one day at a time. Wassup with you? I hear you and Hitta done leveled up. I'm proud of y'all," L.A. expressed, congratulating him.

"Yeah, we done turned up next level, bro. But shit ain't the same without you, my nigga, for real."

"Shit won't ever be the same. P. Rico's gone, Relo's gone, and Murda and Hitta out there tryna kill each other. Shit's all fucked up. But, on the real, I appreciate you and Hitta sending me them money orders. That shows me that distance never destroyed our bond," L.A. said sincerely.

"We family, bro, no matter what. When was the last time you spoke to Murda?" Peso asked him.

"We speak every day."

"I need a favor. Next time y'all talk, try to get him to end this shit with Hitta. We almost got into it at Rico's gravesite. This shit is getting outta hand."

L.A. just shook his head. "I've been tryna end that shit since it started, but that nigga ain't tryna hear me. You know he's stuck in his ways. I'ma keep tryin', though. Fuck all the drama. How's the family?

"Everyone is doing well. Mom is good. Shoota just came home. Him and Heat out there bugging. It's gonna be a hot summer. I got some good news for you, though."

"Spill it. Don't just sit there," L.A. said, excited to hear the news.

"I got a label deal with Royalty Records. The label is throwing a party next week to welcome me."

L.A. smiled broadly. "I'm proud of you, bro. The industry needs more niggas like you. Jay-Z better watch out."

The two men kicked it until visiting hours were over, then said their goodbyes. Peso left with promises of returning soon.

***

Hitta drove around making drops and picking up money on behalf of himself and Peso. His final destination was Boston Road in the Bronx. The sound of his phone ringing interrupted his thoughts. Hitta turned down his music and accepted the call.

"Yo!" he answered.

"Where you at, bro?" the caller asked.

"I'm on my way to you. Why? Wassup? Everything straight?"

"Nah, bro, the boys got me trapped off. I need you to come pick me up," the caller replied nervously.

"You trapped off where, bro? What the fuck happened?"

"It's a long story, but I'm hiding in the backyard of somebody's crib on Trinity Ave. They got the dogs out and everything, bro. I'ma jump out on the back street in exactly five minutes. Just be by the school, bro."

"Kopy! I'll be there," Hitta replied and ended the call.

Hitta was a bit nervous because he had over two hundred thousand dollars in cash along with six kilos of coke in the trunk of his car, but he refused to leave his comrade hanging. The person on the other end of the phone was Santana, one of the Untouchable Gorilla Family's shot callers. Hitta didn't know what was going on, but he was going to stand by his brother right or wrong.

True to his word, Hitta arrived at the destination Santana gave him exactly five minutes later. He became nervous after a few minutes when he didn't see Santana. Looking up the block, he saw that the police had it blocked off.

"Fuck!" he shouted, hitting the steering wheel with his fist.

The sound of Hitta's cell phone ringing interrupted him.

"Yo, bro, where you at?" Hitta asked anxiously.

"I'm under the blue van at the beginning of the block."

Hitta looked for the blue van.

"I see it, bro. The coast is clear. Come out," he instructed, driving up to the van.

As soon as Santana jumped in the passenger seat, Hitta hit the gas and got the hell out of there.

***

It was ten at night, and Reem sat in a Chevy Malibu. He lay back in the driver's seat, waiting on the call from Sho-Tyme. While waiting, he noticed a black BMW pull up and park about a half a block away from him. He watched the Beamer from afar, but nobody exited the car. Reem pulled out of his parking spot and circled the block to see who was inside the BMW.

***

Shoota, Heat, and Caine sat inside the BMW watching the front door of the Brooklyn brownstone. The brownstone was a stash house that belonged to Bricks.

"You sure this the spot?" Caine asked from the backseat.

"Yeah, I'm sure, nigga. We wouldn't be here if I hadn't done my homework," Shoota responded from the driver's seat.

"Ayo, that's the second time that Malibu drove past us tryna peek in here," Heat informed them, putting everyone on point.

Minutes later, the Malibu cruised down the block again. The three of them cocked their guns, putting a round in the chamber of their semi-automatic weapons. Shoota rolled down his window as the Malibu got closer. Seconds later, the car was right beside them.

Reem couldn't help but smile when he noticed Shoota in the driver's seat of the BMW.

"Ayo, put y'all guns down," Shoota told the two young boys in the car with him. "Nigga, you was 'bout to get ate up. What's the word?" he said, greeting Reem.

"I see, lil' nigga. It's the same ol' shit. What brings y'all young'uns over here?"

"Come on, nigga. Don't act like you ain't been hearing about the work we been putting in behind what that fuck nigga did to you. We on these Blood niggas asses, big bro."

Reem heard what had been going on, but he didn't know Shoota was behind some of the bodies that had been dropping.

"So y'all lampin' on this trap down the block?" Reem asked, referring to the stash house.

"Yeah. We waiting for one of them niggas to leave."

"How 'bout we just go inside? Them niggas holding some racks. Whatever we find in there, y'all keep. I ain't come for money; I came for blood. This shit is personal."

The sound of Reem's phone ringing cut their conversation short.

"Yo, what's the word?" Reem answered quickly.

"It's open whenever you ready. Only four niggas in here besides me, and none of them niggas are strapped. The hammers are in the backroom," the caller informed him.

"A'ight, say less. See you in a few seconds," Reem replied, then looked at Shoota after ending the call. "Yo, I'm laying these niggas down. I'ma let y'all get the goods first. It's five of them inside, but one is my man. So, don't get crazy until I give y'all the heads up."

"Kopy! Say no more. Let's roll," Shoota said as he and the others exited the car.

When they got to the brownstone's front door, Reem slowly twisted the doorknob, and the four of them entered quietly. They walked past the kitchen and entered the living room. The five Bloods were playing Call of Duty on the PS4. They were so engrossed in the game that they never heard Reem and the young boys come in.

"What's poppin', Blood?" Reem greeted.

Caught slipping, they all looked like they had seen a ghost. Sho-Tyme was the only one who didn't look surprised.

"Why the long faces? Y'all ain't miss the homie? Oh, let me guess. You bitch-ass niggas sided with that fuck boy Bricks, huh?"

Reem quickly pulled his .9mm, and the three young boys did the same.

"Big homie, you don't gotta do this. We with you," a Blood who went by the name of Venom pleaded.

"Y'all with me?" Reem satanically laughed. "Nah, y'all niggas against me. Now where the fuck the money and the work at?"

"Everything in the back, Blood. Ain't nothing change. Just don't kill us, scrap. We know how you give it up," another Blood pleaded.

"If you knew how I give it up, why would you stupid muthafuckas side with Bricks and B-Gunnz?" Reem asked.

"Blood, we were just following protocol."

"Sho-Tyme, take my lil' homies to the back and clean that shit out. Every dollar and every brick comes with us."

Minutes later, they returned from the backroom carrying duffle bags.

"Yo, Venom, call that nigga Bricks and put it on speaker," Sho-Tyme ordered, now aiming his .40 cal at Venom's head.

"So, you set this shit up, huh, Sho?" Venom asked angrily.

"Nigga, shut the fuck up and make the call!" Reem shouted.

Venom pulled out his phone and called Bricks.

"Suuwhoop!" Bricks shouted from the other end of the phone.

BOC!

Sho-Tyme fired a shot, hitting Venom in the head.

BOC! BOC! BOC!

Reem, Shoota, and Heat finished off the other three Bloods. Not to be outdone, Caine stood over one of the bodies and fired two shots, going for overkill. With their deed done and mission accomplished, the men left the house with duffle bags full of drugs and money and a message well sent.

The whole time, Bricks had been listening on the other end.

"Gotdamn!"

***

Thirty minutes later, Shoota, Heat, and Caine were sitting in one of Reem's spots, smoking Kush and drinking Hennessy while counting their earnings from the lick they just caught. Reem was out making a drop, and he sent Sho-Tyme to link up with some of the Blood homies so he wouldn't look suspect.

"This a nice lick we just hit," Heat said while counting the last stack of money.

"What's the total?" Shoota asked.

"Eighty-two bands," Heat replied with a smile.

"Not bad for a day's work—eighty-two thousand dollars, four kilos of coke, and thirty-one and a half pounds of weed," Caine added, finally breaking his silence.

Reem walked in as they were splitting up the money.

"Ayo, big bro, we got eighty-two thousand in cash, four birds, and thirty-one and a half pounds. Here, that's twenty thousand, five hundred. We about to split the rest of this shit up," Shoota said, tossing him a stack of money.

"Nah, bro, I'm good," Reem responded, tossing the money back to Shoota. "I told you that was personal. Everything ya came up on belongs to y'all three. Y'all was there for the link. I was there for blood. I also wanna thank you niggas for the work y'all been putting in on my behalf."

"No need to get all sensitive. Peso and Hitta said you family, so we gonna treat you as such. I never met you personally before, but I know who you are. I know your work. So, from one gangster to another, you're a legend," Heat said, showing respect.

"That means a lot coming from a nigga who put in just as much work as me," Reem replied with a smile. "But on some real shit, though, y'all enjoy that bread. You niggas earned it. By the way, ya bro Peso on his way, too," Reem said as he sat down and started rolling up.

***

Peso pushed his Ferrari down Mermaid Avenue. For the past six blocks, the same black-on-black Audi had been following him. When he got to 28th Street and took a right, the Audi did the same.

"These niggas got me fucked up," Peso said out loud.

He reached for his gun, putting it in his lap. He made a left when he reached Surf Avenue. The Audi took the left, also. Peso sped up, leaving the Audi behind. When he reached 30th and Surf Avenue, he parked the car and got out. Two minutes later, the Audi sped past him. Peso leaned on the Ferrari and clutched his gun tight. He watched the Audi closely. Once the car was out of sight, Peso waited about five minutes before getting back into his Ferrari and driving off. Ten minutes later, he was knocking on Reem's traphouse door.

"I'm glad to see you back to normal, bro," Peso said once Reem opened the door.

"Come on, Peso, you know a nigga gonna need a rocket launcher to take down a nigga like me," Reem responded arrogantly.

When they entered the living room, Shoota, Heat, and Caine were passing around blunts.

"Gorillas stack six-two," Peso greeted in U.G.F. lingo and saluted them with the U.G.F. handshake.

"No keys, push to start," they all replied.

Peso looked back at Reem. "How the hell you link up with the three stooges?"

"Long story! Let's just say we were all at the right place at the right time. These young boys right here are about business," Reem expressed.

"Yeah, they don't fuck around. Ever since I pushed the button on Bricks and them niggas, they've been laying shit down. I be tryna tell them to just relax and get money, but they wanna shoot shit," Peso said, shaking his head and laughing.

"Y'all talking about us like we ain't sitting right here. And for the record, big bro, we getting money," Shoota stated, defending himself and his crew.

"There is always room for improvement, baby bro. On a brighter note, I got a surprise for y'all niggas. Royalty Records is throwing this big-ass party, and all of y'all are invited. Make sure you niggas are dressed to impress," Peso said, handing Reem two tickets. "Yo, Shoota, I'ma give you some tickets for you and ya team when I see you at Mommy's crib. That bud smells nice. What y'all niggas want for a pound of that?"

"Nigga, ain't nobody charging you for shit we just got for free. It's thirty-one and a half pounds sitting here. Take what you want, bro," Heat told him.

"Nah, I respect y'all hustle. What's the price?" Peso replied as he pulled a stack of hundred-dollar bills from his pocket.

"Ya money is no good here. Take what you want," Heat repeated, killing the discussion.

***

Hitta sat in the living room of Santana's apartment.

"Ayo, what the fuck happened, bro?" Hitta asked.

"I went to make a drop. On my way outta the projects, niggas tried to bust a move, so I fired first. Soon as I let the shot go, blue and whites pulled up on the scene, so I had to get low," Santana explained.

Hitta shook his head. "Good thing I was already on my way to you, bro. Glad yo' ass ain't get jammed up."

"I know, bro. I owe you one."

"Cut it out. Real niggas don't count favors. We family. I know you would've done the same for me. But on some G-shit, ya district been moving shit fast. So, me and Peso decided to add a lil' more. There's fifteen joints in that bag. Just bring back three hundred and seventy-five thousand dollars when y'all done," Hitta told him.

Santana walked to his bedroom and returned seconds later with a Nike duffle bag. He dropped it at Hitta's feet.

"That's two hundred and fifty thousand dollars, bro—the hundred and twenty-five thousand dollars we owe, and I'ma pay for five of those bricks up front. So, that leaves me with a two-hundred-and-fifty-thousand-dollar tab."

"Kopy. That'll work. Here, this is ten tickets to the party that Royalty Records is throwing. Bring some of the bros with you. That shit gonna be lit," he said, handing Santana the tickets. "I gotta slide up outta here. You just lay low and collect money. Let the bros take care of the other shit until you find out what's what."

"I got'cha, bro," Santana replied. "You be safe."

Chapter 17

The night that hip-hop fans had been anticipating finally arrived. Peso couldn't put his excitement into words. This was the moment he had been waiting for his whole life. He stood in the mirror eyeing himself, making sure his attire was on point. Peso was dressed in an all-white Balmain jean suit, a white Balmain V-neck shirt, a Fendi belt that held up his jeans, and a pair of patent leather Balenciaga Arenas. He was draped in diamonds and gold—the jewelry only adding to his swag. The two solid Cuban links that hung from his neck were flooded with diamonds, along with the Cuban link bracelet on his right wrist, which was also busted down. A pair of diamond studs fit perfectly in his ears. He topped it all off with a Presidential Rolex on his left wrist.

Peso sported a dark Ceaser haircut with a tapered shape-up that complemented his waves. After placing a pair of 18-karat gold, woodgrain Cartier frames on his face, he took one last look at himself in the mirror and made his way out the door. For this once-in-a-lifetime occasion, he rented a white Rolls Royce and hired a driver. He got in the car feeling and looking like a million bucks as he headed to pick up his date for the night.

***

Hitta sat in his living room smoking a blunt of OG Kush. He was already dressed and waiting for Ashley. Hitta kept it simple with a royal blue, soft-denim Gucci outfit and a pair of royal blue suede tennis shoes.

"Yo, Ash, hurry up!"

"I'm ready. I'm ready," she replied, entering the room looking like a contestant from *America's Next Top Model*. She wore a blue Alexander Wang open-back mini. The dress fit her so well it could have passed for body paint. Her hair was long and flat-ironed bone straight. It hung down the middle of her back. Hitta draped her in the finest jewels, and Ashley looked flawless.

"You just gonna stare, or are you gonna tell me how sexy I look in this dress?" she asked, twirling around slowly so he could get a good look at her.

"Baby girl, I'm trying not to remove that dress and do you right here and now," Hitta replied, licking his lips.

"Well, maybe you should do me in the dress," Ashley said seductively.

"Don't tempt me, 'cause you know I will. Come on, baby. I don't wanna be late. It's Peso's big night."

***

At 11P.M. sharp, the Rolls Royce pulled up in front of the two-family Staten Island home owned by Princess's mother. The driver got out of the car and opened the door for Peso, who slowly stepped out and made his way through the home's front gate. He rang the doorbell, and seconds later, a beautiful older woman opened the door. She looked like an older version of Princess—only she had a little more hips.

"Good evening! You must be Tyler. It's a pleasure to finally meet you," the woman greeted. "Oh my goodness. You're just as handsome as my daughter described, and your eyes are beautiful."

"Thank you, Ms. Carter. It's a pleasure to meet you. I see where Princess gets her beauty from."

The two hugged, and there was an instant connection.

"Princess, this fine young man is waiting for you!"

"I'm coming!" Princess yelled from upstairs.

"I apologize for not being able to join you two tonight. I was called in for work."

"It's okay, Ms. Carter. Hopefully, we can do dinner sometime this week."

"That would be nice, and cut that 'Ms. Carter' crap. You can call me Vivian."

When Princess finally descended the stairs, Peso felt something move in his stomach. She was breathtaking. Princess looked amazing in her white Alexander McQueen silk chiffon, open-back dress. The dress hugged her body perfectly. The diamond tennis bracelet and matching necklace Peso bought her a few days prior looked as if it was designed just for her. Peso just stared, admiring her beauty.

"Are you gonna keep undressing me with your eyes, or are you gonna say something?" Princess asked, smiling as she stood in front of him.

"You look amazing," he replied, then kissed her lips.

"Before you two leave, let me get a picture."

Ms. Vivian took a few pictures. Then Peso and Princess headed out the door.

As they arrived at the party, it was clear the place was packed, and the paparazzi were everywhere snapping pictures. When the white Rolls Royce pulled up in front of the club, it grabbed everyone's attention. The driver got out and held the door open for Peso and Princess to make their grand appearance. While everyone tried to figure out who this lovely couple was, photos were snapped by the second.

Peso walked straight to the entrance and gave the host his name. The host unhooked the velvet rope, letting Peso and Princess in without a pat-down. Then they were quickly escorted to the VIP section.

When they reached the reserved area, every one of the people Peso gave a special invite to sat drinking, smoking, and having a good time. Peso greeted all of his comrades, then took a seat next to his lady.

"Ayo, Hitta, where that nigga Reem at?" Peso asked.

No sooner than the words left his mouth, he noticed Reem walking toward them with his girlfriend, Sonia, on his arm. Reem was guccied down to his socks—rocking a red suit, a pair of black and red loafers, and matching glasses. The King of Diamonds playing card pendant looked too heavy as it hung from his neck, but it complemented his swagger.

"What's poppin'?" Reem said, greeting everyone.

"You poppin', nigga. I see you shining," Peso commented with a smile.

"Nigga, I'm tryna keep up with y'all," Reem replied.

Before they could respond, Katrina entered their section looking gorgeous as ever. She greeted everyone, then reached for Peso's hand. He stood and kissed her cheek.

"Are you ready to show the world that talent you have?" she asked him.

"I was born ready," Peso replied arrogantly.

"Glad to hear that, 'cause this event is streaming live. You will be going on stage in about seven minutes. I'ma give my intro, and then the deejay is gonna drop the bomb. Peso, you better turn this shit the fuck up," she said, grinning at him.

It wasn't lost on Katrina that Hitta had shown up with a woman. Even though there was no relationship between them, she felt a twinge of jealousy, knowing that the young lady would later get the "dick" she desired. For Hitta's part, he looked at Katrina, then looked away quickly. His dick jumped in his pants when he thought about her giving him head.

Katrina made a beeline for the deejay's booth and requested that the deejay cut the music.

"How are you people feeling tonight? I'm Katrina Royal, the acting CEO of Royalty Records. For years, my label has been giving you hit after hit. It's time for the world to meet my newest artist. This young man is extremely talented, and

I can't wait for y'all to experience his gift. So, please, help me welcome and give it up for PESO!"

The crowd went crazy as the deejay dropped the beat. Peso felt like he was moving in slow motion as he headed to the stage. With each step, he wondered if he was going to blow his big moment. He heard the beat drop, and while looking at the faces in the crowd, it was like a switch turned on his head. Everything clicked. The nervous feeling instantaneously went away, and he started spitting the lyrics. The crowd went wild as he flowed on the beat.

Peso performed two songs, then made his way back to the VIP section. His people were on their feet to congratulate him.

"Yo, bro, you did the damn thing! The crowd is loving you," Shoota said, hugging Peso.

Mariah walked over to Peso, and with tears in her eyes, she hugged him tight. She knew how much this night meant to him.

"Tyler, I'm proud of you."

"Thank you, baby momma. Now wipe those tears, and let's turn up."

The deejay played Peso's first single, "The Real is Back", and the crowd went crazy again. Peso walked to the middle of the VIP section and held up his glass.

"Can I please have everyone's attention?"

Everyone in the section gave Peso their undivided attention.

"I just wanna thank all of you for coming out to show a nigga love. Some of you may feel like this is my big night, but this is *our* big night 'cause when I win, my family wins. I'm nothing without y'all. Now, everybody raise ya glasses, and let's toast to more life."

"To more life!" the group said in unison as they all touched glasses.

After the toast, Peso walked over to Katrina's VIP section, which was packed with artists and staff of Royalty Records, along with the Royal family. Richie Rich, Ray, and Roxy were all in attendance. Richie Rich and Ray greeted Peso, but Roxy just stared at him. He locked eyes with her and smiled. Then his eyes almost popped out of his head when he saw actress/model Nautica Taylor.

"Keep ya eyes off my lady, nigga," Ray joked.

"No disrespect, bro, but she's beautiful," Peso said, offering the compliment.

"Come on, let me introduce you to her. Babe, this is a close friend of the family and newest artist to Royalty Records, Peso."

"Nice to meet you, Peso. You burned that stage down. The crowd loved you," she said as the two shook hands.

"Ayo, Peso, let's take this pic for the 'Gram!" Richie Rich yelled out.

Peso walked over and took a few pictures with him and Katrina. After shaking a few hands and meeting a few of his labelmates, Peso headed back to his section. For the remainder of the night, Peso celebrated with his woman and closest friends. It felt good to have his lady by his side to enjoy this moment, and he knew music was his calling. Even with all that he had "achieved" in the streets, there was NOTHING that could compare to the way he felt that night. This was his true definition of The Level Up.

Two Days Later…

Hitta and Peso sat at the dining room table of the Royal Estate drinking D'usse.

"Yo, bro, my single dropped yesterday, and that shit is already platinum," Peso said with a smile.

"You about to take the industry to a new level. I'm glad you're finally able to live ya dream, bro."

Their conversation was interrupted by Roxy, who walked into the dining area.

"Hey, y'all," she said, greeting them.

"Wassup?" they both replied.

"Peso, you did ya thing the other night," Roxy said, congratulating him.

"Oh, so you were watching me?"

"Don't flatter ya'self," she told him before leaving the room.

Hitta sat back in his chair and laughed. "She's feeling you, bro. I see that shit all in her eyes."

"She wants to give it to me bad," Peso responded, and Hitta laughed again.

Katrina walked into the room next.

"Peso, did you get the news about ya single going platinum?"

"Yeah. I was just telling Hitta about that."

"Looks like you're gonna be getting another check in a few days. I told you the event was streaming live. My phone hasn't stopped ringing yet. Every radio station and magazine wants to interview you."

"So, whose interview are we taking first?" Peso inquired, smirking.

"I'm thinking *XXL Magazine* because they are dying for you to be on the cover of the freshmen issue. I'll sort everything out and get back to you. Oh, before I forget, you have full access to the office building. Studio 6 on the 12th floor is all yours. Also, how are we gonna go about your management? Do you want to sign a management contract with us?"

"Nah. No disrespect, but I rather give that fifteen percent to someone who has been in my corner from day one. I wanna change the lives of those around me, but they gonna work for it."

"Understood. That's smart. I love your mindset."

Their conversation was interrupted by Peso's phone ringing. He took the call, spoke briefly, and ended the call.

"Sorry to cut this meeting short, but I gotta go."

Peso dapped Hitta, hugged Katrina, and then headed for the door. When he got to his car, he looked up to see Roxy standing in the doorway watching him.

"What you looking at?" he joked.

"I'm looking at you," she replied while walking towards him.

"You been doing a lot of looking lately. You see something you like?"

"Maybe, maybe not," Roxy replied, openly flirting with him.

Peso reached for her phone, taking it out of her hand. He put his number in it and handed it back to her.

"You got the number now, shawdy. Hit me when you're done playing games," he said, then got in his Ferrari.

Roxy stood watching him leave and at a loss for words.

***

Reem pulled up outside of Red Hook Houses, parked his car, and walked through the projects. There was a group of dudes standing in front of one of the many buildings. Reem approached the group.

"What's poppin'?" he said, greeting them.

The leader of the group, who went by the name 2-Gunnz, stepped up. He was the godfather of his Blood set and once a powerful ally to Reem.

"You got some big balls showing up around here when B-Gunnz gave the green light to off yo' ass *on sight*," 2-Gunnz said, the look of death in his eyes.

"You've known me since I first came up in this thang, 2-Gunnz. When have I ever been afraid of anything?"

Reem paused to allow 2-Gunnz to object. When he didn't, Reem continued.

"Exactly! Now, I came to have a word with you, but if you ain't feeling what I'm about to say, then you can shoot." Reem matched his stare.

"C'mon, let's take a walk, Blood." 2-Gunnz turned to his homies. "We gonna walk to the store. Be right back."

As the two men walked off, 2-Gunnz told Reem, "Speak ya peace, Blood."

"The two of us have history with B-Gunnz—all good history at that. But you and B-Gunnz go back way before my time, so the bond y'all share may be more sacred. You know me, big bro. I've always been solid. I dedicated my life to this Blood shit. Never once did I break the code. This issue me and B-Gunnz got is personal."

"Why is it personal? Why can't two brothers come to a common ground instead of going to war?" 2-Gunnz asked, trying to make sense of the situation.

"I took an oath, and I don't break or bend the rules for *nobody*! Dame was working with the police, so I touched him. In turn, B-Gunnz pushed the button on me and had Bricks try to take me out. But, as you can see, them shots couldn't stop me," Reem said with a hint of arrogance. "I don't know what B-Gunnz been telling you or the other members of the roundtable, but I did nothing wrong. I took out a rat. The rat just happened to be B-Gunnz's brother. Was I supposed to change the rules of the game because of that?"

He paused before answering his own question.

"No, I wasn't, because I would have given my own brother the same fate."

"How did you know Dame was a rat? Did you have proof? Or did you go off of assumption?"

Reem pulled out his phone, pulling up the recording he had of Dame getting out of the unmarked police car. 2-Gunnz watched the video in disgust. After the video ended, he looked up at Reem.

"B-Gunnz is wrong for what he's doing. He voted you out when you did nothing wrong. He expected you to change the laws of Blood because Dame was his brother. I understand he's hurting, but a rat is a rat. A lot of blood is being spilled because the nigga is in his feelings. I'ma call a meeting with the roundtable and let them know what's up. But you know they're not gonna vote him off. That nigga paved the way for a lot of homies, and he has a lot of soldiers in his corner. The green light will be removed off ya head, though, and as far as I see it, you're good in my book. But let's be clear. B-Gunnz is not gonna want you pushing his set behind this lil' situation y'all having."

"It's just as much my set as it is his. Yeah, he's been around longer, but we share the hood. I put in a lot of work, and you know that shit, 2-Gunnz," Reem retorted.

"I know, bro, but that nigga is the one who gave you ya start. He put you in position, so he can take it from you. Remember, the roundtable can't tell the nigga how to run his set. What you *can* do is come fuck with me. I'll give you ya own subdivision under my banner."

"I don't know, Blood," Reem replied after thinking about the offer for a moment.

"What is there not to know? Why stay somewhere where you ain't wanted?"

"A man who makes the same bad decisions is a fool. I may just pull out and start my own banner on some 'salute me or shoot me' type shit. I ain't tryna repeat the process. I rather not answer to nobody when it's time to make critical decisions for my set."

2-Gunnz looked at Reem and smiled. He finally realized that Reem wasn't the same young boy they accepted into the nation years ago. Reem had grown into a man.

"So what you come here to get, my blessings?"

"No disrespect, but I don't need the blessings of another man for anything I wanna do. You didn't ask for nobody's blessings when you pulled out of the council and started ya own banner. I believe you once told me a gangsta does what he wants, and a bitch nigga does what he's told to do. I came here as a sign of respect. I also came here to show you the facts."

"You sure you can handle what may come ya way? A lot of drama may come behind this."

"I live for drama, homie. You know me. Ain't nothing changed. I just pray you don't pick a side, because this shit with me, B-Gunnz, and Bricks is personal."

"Listen, Blood, I don't agree with what B-Gunnz did, and I respect your gangsta. So, I'ma make sure all sets under the banner stay outta this shit, but you have thirty-one days to clean this shit up."

"That's all I need. Check this, though. I got some good coke, grade A shit. Nobody in New York is fucking with this work I got."

"What's the tag on a whole thing?"

"For you, twenty-eight."

"That's not bad, not bad at all. If that shit is as good as you say it is, I'ma need ten. How fast can you take care of my order? 'Cause I'm about to run out."

"I'll hit you in the a.m," Reem replied.

The two men then embraced each other before going their separate ways.

***

Hitta was leaving the Royal Estate when he saw Ray choking a female. Hitta ran over to him, grabbing his arm to stop the assault.

"Yo, Ray, what the fuck are you doing, man?"

Ray let the girl go and turned to Hitta.

"Mind ya business, bruh. This shit has nothing to do with you."

"You're right. It ain't my business, but you're wrong. That's a female. I'm pretty sure you ain't out in the streets beatin' on niggas how you beatin' on her."

"Like I said, mind ya fucking business," Ray said and then stormed off, leaving both of them standing there.

Hitta turned to the young lady, and that's when he realized who she was.

"Hold up. Ain't you that actress chick?"

"Yes, I am, and thank you for helping me."

"Don't thank me. I did what any real nigga would do. For the record, you're too pretty to be letting a nigga beat on you."

"I'm used to it," she replied, putting her head down.

Hitta gently put his finger under her chin and lifted her face until their eyes met.

"Listen, love, the only thing you should be used to is a man treating you like the queen you are. No woman should be used to getting beat."

She began to cry, her tears falling freely. Hitta wiped them away.

"Don't cry. It's gonna be alright. You're beautiful; remember that. I have to get going. Are you gonna be okay? Can I take you somewhere?"

"No, I'll be alright. Thank you."

"I'm Hitta, by the way," he said, extending his hand.

"Nautica," she replied. "I better get inside before he comes back out here. Once again, thank you very much."

As she walked away, Hitta couldn't help but watch her every step, admiring her perfect frame until she was no longer in sight. Nautica Taylor was by far the most beautiful woman Hitta had ever seen.

Chapter 18

Peso sat on the couch in his 12th-floor penthouse. The elevator door opened, and Princess got off, entering the penthouse.

"Hey, bae," she said, greeting Peso with a smile.

She set the bags in her arms on the kitchen counter, then joined Peso on the couch. She leaned over, kissing his lips.

"Wassup, love? How was your day?"

"It was okay. Just another long day at work."

"So quit. You don't have to work."

Peso's phone rang, interrupting their conversation.

"We gonna finish the conversation in a second. I have to take this call." Peso pushed off the couch, walking to the kitchen.

"Hello?" he said, answering the phone.

"Yo, Peso! X just got hit, bro!" the caller yelled into the phone.

"What?! When?!" Peso shouted.

"A lil' while ago, bro. Niggas just came through the block spraying. It's looking bad for him, bro. We all at Brookdale Hospital."

"I'm on my way now," Peso informed the caller and hung up. "Fuck!" He slammed his fist on the counter. "Bae, I gotta go. My friend has been hurt."

Peso moved quickly around the room, preparing to leave.

"Okay, I'll stay here until you come back. Do what you need to do, bae," Princess responded.

Peso walked over to her. She stood and embraced him. Peso held her in his arms, looking in her eyes.

"You be safe out there," she told him, then kissed his lips.

***

Peso jumped in his Ferrari and headed straight for the Brooklyn Bridge. Several minutes into the drive, he noticed a smoke-grey Infiniti following him. He sped up, making a few turns and losing the driver. Thirty minutes later, he pulled up to Brookdale Hospital. After finding a parking spot, he rushed inside.

The emergency room was filled with X's friends and family members. Hitta stood in the corner of the room holding X's mother, who was crying in his arms. Peso and Hitta went way back with X. The three of them had been friends since grade school. X's family moved from Coney Island to East New York when X reached the seventh grade, but the three stayed in contact throughout the years.

Peso walked over to Hitta.

"Miss Evette, Xavier's gonna be fine. He's a warrior," Peso said as he hugged her.

"I hope so, Tyler. I hope so," she cried.

Peso hated seeing his friend's mother in tears. On his way to the bathroom, he bumped into X's little sister, Zimora.

"Oh my gosh, Tyler. How are you?" She greeted him with a hug.

"I'm okay. I almost didn't recognize you. Damn, you grew up," he said, looking her up and down.

Zimora had grown up to be a beautiful young lady.

"Thank you. I couldn't stay young forever," she said, chuckling. "How's the family? I haven't seen you in forever."

"The family is well," Peso responded. "And yeah, it's been a long time. I just hate that I have to see you under these circumstances."

Sadness came over Zimora's face. "He's gonna be okay, Ty. Xavier is a fighter—he always has been."

"I know. C'mon, let's go back and check on ya moms," Peso said as he led her to the waiting area in the emergency room.

***

Six men sat in front of the building, smoking blunts and drinking Ciroc. This was an everyday thing for them. They hustled all day to party and bullshit all night. A group of females was also kicking it with them. Amongst the group was Dawg, the five-star general of B-Gunnz's Blood set, Reem, Sho-Tyme, and a homie named Dolla, who Reem put on the set a few years back. Red bandannas covered their faces, so Dawg and his crew weren't alarmed.

"Suuwhoop!"

One of the Bloods sitting with Dawg stood up and started throwing up gang signs. Reem quickly pulled his .9mm off of his waist and unloaded on the group. Sho-Tyme and Dolla followed up.

BOC! BOC! BOC!

The sound of gunshots caused bystanders to flee in different directions. Dawg fell to the ground, blood pooling from his chest. Reem stood over him, unloading his .9mm until Dawg was lifeless.

***

Peso exited the hospital and began walking to his car. He heard the screeching of tires. The smoke grey Infiniti caught Peso's attention. He quickly turned around and saw a masked man hanging out the back window, aiming a handgun at him.

BOC! BOC! BOC!

Peso got low, taking off down the sidewalk in an attempt to get away. Shots were still ringing out as the car attempted to catch up to Peso, who ran full speed in the opposite direction of his car. The shooter hopped out of the Infiniti and began chasing Peso on foot.

The gunman fired two more shots at Peso—both shots missing their intended target. Sirens could be heard in the distance as Peso got closer to the hospital entrance. Hearing the sirens, the shooter stopped and turned to run back to the Infiniti.

***

The three men got out of the Infiniti and quickly entered the basement of a Brooklyn brownstone. Matt Murda and Rah-Rah were involved in an intense game of pool when the three men entered.

"Tell me something good, fellas," Matt Murda said.

"Don't got nothing good to tell you, boss."

"Fuck you mean, y'all don't got nothing good to tell me?"

"We missed. That lucky bastard got away."

Matt Murda shook his head.

"See, Rah, if you want something done, you gotta do it yourself," he said, turning to the three goons he hired for the hit on Peso. "The job is canceled. Y'all can keep the upfront money. Now get the fuck out before I put a shell in one of you niggas."

***

When Peso stepped inside his penthouse, Princess was asleep on the sofa with the TV still playing. He walked over to her, admiring the beautiful sight. He didn't want to wake her, so he walked over to the minibar, pouring himself a drink. Hennessy was his drink of choice. He threw the shot back quickly and poured another. Then he sat on the stool and began thinking about the day's chain of events. X was shot. He himself was followed and shot at. Peso's mind was still racing when the vibration of his phone interrupted his thoughts.

"Yo!" he answered.

"I'm on my way up now," Hitta replied from the other end.

"Cool. Just be quiet when you walk in. Princess is asleep on the sofa," he informed Hitta before ending the call.

Minutes later, the elevator door of the penthouse opened, and Hitta walked in with Ashley. Both were carrying duffle bags. Peso hugged Ashley, then greeted Hitta.

"What's the word on X?" Peso asked.

"He's fucked up, bro. The doctor is saying he might not pull through. Shit is happening way too fast, bro. What the fuck happened when you left the hospital?"

"I don't know, bro. Whoever it was followed me from this area. I shook them before I got to the hospital. Then they popped up at the hospital. I don't get how they knew my exact location. Something ain't right, bro. I'm telling you."

"Whatever it is, we gotta get to the bottom of it ASAP, but I got the shit you asked for in them duffle bags," Hitta told him.

Peso walked over and unzipped the duffle bags. He smiled as he pulled out one of the uniforms, which was for his basketball team.

"Those lil' niggas gonna love these shits," Peso said.

"They might like the Jays more. I got them the Olympic 7s."

Their feeling of excitement was short-lived when Hitta's phone rang.

Chapter 19

Reem sat in the passenger seat of the tinted BMW. Sho-Tyme was the driver. Bricks called Sho-Tyme and told him that they needed to talk face to face. When Sho-Tyme received the call, he texted Reem. Now the two of them sat together in his car, plotting how they would take out Bricks. Sho-Tyme's phone vibrated. After answering the call, he put it on speaker.

"Yo, Blood!"

"What's poppin', skrap? Where you at?" Sho-Tyme asked Bricks.

"I just pulled up to the hood. I'm getting out my car now. Be at the spot in a minute."

"Nah, don't go to the spot. I'm in building twenty-one at Toya's crib. Meet me in the lobby."

"Heard, bro. I'll see you in a few," Bricks said, hanging up.

Sho-Tyme turned to Reem. "You heard that, right?"

"Yeah, I heard him. You meet the nigga in the lobby, and I'ma creep through the back on him."

The two waited for a while, giving Bricks a chance to get to the meeting location. Then they got out the car, walking in different directions towards the building. Sho-Tyme took a shortcut. When he made it to the building, Bricks was already waiting for him in the lobby. They greeted each other with the Blood handshake.

"What the fuck is going on, Blood?" Sho-Tyme asked.

"I don't know. Shit's crazy for the home team. We been taking hits left and right. Somebody's been giving Reem the drop on us. We gotta get to the bottom of this shit before it's too late."

"Who you think it is, bro?" Sho-Tyme asked.

"You!" Bricks replied, pulling his .40 cal.

"Come on, Blood. You can't be serious. Put that gun down," Sho-Tyme pleaded.

"Nah, I ain't putting shit down. Unlock ya phone and hand it to me," Bricks ordered.

He was so caught up in his own rage that he never heard Reem creep up behind him.

"Nigga, I said unlock the phone and hand it over."

BOC!

Reem fired the first shot, the bullet hitting Bricks in his skull. The impact sent him crashing to the floor.

"Told you I was gonna catch you, pussy," Reem said, then fired two more shots into Bricks' already dead body.

***

For the past six hours, Peso had been in the studio recording track after track. He had been in studios before, but nothing topped this studio. Royalty Records was the real deal. Everything about the studio was top of the line. Instead of using one of the label's engineers, Peso brought Lee with him. Lee couldn't hide his excitement when they first walked through the door. Peso was finishing up his last track of the day, "Bossed Up", when an artist named Swagger B stepped into the room. Swagger B was a platinum-selling artist who currently had the rap game on smash.

"Pardon my intrusion, fellas. Don't mean to interrupt you guys, but I had to come see who was in here burning the booth down," Swagger B said, extending his hand.

"I'm Peso, and this is my engineer, Lee."

"Ya name has been buzzing a lot. Sorry I missed ya welcoming party. I was on tour, but I saw the footage. You did ya fucking thing," Swagger B said, smiling. "Where you from?"

"Same place you're from, homie."

"Word? You from the jungle? What part?"

"Coney Island," Peso proudly replied.

"About time they signed another Brooklyn nigga. Ayo, I got this track you would be perfect on. I had another artist in mind, but to be one hunnit, I'd rather rock with you if you're up for it."

"You dead ass or you playing?" Peso's head was spinning.

Swagger B, who was in heavy rotation on the radio and already had three Grammys, asked him to jump on his track. The whole ordeal felt unreal to Peso.

"Hell yeah, I'm dead ass. You with it?"

"Let's go make history, my nigga," Peso said, grinning.

Peso was nervous as he and Lee followed Swagger B to the next studio, but he wasn't going to let an opportunity this big get away from him. Peso had been a fan of Swagger B's work since he was an underground artist. Now, they were about to record a track together, which might prove to be a major move forward in Peso's career.

***

Hitta cruised through the Brooklyn streets in his Ferrari. Melly sat in the passenger's seat in complete shock. It was the first time he had ever been in a Ferrari. The stereo played at a decent volume as he rapped along with Yo Gotti as he spit his track "I Am".

I have bricks down, choppas up
It wasn't no nigga real as us
City fuckin' with me 'cause they know a nigga real as fuck
Yea, then the shit got easy

Told my dawg I had a million and he didn't believe me
I told him cool, roll a brick, bringing 22 easy
I would live it up and die before I heard about Jeezy
For real

"Damn, this shit rides smooth as fuck!" Melly shouted with excitement. "This shit must've cost you half a mill."

Hitta smiled modestly as he drove.

"Damn near, but soon enough, you gonna be riding 'round on a half a mill yourself. Just stay focused and loyal."

"Loyalty ain't no slogan for me, big bro. It's my way of life. Through good and bad, a nigga's all in with you. Hitta, you put in work with a nigga when the nigga I grew up with left me dry. When it was time to get busy with them Crip niggas, the niggas chose a color over loyalty. I'm forever grateful for what you did, bro. I'll never forget that," Melly expressed from the heart.

"I don't get no pat on the back for that. Don't ever feel like you owe me anything. Niggas you eat with are niggas you go to war with. I ate with you every day, baby bro. So, the way I see it, getting busy with you that day was a must," Hitta replied as he pulled up in front of the parole office.

"I'ma be right here, bro. Do ya thing."

"Kopy. Hopefully, this bitch don't have me in here all day," Melly said as he exited the car.

As soon as Melly made it inside the building, a cherry red BMW pulled up behind Hitta's Ferrari. The Ferrari had dark tint, so he wasn't worried about being seen. Hitta's eyes lit up when he saw Supreme get out of the passenger seat.

Gotchu now, you bitch-ass nigga, Hitta said to himself.

Supreme was the ring leader of the group of Crips who jumped him and Melly on Rikers Island. Pulling out his phone, Hitta placed a call.

***

Heat and Caine were driving around in an Audi A8, blasting music and smoking weed. When Heat's phone rang, he lowered the volume of the stereo before answering the call.

"Yo, what's the word?"

"Ain't shit. Where you at right now?" Hitta asked from the other end.

"Me and Caine are on our way to get Shoota from parole. We like ten minutes away."

"I got him. I'm already here. When he comes out, I'ma have him jump in with me. I need you and Caine to handle something for me. Y'all strapped?"

"Hell yeah. Wassup?" Heat asked.

"Pull up to the building. It's a red beamer parked behind me. Watch it closely. I'ma text you when I see my boy walking out. Stay by your phone."

"Say less. I'm on my way."

***

Melly strolled out of the parole office with a big Kool-Aid smile on his face and hopped into the Ferrari.

"Fuck you cheesing so hard for, nigga? Ya PO just sucked you off?" Hitta joked.

"Shit, I wish she would have, but shawty just put me on once a month. So, I don't gotta report until next month," Melly explained. "But yo, why I just seen that fuck nigga Supreme in there?"

"I know. I watched him walk in. I got something for your boy, though," Hitta replied, rolling down the window.

***

Supreme lit a Newport as he left out the parole building. He inhaled and blew out thick rings of smoke. Just as he reached his BMW, he was greeted by a masked gunman.

Supreme's eyes widened with fear. Two shots hit Supreme, killing him instantly.

The gunman took off running down the block until he reached the Audi A8. He snatched the door open and jumped in the passenger seat. The car peeled off before he got a chance to close the door.

"I picked that nigga!" Caine said, sounding excited as he pulled the mask from his face.

Heat looked at Caine and smiled when he saw the rush his friend got from putting in work.

"You sure that nigga parked?" Heat asked from the driver's seat

"C'mon, bro, don't question my gun game," Caine responded with a smile.

***

Hitta pulled off after the last shot. He smiled to himself as he thought about how easily he was able to execute his plan. Shoota had gotten in the car before Caine showed up.

"Play well called, Coach," Melly said, admiring Hitta for the way he took care of Supreme.

"My plays are always well called, nigga," Hitta replied, looking over at him before he began to laugh.

"Yo, big bro, tell me you got some bud on you," Shoota said from the backseat.

Hitta tossed him a Ziploc bag full of weed.

Thirty-five minutes later, they pulled up in front of Melly's mother's house.

"I'll be right back," Melly said before getting out of the car.

Hitta turned to Shoota. "Hop in the front, baby bro."

Just as Shoota got in the passenger seat, Melly walked to the driver's side and handed Hitta a brown paper bag.

"It's all there, bro."

"I'll take ya word for it. I'ma have somebody come drop you off something in the next hour. Just be by ya phone, bro."

"Say less. Y'all niggas be safe."

Hitta pulled off, heading for the interstate. They reached Coney Island in minutes. It was a beautiful day. All the hustlers were out; the females, too. The kids were running to the ice cream truck. After Hitta and Shoota got out of the Ferrari, Hitta walked to the ice cream truck window. The kids surrounded him.

"Yo, Mr. Softy, wassup? How you been?" Hitta said, greeting the elderly Puerto Rican man.

Mr. Softy had been around since Hitta was a kid.

"I'm well, Amir. How's the family?" Mr. Softy replied.

"Everyone is well. Aye, Mr. Softy, how much money would you make today driving on ya routes?"

"I'd say about five hundred."

"Bet. I'ma help you help the kids. I will give you a band if you stay here for the day and serve them ice cream."

"That won't be a problem."

Hitta pulled out a stack of money from his pocket and handed it to the elderly man.

"Thank you. Thank you so much," Mr. Softy said sincerely.

Little did Hitta know he had helped Mr. Softy out tremendously.

"Free ice cream all day for everyone!" Hitta shouted to the kids.

More and more kids surrounded the truck. Hitta ordered a vanilla milkshake for himself before walking off.

Chapter 20

"Listen, baby girl, quit that fucking job!" Peso shouted, furious about having to have this same conversation again.

This was the first real argument he and Princess had since they met.

"Quit my job and live off you? Tyler, you must be crazy," Princess shot back.

"Princess, I'm a legal millionaire now. I don't want my lady working in some funky-ass hospital. How about this, you can focus on your hair and eyelash line, fuck working! You could put a hundred percent into that and start another business I'll invest! You could be your own boss and make your own money and we'll level up together.

"Anything?" she asked, a huge grin on her face.

"Yes, babe, anything. Now call that hospital and tell them you quit."

Peso's phone rang. He looked at the screen; it was from Mariah. He answered it quickly.

"Why are you just now calling me back?" Peso asked, his tone dripping with frustration.

"'Cause I have a life, Tyler. The world doesn't stop when you call. Now, what's so important?"

"You always said that when I get on, you wanted to be my manager, remember? Well, if you still want the job, you got it."

"Oh my God, baby daddy! Yes! Thank you. I promise I won't let you down. Where's Princess? We have to celebrate.

Drinks are on me," Mariah said without stopping to catch a breath.

"She's right here, but I gotta end this call. See you tonight," he replied.

"Tyler, you really have a great soul. You work so hard to make everyone around you happy," Princess said, wrapping her arms around him.

Peso lifted Princess to sit on the countertop.

"Do I make you happy?" he asked while standing between her legs and with his hands on her thighs.

"Yes, you do. I've never been so happy in my life. What did I do to deserve such a good man?"

"Nah, what did I do to deserve such a wonderful woman? Do you know what will really make me happy?" Peso asked, looking Princess in her eyes.

"Tell me, bae," she responded.

"You quitting that damn job!"

"Okay. I'll quit, Tyler," she said, conceding.

Peso kissed her lips.

"You won't regret it, baby. I promise. Just pick something you wanna do, and I got you. I want you to be a boss, P, that's all," he said before kissing her deeply.

***

The Crown Heights backyard was filled with a ton of Blood gang members—all their attention focused on Reem, who stood in the middle of the group. He spoke loud and clear so everyone in attendance could hear him.

"I called all of you here because a few things need to be addressed. As you all may already know, an attempt was made on my life. B-Gunnz tried to push the button on me and have all of you vote me out because his brother was a fucking rat."

Reem looked around at all the members before continuing.

"He sent Bricks at me, then tried to get y'all to ride with him. I harbor no ill feelings towards anyone. Y'all was just following protocol. However, let me be the first to tell y'all today is a new day. Today is the day we gain our independence. We no longer answer to B-Gunnz or the members of the roundtable. We are now an independent set. Anybody under B-Gunnz is food. When we see food, we eat it. So, I expect nothing less. If they not with us, they're against us. Any of you not feeling anything I just said? If so, speak now."

Everyone remained quiet. None of them wanted a war with B-Gunnz or any other member of the roundtable, but the call had been made. So, they were all ready for war.

"As you niggas already know, we can't play around. There is no room for error. I will have B-Gunnz taken care of behind the wall. You niggas focus on the soldiers that he has in the streets. Anybody who didn't show to this meeting is food. That means B-Gunnz has their loyalty, so it's on sight. This meeting is now concluded."

***

Hitta was running late for the basketball game, so he texted Peso and told him to warm up with the young boys until he got there. He left the barbershop, making his way to his car. Hitta didn't notice the smoke-grey Acura parked three cars down from his vehicle. As he reached for the door, two masked gunmen jumped out of the Acura. Hitta's instinct told him to look up. The first shot missed his head by an inch.

BOC! BOC! BOC! BOC!

More shots rang out. Hitta quickly pulled his .40 cal and returned fire. The two gunmen ran for cover, but Hitta wasn't letting them get away this time.

BOC! BOC! BOC!

He chased them down, emptying the clip. He reloaded quickly as he continued to chase them. A slug hit one of the gunmen in the back, causing him to hit the pavement hard. Hitta ran until he was standing over the gunman, putting two more bullets in him and silencing the dude for good before running back to his car. He jumped in his Ferrari, peeling off recklessly.

By the time he made it to Kaiser Park, it was packed for the Starbury Basketball Tournament opening day. Peso stood with the young boys, giving them the pep talk he thought they needed. The young men were dressed in the uniforms and Jordans purchased for them a few weeks earlier.

"Ayo, Peso, the game starts in a few minutes. Is Hitta gonna be here?" one of the kids asked, looking sad.

"I'ma call him now. Y'all just get warmed up. Start a layup line," Peso replied, pulling out his phone. He had a text from his partner.

Hitta: *Yo bro, I ran into a lil' situation. Had to change clothes. I'll be at the park in a minute!*

Peso realized the message was sent twenty minutes earlier, but he still responded. He wondered what "lil' situation" Hitta had run into.

Peso: *Say less, bro. Just get here quick. These lil' niggas looking all sad and shit. We can't let them down.*

As soon as he pressed send, he looked up and saw Hitta making his way toward the court.

***

Katrina's phone had been ringing non-stop since Peso's welcoming party. Everybody wanted to interview him, book him for shows, or have him as a feature on their tracks. She checked her text messages and saw she had a message from Peso, giving her the name, phone number, and email address of his manager. Katrina sighed in relief. Now she could forward all the emails she had been getting about Peso to Mariah.

Roxy walked in with shopping bags in both hands.

"Hey, Mommy!" She greeted Kat full of excitement.

"Hey, baby," Katrina responded, hugging her daughter. "What's in the bags?"

"A bunch of the good stuff, but here, this is for you."

Roxy handed Katrina one of the shopping bags, and she ripped through the bag quickly.

"Oh my God! How did you know I wanted this?"

She was ecstatic when she saw the Chanel bag.

"You're my mom! We have the same taste. But how are you feeling? Did you talk to Dad? He hasn't called me in a few days," Roxy commented.

"Yes, I spoke to him a little while ago. I have to meet with this new attorney on Monday. Enough about family stuff, though. How was the photo shoot and fashion show?"

"It was fun. You know your daughter slayed on that runway."

Just then, Katrina's phone rang. She looked at the screen and saw her assistant's name.

"Hey, Shanice, what's going on?"

"I'ma tell you what's going on. That sexy muthafucka Peso is what's goin' on. His single is number one on the Billboard, bitch!" Shanice shouted. "And the new joint he just did with Swagger B got the internet in a frenzy."

"What? I didn't even know they did a song together."

"Them boys are lit, girl. I'll be over there later tonight. I just wanted to be the first one to tell you that fine-ass nigga Peso is gonna take your label to a whole other level. Love you, sis. See you soon."

"Love you, too." Katrina couldn't hold back her smile.

"Why you cheesin', Ma? Talk to me," Roxy said.

"Things are going well for the label. Peso's single is number one on the Billboard Top 100, and he has a track with

Swagger B that has the internet going crazy, according to Shanice," Katrina told her.

Now Roxy was the one smiling.

"Why are you cheesing so hard? You like him, don't you?"

"I'm not even gonna front, Ma. Yes, I like him. He's so damn fine, and his swag…OMG! Everything about that boy is amazing. I'ma text him and say congrats," Roxy said, reaching for her phone in her YSL bag.

***

Peso paced back and forth on the sideline of the basketball court.

"Come the hell on, Ref! Let the kids play ball!" he shouted to the referee who just called a foul that Peso didn't agree with.

"Good call, ref! Good call!" the coach of the opposite team called out.

"Nigga, that was a bullshit call, and you know it!" Peso shouted to the coach. He shook his head as the kid went to the foul line.

Peso was super competitive. He hated to lose at anything. He had been that way since he was a child. His team was down by three points, but he looked over at the clock and realized his team could still make something happen. It was the fourth quarter, and there was a little under one minute remaining. The kid missed the free throw, and the center on Peso's squad snatched the rebound.

"Zaya, get on the ball!" Peso called out to his point guard, who was also the star player.

Zaya quickly broke free from his defender and got the ball. He swiftly dribbled past the half-court line and dished the ball to a teammate who was open at the top of the key. He was instantly double-teamed. So, he dished the ball back to Zaya, who was now at the wing of the three-point line. He took a step back, jump shot, and dished a lead pass to another teammate who was cutting to the basket. The kid managed to lay it in, and everyone in the crowd went crazy.

Peso's team was down one point with twenty-eight seconds left.

"Full court press! Full court press!" he yelled out to his team, who immediately started applying pressure on the offense. The point guard tried to dish a pass, but the ball was tipped away and stolen by Zaya. He quickly dribbled to the basket and did a behind-the-back layup, putting his team up by one point. The other coach called a timeout. Peso's team huddled around him.

"Y'all played great defense, but the game ain't over until the clock reads zero. We need some more of that great defense. Just don't foul. Giving them a trip to the free-throw line can really damage us. It's showtime! Give me a 'hard work' on three, two, one…"

"HARD WORK!" the kids chanted.

***

An unknown man stood in the lobby of a building located directly across the street from the Kaiser Park entrance. He watched the crowded park impatiently as he smoked a blunt. The sound of his ringing cell phone got his attention.

"Yo!" he answered.

"The game just ended. They should be heading to the entrance any minute now. Don't fuck this up, homie," the caller said.

"Come on, man. When don't I get the job done?"

The caller didn't respond.

"I figured you wouldn't be able to answer that. I got a situation to attend to. I'll hit you when I'm done."

After ending the call, he saw several people leaving the park, but he didn't see the men he was looking for.

***

Peso's team won the game, and everyone surrounded him, trying to get pictures with him. He wasn't used to his newfound celebrity status, but he enjoyed every bit of love that he was getting.

"Peso, let me get a picture of you and the boys," Ashley said.

All ten of the boys gathered together with Peso to take a picture.

"Come on, bae. You get in the pic, too," she said, looking at Hitta.

"You know I ain't the picture type," Hitta replied, smiling at her.

"Hitta, come on, bro. Take this one flick for the young boys. They did a great job," Peso encouraged him.

"Yeah, Coach Hitta, do it for us."

"A'ight, I got y'all," Hitta conceded, joining the group.

Ashley took a few pictures of the group, then handed her phone over to Peso. He looked through the pictures and smiled.

"Litty!" he said, handing Ashley back her phone.

"Ayo, sis, text these to me ASAP so I can throw them on my 'Gram."

"I gotcha, bro. I'ma do it right now," she replied.

"Coach, can you text them to me once you get them?" Zaya asked.

"Zaya, call me Peso. Cut that 'Coach' shit, lil bro," Peso said, not quite comfortable with his new title.

"Gotchu. I'm just glad you didn't leave us hanging today."

"I will never do that. I'm a man of my word. Long as I'm alive, I'll be here to coach every game."

"What if you're booked for a show or something?"

"I'll still be here. Don't you worry about that. Trust and believe, I gotcha, Zaya."

"Ayo, Peso, I'll meet you at the front of the park. Let me holla at Heat real quick!" Hitta yelled out.

Peso nodded his head, acknowledging Hitta as his team headed to the park's entrance. As they reached the front, Peso's phone vibrated. He looked at the screen. It was his mother FaceTiming him. Peso answered the call.

"Hey, beautiful." He smiled when her face appeared on his screen.

"Hey, baby boy. How are you?" she asked, holding back tears.

"I'm fine. Just got finished coaching the young boys. Our team won. The boys did great!"

"Baby boy, I'm so proud of you."

Peso noticed the tears falling from his mother's eyes.

"Ma, what's wrong?" he asked, becoming alarmed.

"I'm just so proud of you, Ty. You grew up to be a great man. I love you so much."

"Those aren't tears of joy, Ma. I know you. Now, what's wrong? Talk to me."

"Ty..."

She paused for a moment, trying to find the right words to break the news to him, but then realized there were no "right" words for what she had to tell him.

"Ty, the doctor just told me that I have cancer."

She hadn't planned to break the news to him this way, but at the same time, she was scared and needed someone to comfort her.

"What? No, Ma, this can't be happening. I'm on my way to you now. I'll be there in a few."

Peso's heart was beating hard and fast like a jackhammer in his chest. Peso had been running from bullets for the last few months. It would have been easier to do that than to receive this news about his mother.

BOC! BOC!

Two shots rang out; two bullets penetrated Peso's chest. His body dropped to the pavement as the crowd ran for cover. The hot lead melted away in his chest, and he began coughing up blood. The gunman approached closer, pointing his weapon at Peso, who lay there fighting to breathe. He pulled the trigger once more, hitting Peso a final time.

Hitta heard the gunshots from where he was standing talking to Heat. His heart began to pound with fear. His first thought was Peso being on the opposite end of someone's gun. He was in a full sprint as he raced to the front of the park with his gun drawn. When he reached the entrance, he saw Peso lying in a pool of blood and the gunman running in the opposite direction. Hitta aimed his cannon and fired.

BOOM! BOOM! BOOM!

The gunman spun around in a swift motion and fired back two shots.

BOC! BOC!

The bullets missed Hitta but hit an innocent bystander.

BOOM! BOOM!

This time, one of Hitta's bullets found its target, hitting the gunman in the back of the head. Hitta watched him fall in slow motion, hitting the pavement face first. He then ran over to his lifeless body and pumped several more bullets into him before searching the man's pocket for his phone.

***

The ambulance pulled to a stop at the emergency entrance of Lutheran Medical Center. A doctor and several nurses were waiting for them. Inside the ambulance, a female paramedic was doing her best to keep Peso alive; he had lost a massive amount of blood.

The ambulance's back doors flew open, and the stretcher carrying Peso's listless body was pulled from the truck and quickly pushed through the hospital's doors. He was drenched in blood; his eyes were closed, and he appeared to be dead. The doctors and emergency room medical staff worked quickly to stabilize Peso so they could get him to surgery.

$$***$$

Shoota sat in a corner chair in the emergency room's waiting area, crying openly. Earlier that day, he found out his mother had cancer. He hadn't had time to process that news, and now his brother was fighting for his life. Shoota's anger was palpable. At the moment, the only thing on his mind was revenge.

Princess walked into the waiting room and saw Shoota. She had been on a break and was headed back to her nurse's station. When she saw him, she immediately knew something was wrong. A feeling of anxiousness came over her as she approached him.

"What's wrong, bro?" she asked. "What you doin' here?"

"It's Peso. He got shot. You didn't know?"

Princess's legs went weak, and Shoota caught her before she hit the floor. Shoota pulled her into his arms, trying to console her, but she was inconsolable.

"It's gonna be okay, sis. Don't cry. Please don't cry."

Hitta walked into the emergency room with purpose. Heat and several other members of the U.G.F. were behind him. He was on some whole other shit now. Someone had harmed his brother, and if he had to fuck up the whole city to get to the bottom of it, then that was what he was going to do.

The ER began filling up with people who were concerned about Peso and praying for him to pull through. It's like once the news got out about him being shot, the whole hood showed up to show their love and support.

When Shoota saw Hitta, he walked over to him.

"What the fuck happened, bro? Who did this?" he asked Hitta.

"The nigga who shot him is gone, bro, but we gotta do somethin' about the nigga who sent him 'cause this nigga ain't gonna stop," Hitta replied.

"Who sent him to do this, bro? Was it that nigga Murda?"

Hitta nodded his head, confirming Shoota's suspicion.

"Are you sure it was him?" Shoota asked, narrowing his eyes.

"Yeah, I'm sure! I took dude's phone and read through all of the messages. Matt Murda was behind all the attempts on Peso's life recently. The nigga put a tracker on—."

Before Hitta could finish speaking, the doctor walked into the waiting room. Those who had been sitting were out of their seats in seconds, surrounding the doctor.

"Who's here for Tyler Carter?" the doctor asked, looking around at all the people in the room.

"That would be us, Doc," Hitta answered anxiously, wanting to know if Peso was still alive.

"What is your relationship to him?"

"He's our brother," Shoota said quickly.

Mariah walked in holding Mya's hand, her eyes full of tears.

"Well, your brother is a very strong man. He took some bad shots, so I can't make any promises. However, he's young and strong. The next twenty-four hours will be crucial, though."

"Can we see him?" Shoota asked, wanting to lay eyes on Peso.

"They're closing him up, and then he will be taken to recovery. Once he's in ICU, I'll have the nurses come get you."

"Thank you, Doc. Thank you so much," Shoota said, shaking the doctor's hand.

They all felt a sense of relief, everyone but Princess. She wouldn't be okay until she could see Peso.

***

On the other side of Brooklyn, Matt Murda sat inside Peter Luger's Steakhouse. Across the table was Timah, his fiancée and the love of his life.

"Babe, Tyler got shot today. I hope you didn't have anything to do with that," she inquired, feeling the animosity between Matt and Hitta had gone too far.

"How can I have somethin' to do with that when I'm sitting here with you?"

"Matt, I'm not stupid. You may be here with me, but your arms reach very far. You and Amir need to dead this madness. Y'all have too much history. It's fucked up how Tyler is stuck in the middle of y'all stupidity. The boy gets one of the biggest record deals in history, and now he's laid up in a hospital bed fighting for his life," Timah stated.

"Babe, I didn't have anything to do with that," he lied.

"So you gonna sit and lie to my face?"

"I'm not lying. I said I didn't play no fucking part in that! Now leave it alone!" he said, raising his voice.

Timah shot him a look that bled venom.

"Who the *fuck* do you think you talking to? One of them lil' birds you fuckin', nigga? Ain't no fucking 'leave it alone'. Do you think about how ya actions can hurt my family or me? My mother still lives out there, Matt! What if they do something to me when I'm out there? Huh? Have you ever thought about that?"

"Timah, they not that stupid. Besides, this beef don't have anything to do with family members. It's personal. I ain't involve they families. I'm only aiming for them. I know them, Tee. You're safe."

He reached across the table for her hands, but she pulled them away, not wanting him to touch her.

"I'm not safe until you dead this shit with them. They are ya friends, Matt," she replied, not understanding what was driving his decisions.

"No! They *were* my friends. Hitta shot me, and Peso picked a side. I ain't deadin' shit. Now, just drop this convo," Matt said firmly.

"And YOU shot them both! Rico must be turning in his grave right now. Maybe if ya damn ego wasn't so big, y'all would be able to fix this."

"Timah, stop. I said drop it!"

"I'm not dropping shit. Ya ass gonna listen to me."

"You know what, enjoy ya dinner. I ain't hungry no more. Here, take the car. I'm out."

Matt Murda pushed out of his seat, dropping the car keys on the table. Timah watched the back of him as he walked out of the restaurant.

Chapter 21

Hitta walked into Rick's dealership accompanied by Shoota and Heat. This was one thing Hitta knew he could take care of quickly. He would not tolerate a spy in his camp. Seeing Hitta, Rick stopped what he was doing and quickly walked over to the young men.

"Hitta, my friend, how can I help you today?"

"Let's go to ya office. We need to talk," Hitta told him.

"Sure, no problem," Rick said, leading the way to his office.

Hitta turned to Shoota and Heat. "I'll be right back."

Rick and Hitta went into the office. Hitta closed the door behind them.

"So what brings you here?" Rick asked, taking a seat behind his desk.

"What brings me here, huh?" Hitta laughed. "Your actions caused this visit. Do you have something you wanna tell me, Rick?"

This question made Rick nervous, but he tried to mask his features hoping that he wouldn't give himself away. It was too late, though. Hitta knew everything he needed to know.

"What would I have to tell you, my friend?" Rick asked, trying to play the odds.

"Tell me how you set my brother up!" Hitta shouted.

"I would never do such a thing, Hitta," he lied.

"So you didn't place a tracking device on my brother's Ferrari?" Hitta asked point-blank. He was done dancing with Rick.

Rick put his head down, his mind racing a mile a minute. He was contemplating denying the accusations, but he knew Hitta was crazy enough to kill him right there in his office. So, he decided to be honest, hoping it would save his life.

"Hitta, listen, I'm gonna be completely honest with you. I had to place a tracker on the car, or Matt would have killed me. I'm sorry, man. He forced me to. I didn't wanna die. I have a family."

He began weeping like a child.

"So you didn't think I would kill you once I found out?" Hitta asked, wanting him to know the consequences of his decision.

Rick wept harder.

"Ohhh, lemme guess. You thought I wasn't gonna find out."

"Hitta, please don't kill me, man. I have money, lots of money. I'll pay you. Please just don't kill me," Rick begged.

"If my brother would've died, money wouldn't have brought him back, Rick."

"So what can I do to fix this? I'll do anything, man."

"I'm glad you're willing to do anything," Hitta replied, handing Rick the manilla envelope he had in his hand.

"What's this?" Rick asked, confused.

"It's your ticket to stay alive. Open it."

Rick opened the manila envelope, pulling out the stack of papers. He started reading the documents and then looked up Hitta.

"I can't sign over my dealerships."

"You can, and you will. Besides, it's not like we're taking over the whole thing. Just half of ya business is ours. I mean, you did play a part in getting my brother shot. Consider it a payment for our troubles."

Rick dropped his head in defeat.

"Rick, I know you're thinking about snitchin', but you can't go to the police because you're an accomplice to an attempted murder."

Hitta chuckled at the irony of it all.

"Hold up. I have something that will make this easier for you."

Hitta pulled up a few pictures on his phone. The pictures were of Rick's wife, daughter, and mistress. When Rick saw the photos, he quickly signed the documents.

"Thank you, man. I'm glad things didn't have to get messy around here. Now that we're partners, I want my first payment."

Despair was all over Rick's face.

"Don't make that face, Rick. No need to be all sad and shit. I don't want it in cash. My lil' brother has been lookin' at those Maseratis since they got here. Do the paperwork on the black one and the smoke-grey one."

Hitta sat looking out of the window, watching the way Shoota and Heat were admiring the Maseratis.

"I'ma smoke a blunt while I wait. And don't take all day, man. I got shit to do."

"You can't smoke in here, Hitta. C'mon, this is a place of business, bro," he replied as Hitta lit up the blunt.

"Yeah, a business that's half mine. Man, get the damn paperwork ready."

Hitta took a phone call while he waited.

"Yo, wassup, brodie?" he answered.

"What's the word, bro? How's Peso?"

"He gonna be a'ight. He's the strongest nigga I know. You know bro been through worst shit."

"Yeah, I already know. Sorry for taking a few days to get to you, but I found out what happened. That shit is all over Facebook, the 'Gram, TMZ, and a bunch of shit now. I'm actually about to get off the belt now. You in the hood?"

"Kopy. Nah, I'm at the dealership. I'll talk to you when I get to the hood. Peso is in Lutheran. I'll meet you there, bro. Be safe," Hitta said before ending the call.

"Always, bro. You too."

***

Back at Coney Island, Breeze got off the Belt Parkway and saw the police were behind him, flashing their lights for him to pull over.

Fuck! he said to himself.

His first thought was to take off on them because he had two hundred and fifty thousand dollars cash in the trunk, but he quickly went against his first instinct and pulled over. To his knowledge, he hadn't broken any laws, but a black man was never truly safe in the hands of the police. Thinking on his feet, Breeze turned his phone on audio record. The officers were approaching his car—one to the left of the car and the other on the right. He sighed when he saw Detective Brown, the dirty cop who killed his friend a few years prior.

"Oh shit! If it isn't the one and only Breeze. What's wrong? You made enough money outta town you decided to come back home?"

"Enough with the small talk, Brown. Why did y'all pull me over?" Breeze asked.

"Ya tints. Now, step out the car!" Detective Brown ordered.

"Man, you just said I was pulled over for tints. Give me my ticket and let me go about my business."

Detective Brown laughed. "Step out of the car now. I ain't gonna repeat myself again."

He snatched the door open, and Breeze got out.

"Do you have any weapons on you?"

"Nah, just a few dollars and my cell phone," he responded.

Detective Brown patted Breeze down, but he didn't find anything.

"What's in the car?"

"Nothin'. I don't have shit, man. Now gimme my ticket so I can go about my business."

"Pop the trunk," Detective Brown ordered.

"No, I ain't poppin' no trunk. Y'all need a warrant to go in there."

"Nigga, I don't need a warrant for shit. I'm the law. Cuff this nigga," he told his partner, who quickly placed the handcuffs on Breeze.

Detective Brown popped the trunk, then began searching it. After moving a few things around, he noticed a Gucci duffle bag. He unzipped it, and a big smile appeared on his face.

Fuck! Breeze shook his head in disgust. He couldn't believe his luck.

"Look what we have. This has to be about a quarter millie, huh, Breeze?"

"Brown, just take the money and let me go."

"Oh shit, you trying to bribe an officer? That's another charge. What else is in here?"

"Nothin', man. Just take the money," Breeze repeated.

"I'm gonna take the money, nigga, but I'm also gonna take some of this shit and charge you for it. It's enough money to go around. What you think, partner?"

"I think we should collar him for some of it, then keep the rest for ourselves."

***

Peso lay in the hospital bed, Princess and Mya by his bedside. There had been non-stop traffic in his room all day with people paying him visits.

"Daddy, when can you go home? Granny is real sick, and we need to go see her," Mya said.

"I don't know, baby girl. Hopefully, they let me out today so we can go see Granny," he replied, then turned to address Princess. "Babe, I thought I told you to quit," he said, referring to her employment at the hospital.

"I know, babe. I gotcha," she told him.

"Cool. Since you got me, today is your last day."

Just then, Mariah walked into the room. Her eyes were red and puffy. Peso could tell she had been crying.

"Riah, I'm good. You don't need to be stressing ya'self anymore," Peso informed her, assuming she was stressing over his condition.

"It's not you, Ty. It's ya mom. She…she passed away."

The news of his mother stunned him. Peso couldn't believe what he was hearing. He thought he had more time.

"Please tell me you're lying, Riah! Please tell me she didn't die!" he cried, his eyes squeezed shut.

"I wouldn't lie about nothing like this, Ty. She gave me this letter to give to you," she responded, handing Peso a sealed envelope.

"I need a minute. Y'all mind steppin' out the room? Mya, go with Mommy and Princess. Daddy needs to clear his mind. Okay, baby?"

"No, Daddy! I wanna stay with you."

"Mya, please go with them for a few minutes. You're coming right back. Daddy is gonna be okay," he assured her.

"Come on, baby. Daddy needs to be by himself. It's okay, I promise," Mariah told her.

Once Mariah, Mya, and Princess left the room, Peso looked at the envelope in his hand. He took a minute to decide if he was going to open it. He wasn't sure he could handle what his mother would have to say. Finally, Peso opened the letter.

To My Handsome Baby Boy!

I pray this missive finds you in the greatest stages of health in all aspects…Mind, Body, and Soul! If you are reading this letter, it means I did not make it. My battle with cancer got the best of me. Do not be sad, son. Momma was tired, so God called me home. My work on Earth was done. I overcame my addiction to crack cocaine and became strong enough to become a great mother again. I see that despite all the bad I've done, I did a great job with you and Tymel. The two of you are the best sons a mother could have. Y'all are some amazing young men. Both of you finished school as I asked. Then you bought me my dream home. Not too many mothers get this lucky. ☺

Tyler, live your life to the fullest. Take over that music industry, win some Grammys for Momma, and bring home some platinum plaques. Show the world that you are GREAT! Do not worry about me, son. Don't cry for me either. I am at peace. I am alive through you, Tymel, and Mya. Just continue making me proud, son. Continue being a great father, a great son, a great brother, a great friend, a great rapper, and a great man. Change lives while you can. Use your voice for something positive, not just rap music. God gave you that talent, so in the process of being one of the world's greatest rappers, do a little of God's work.

Son, when I heard those gunshots, it broke my heart, but you are a strong man. You will survive and get well. Maybe God called me home to save you. Thank Him, Tyler,

Well, I'm not gonna talk ya ears off (LOL). Just know that I love you with all my heart. I'm so proud of you, Tyler. Take care of your brother for me. Oh, by the way, you better take care of Princess. Make her happy. She is the one for you, trust me. Sooner or later, you will see why. Momma knows best. Tell my baby Mya not to be sad. I am watching over her. Kiss her and let her know that I love her sooo much! Now wipe those tears and go continue to be great!

Love Always,
Mommy (XOXO)
Your #1 Fan

Peso was in tears when Hitta walked into the room. Hitta approached his best friend, and leaning over, he hugged him.

"Let it out, bro. She is in a better place now."

"She's gone, bro. My mom is really dead," he said, continuing to cry.

"I know, bro. Nothing is gonna bring her back, but we can share my mom. You know she prolly loves you more than she loves me," he said, trying to get Peso to laugh.

"You're a real friend, Hitta, for real. I love you, my nigga." Peso expressed sincerely.

"I love you more, nigga. It's time you get out the streets and be great for her, bro, real shit! You don't have nothing holding you back. You paid ya dues, big homie."

Chapter 22

Peso sat on one end of a twelve-man roundtable, and Hitta sat on the other end. They were accompanied by ten of the most loyal members of their organization—Shoota, Heat, Santana, Eazy, Slim Goon, Melly, Kavali, Breeze, Wopo, and Reem. Peso and Hitta handpicked each man prior to the gathering.

"To a New Year and new money, but to the same love and loyalty," Peso said while holding up his glass.

Everyone at the table did the same.

"I love y'all niggas, man, for real. Y'all the realest niggas I know. We took some losses, but we won way more. So, I'm grateful. We should all be grateful. We leveled all the way up, and we're still here. We could all be dead, but we're very much alive and living! We could be locked up, but we're free. We could be broke, but we all muthafuckin' rich."

Peso laughed, then continued.

"When the ball drops, my first album drops. I'm happy as a bitch right now. I got two multi-platinum singles, four songs on the Billboard charts, two of the hottest mixtapes in the streets, millions of downloads, millions of views, and millions of people who love me. Life is great. On the real, though, none of this shit would mean anything without y'all because family means everything to me. I pray we continue to level up. Anything in the way of our success gets knocked down. If they ain't with us, they against us. I'ma let Hitta take the floor."

Peso took a seat, and Hitta stood.

"I love all you niggas in this room like my momma birthed y'all. Words can't express how sacred our bond is. Reem, you're the only nigga in this room who isn't a part of the U.G.F., but you're family. So, you still get a seat at the roundtable. As you all may know, the U.G.F. has an alliance with Reem's nation of Bloods. So, I expect for you all to treat them as you would treat one of ours because they are one of us."

Hitta looked around at the men before continuing.

"I got a new plug. I'm getting better numbers, which means y'all will get better numbers. How does twenty a bird sound?" he asked, waiting for a reaction from the group.

"That sounds damn good to me," Hitta said, answering his own question.

"Those of you who pulled away from the drugs and found y'all way with fraud, I'm loaded with numbers, top-of-the-line card info. My pieces don't decline. Each man here will get a packet with a hundred thousand numbers—some credit and some debit. Y'all should make about nine mill or better. All we want back is a mill a piece. If you not with it, then leave the packet on the table. Oh shit, I almost forgot. I got a surprise for y'all."

Hitta stopped talking to send a text message. Seconds later, Ashley and Princess walked through the door carrying silver trays. Ashley's tray carried five Audemars Piquet jewelry boxes. The tray Princess was carrying held five Rolex jewelry boxes. The tray that had the Audemars was placed in front of Hitta, and the Rolexes were placed in front of Peso. The ladies left the room, leaving the men to their business.

"Once the ball drops and midnight, the U.G.F. banner called The Jewelry Box will be official. Only the twelve of us will know about this banner. This is our own lil' members-only club. We on some real secret society shit. Peso's line is Rolex Diamonds, and my line is Cuban links. Bro and I handpicked the ten of you. Now we're gonna pick our starting five. Take ya first pick, beloved," Hitta said, looking to Peso, who picked Reem.

Hitta picked Santana, and the two men continued going back and forth, respectively choosing members.

Once they finished, Hitta told the men, "Y'all can open the cases."

Each man Hitta picked received an 18-karat gold Audemar, and every man Peso picked received an 18-karat gold Presidential Rolex. Both styles were flooded with diamonds.

"Happy New Year, gentlemen, and welcome!" Peso said, raising his glass.

***

Matt Murda and Timah sat in the backseat of the Rolls Royce. They were heading to Jamie Estrada's New Year's party. Also in the Rolls Royce was Rah-Rah and his longtime girlfriend, Cola. As they made their way to the event, the quartet popped bottles and passed around blunts. Matt Murda suddenly remembered the letter he had in his pockets. Pulling it out, he began to read it.

12-27-2013
Song: Ain't No Click
Artist: Lloyd Banks
Mood: G-makkin

Beloved brother,
I pray this missive travels its proper channels and finds you in the greatest stages of health in all aspects—mind, body, and soul. As for self, I'm elevating through my current endeavors, remaining firm against all odds as I'm forced to endure these inhuman circumstances behind these

oppressive walls. First and foremost, East Coast G'Z Blood! Long time no speak, Komrade. I know you not still tripping over that Puffy & J.Lo shit. (LMAO) Let it go, Blood. We bigger than that. Anyways, we do have a common enemy.

Yeah, I'm aware of ya little beef with Hitta and the U.G.F., and I'm pretty sure you know about my issue with Reem. To be honest with you, Blood, I'm in dire need of your assistance. I can't lie to you, these young niggas feasting. They real powerful. All the other homies talking about they not supporting niggas personal beefs, but you, Murda, are a renegade like me—Blood in, Blood out. We do what the fuck we want. I'm asking you for ya assistance, beloved. Even if you can't stand side by side with me in this war, a few of your soldiers will be appreciated, and I will owe you a favor. Get back at me, Blood. Signing off but never out!

Respectfully,
Your Komrade
OG B-Gunnz

Chapter 23

Two days after the ball dropped, Peso's album titled *Mary's Son* was certified Platinum and number one on the Billboard chart. He was feeling good, really good! So good that he was driving around in a snow white Bentley GT. In the backseat of the Bentley sat a duffle bag filled with one-hundred-dollar bills that totaled one million dollars.

Peso cruised the streets of Brooklyn with no set destination. After stopping at a supermarket in the heart of Brownsville, he grabbed thirty thousand dollars out of the duffle bag and walked inside.

"Excuse me, sir. Where's the owner or manager?" Peso asked one of the workers.

"The owner isn't here, but I'll go get my manager," the worker replied, then walked off to find the manager. Minutes later, he returned with a pretty woman who appeared to be in her thirties.

"Good afternoon. My name is Peso."

"I'm Karen, and I know who you are. My daughter is crazy about you. How can I help you?" she asked, smiling.

Peso handed her three stacks of crispy bills.

"That's thirty thousand dollars. I want you to let people shop until it runs out. Can you do that for me?"

"Sure! That won't be a problem. I'll go announce to the shoppers that all items are free," Karen replied.

By the time she made it back, Peso was walking out the door. Somebody must have tipped off the media that he was around because Brooklyn 12 News was already outside. Peso went to his Bentley and left the scene. Next, he pulled over at a nearby housing project. Before stepping out of the car, he lit a blunt that was in his ashtray. He pulled more money out of the duffle bag, placing it in the front seat. A teenage girl was walking by pushing a shopping cart. She had a young boy on a scooter with her. He was no older than nine.

"Boy, yo ass better slow down before you fall and bust open that big ol' watermelon head of yours." The girl laughed at her own comment.

"My head ain't no melon. Yo' daddy got a big ol' lemon head," the little boy retorted. He couldn't stop laughing.

"Oh my God!" the girl screamed, recognizing Peso.

"Ssshhh!" Peso said, putting his finger to his mouth.

"It's really you. Oh my God! Oh my God." She was now jumping around.

Peso laughed, turning his attention to the little boy. "Wassup, lil homie? What's ya name?"

He held out his hand for the boy to slap it.

"My name is Romeo."

"You doing good in school?"

"Yeah, I get good grades," the little boy replied honestly.

The girl was now in tears.

"And what's your name?" Peso asked, turning to the young girl.

"My name is Kirra," she responded. "Oh my God! Can I hug you? Can we take a picture?"

"How old are you?"

"I'm seventeen."

"Did you finish school?"

"No. I'm in my last year now."

"Make sure you finish," Peso told her. "Don't let nothing stop you. Never let no man disrespect or take advantage of you. And you, little homie, stay out the streets! Finish school and take care of your family. A real man takes good care of his family."

Peso grabbed the money from the front seat and dropped it in the girl's shopping cart.

"Happy New Year!" were his last words before he jumped back in his Bentley and pulled off.

***

Breeze drove around collecting the money. He had Peso's new album knocking in the speakers. When his phone rang, he lowered the music and accepted the call.

"Yo!"

"Hey, Mr. Davis. Happy New Year," his attorney, Kenneth Rich, said on the other end.

"Same to you, my guy. What do I owe the pleasure of this phone call?" Breeze asked.

"I have some disturbing news."

"Wassup? Talk to me."

"The feds picked up your case after the grand jury dismissed it. You have seventy-two hours to turn yourself in, or the government will issue a warrant for your arrest," Mr. Rich explained.

"What about my bail?"

"Your money will be returned to you. Now that the feds have the case, that bail means nothing. Don't worry, though. I will get you a new bond when we go in front of the magistrate judge."

"A'ight bet. In seventy-two hours I'll be at ya office," Breeze promised before ending the call.

"Fuck!"

He hit the steering wheel and pulled over in front of his trap on Fayette Street. Before getting out of the car, he lit a Newport and took a drag of the cigarette. Then he approached the door of the traphouse and knocked. Several seconds later, a blonde, blue-eyed white chick named Dee opened the door.

"Hey, Breeze!" she exclaimed, hugging him.

"Wassup, Dee? Where's that nigga Black?" Breeze asked.

"He's in the room. You know where it is."

When Breeze entered the bedroom, Black was counting up a bunch of money.

"Black, what's the word, big dawg?"

"Ain't shit, homie. Just tryin' to eat," Black replied, not missing a beat on counting the money.

Black was Breeze's top worker. He had been working for Breeze since he started hustling in Binghamton.

"Listen, bro, I gotta go out of town for a few weeks, so I'ma leave you sitting pretty with ten birds. I need back thirty-two grand a joint, though."

"Say no more, but yo, that's two hundred large in that Champ's bag."

"Kopy. I'll swing through later with the work, or I'll send Freaky," Breeze said, reaching for the bag.

He gave Black some dap, waved goodbye to Dee, and walked out the door. For the next hour, Breeze drove around collecting more cash before heading to his crib. The house didn't actually belong to him. It belonged to his longtime girlfriend Amina, but whenever Breeze wasn't at his home, he was there. He loved her, but he didn't appreciate her. Breeze constantly took her for granted, but she continued to love him through all his imperfections.

When Breeze walked in the house, he was greeted by the prettiest little girl he had ever seen—Amina's three-year-old daughter, Ivy. Breeze and Amina had been together for six years, but during their split, Amina got pregnant by some square dude who couldn't handle her. Amina was too raw for him, was what Breeze always said when people asked him how did he steal Amina back from her daughter's father.

"Hey, lil' momma!" he said, picking Ivy up and smothering her with kisses. She wasn't his biological daughter, but he loved her like she was his.

"Breezy, stop," she giggled, pushing his face from hers.

Breeze chuckled before putting her down.

"Where your mama at?

"In the bathroom," Ivy responded, pointing in that direction.

He headed to the master bathroom where Amina was in the mirror curling her hair.

"Hey, baby girl." He kissed her on the lips.

"You look like you're having a long day," she told him.

"Damn, it's that obvious? I got some bad news, Amina," he said, trying to figure out how he to tell her his news.

"What's wrong, baby?" she asked, putting down the curling iron to caress his face.

"In less than seventy-two hours, I have to turn myself in to the feds," he explained while looking down at her.

"To the feds? For what? Oh my God, Breeze, people don't come home from the feds." Amina began to cry. "I'm here, though, no matter what. I swear, bae. What do you need me to do? Just tell me, and it's done," she said, rambling.

"Bae, relax. I got locked up with money and a gun. I ain't kill nobody. But check it, though. I got seven hundred grand in the trunk of my Beamer. Take that somewhere safe and stash it. I also got two toy chests in the attic—both of them filled with money. And don't worry; your crib is safe. I keep my business away from home. Just hold all this bread for me. No matter where I'm at, you will never need for nothing," he promised.

"I got you, bae. I'm here. I ain't going nowhere."

"Good, 'cause I got a plan. Don't worry, I'll be home soon."

***

Peso had been driving around all day passing out money to random black people in the streets. He now had a hundred thousand left in his duffle bag, and he was crossing through the neighborhood that he grew up in. Gravesend Houses would always be home no matter how far he went.

Peso parked the car and jumped out with the duffle bag, walking through the projects. The weather was kind of chilly, but it wasn't too bad for January. He walked towards the building that he grew up in but stopped in the parking lot because a couple who was arguing caught his attention.

"Please don't do this, Chad," the girl cried.

"Bitch, it's over. Go upstairs to ya momma's house. You lucky I dropped you and this nappy headed lil' nigga off."

"Can we at least come get our things out of your house?" she begged.

"What things? I paid for all that shit. Bye, bum bitch!" the dude barked, then jumped in a Benz and pulled off.

Peso watched the girl flop on the ground, in the cold, with her kid, who looked no older than five. Peso walked over to the girl and her son.

"Don't cry, sweetheart. You are stronger than that."

"I don't feel like it," she responded with her head down. "I feel weak."

"Pick your head up, shawdy. Life isn't over 'cause that nothin' ass nigga left you."

"Life *is* over for me. I have nowhere to go, and I have my son with me. It's cold," she said, continuing to cry.

"Don't worry. I got you."

"You got me?" she responded with an attitude, finally looking up. Despite her face being wet from crying, she was extremely pretty.

"Oh shit! You're that rapper kid!" she said with excitement, shocked to see him in the hood with no security or an entourage.

He smiled at her.

"I'm no kid," he retorted, picking at her to get her to crack a smile.

"You know what I mean," she responded.

The little boy stood next to his mother and mean-mugged Peso.

"What you doing sitting on the ground? Do you have family here?"

"Not anymore. My mom died two years ago."

Without responding, Peso pulled out his phone and placed a call. When he hung up, he looked at the girl.

"In ten minutes, a white car is gonna pull up. My driver is gonna take you to the Marriot downtown. Enjoy a penthouse for the weekend so you and lil' man can relax. You wanna get out this cold, right, lil' soldier?" he asked the little boy, who nodded his head.

"Here, take this bag. Don't spend it all in one spot. Use it to get your life together. Then one day, help someone else how I'm helping you. That's a hunnit grand in the bag. Spend it wisely."

Peso handed her the bag and then walked away.

Chapter 24

Shoota, Heat, and Caine stood in the lobby of one of fifteen buildings in Gravesend, smoking purp and drinking lean. Caine pulled out his phone and began recording his surroundings.

"Niggas out here sipping this drank and smoking this gas," Caine said into the camera.

"U.G.F., we like the new B.M.F. Fuck with us," Heat said into the video.

Soon as Caine posted his video on Facebook and Instagram, the elevator door opened, and a woman stepped out. She was gorgeous and had the most beautiful chocolate skin.

"Hey, Tymel," she said, greeting Shoota.

"Wassup, Timah? How you been?" Shoota asked, hugging her.

"I been alright. Look at you, though. You done grew up," she replied, touching Shoota's face.

"Yeah, I'm finally old enough for you," he flirted.

"Boy, stop." She smiled and headed out of the building.

"Yo, ain't that Matt Murda's wifey?" Heat asked, watching as Timah exited the building.

"Oh shit! Hell yeah!" Shoota quickly walked out of the lobby, catching Timah as she was getting in her BMW.

"Aye, Timah! Hold up!" Shoota called out, jogging toward her.

Hearing her name, she turned around. "Yeah, wasssup?"

"Timah, I really hate that I have to do this, but ya husband almost got my brother killed," he said, pulling her from the car and closing the door.

Timah's heart was knocking against her chest.

"Don't scream, don't run, and don't reach for that little ass gun in your purse. Just act normal and walk in the building. Anything other than normal, I will shoot you," Shoota warned her.

Timah was nervous, her mind racing a mile a minute. Part of her wanted to pull out her .380 Keltek and shoot, but she knew that was impossible to do without dying in the process. Following the orders she was given, she walked into the building.

They took the elevator to the third floor and led Timah inside one of many stash spots. Only the three of them knew about this spot. The apartment didn't look like a regular stash spot. It had new furniture, an aquarium filled with exotic fish, and a large flat-screen TV mounted on the wall. Shoota offered Timah a seat on the sofa and promptly asked her to relinquish her gun, cell phone, and shoes.

"Fatimah, thanks for not making us have to do this the hard way," Shoota told her.

"What do y'all want from me? I have nothing to do with the beef y'all have with my husband. Tymel, you know your brother is my childhood friend. I would never wanna see him hurt."

"Unlock ya phone and call Murda," Shoota ordered.

"That's not gonna happen," Timah said defiantly, lifting her chin.

"Don't matter to us, shawdy. We got all day," Caine said, putting a bullet in the chamber of his piece.

***

Great Meadows Correctional Facility aka Comstock…

The winter basketball tournament was in high gear inside of the facility's gym. B-Gunnz coached his team of Bloods, with thirty seconds left on the shot clock. His team took the W, winning by seventeen points. While the second game got ready for tip-off, B-Gunnz stood around kicking it with a bunch of his homies.

"Yo, what's the word with them U.G.F. niggas? They valid or nah?" one of the homies asked.

"They good…for now."

"Kopy. You know their big homie just pulled up, right?"

"What big homie?" B-Gunnz asked.

"That nigga Tye-Murda."

"You know what…when we get back, spin that nigga. It's time to show niggas we running shit. Hold up real quick. I gotta piss," he said, heading to the bathroom.

Tye-Murda was watching B-Gunnz's every move. Soon as B-Gunnz entered the bathroom, Tye-Murda followed behind him with a ice pick in his hand.

B-Gunnz stood at the urinal. He turned around when he heard someone come into the bathroom. Tye-Murda quickly moved to swing the ice pick at B-Gunnz and stabbed him in the chest. B-Gunnz tried to stop the assault, but Tye-Murda repeatedly rammed the ice pick in and out of B-Gunnz until his body collapsed to the floor.

***

Hitta had just left from a meeting with his new connect, Juan Calle-Serna—the two sealing the deal on a thousand kilos of pure Columbian cocaine.

Before Rolex Rich retired from the drug game, Juan had been his connect. So, it was nothing for Rich to get Hitta plugged in. Juan met the young man and quickly took a liking to him. The two of them had been doing good business ever since.

Hitta pulled up on 36th and Neptune Avenue, parking his car across the street from the corner store. As he exited the vehicle, the cold air hit him, forcing Hitta to zip up his Pelle-Pelle leather coat. He crossed the street to where a few young boys were standing in front of the store. He greeted them with some dap before going inside.

"Yo, Ock, lemme get a pack of Woods!" he yelled while grabbing a bottle of water out of the cooler.

After paying for his items, Hitta left the store.

"Yo, Flee, take a walk with me," he told one of the boys as he passed by the group of teenagers.

Flee was eighteen years old and had recently come home from doing a short bid on Rikers Island. His Puerto Rican and African American mix gave him a pretty boy look that girls couldn't resist, but he was as deadly as any other gangster walking around Brooklyn. Flee was polished and mature beyond his years. He was also one hell of a hustler, and most importantly, he wouldn't hesitate to let his thang go.

"What's the word, big homie?" Flee asked, giving Hitta a pound as they walked toward the Sea Rise housing complex.

"Nothing major. I just wanna holla at you. Come sip with a nigga. I got a bottle in the spot," Hitta told him as they entered the building's lobby.

"Yo, Ke!" Hitta called out after they walked in the apartment.

"I'm in the room getting dressed. Give me a second," Ke-Ke yelled back from her bedroom.

"Say dat. I'm down here with the lil' bro."

Hitta grabbed a bottle of Hennessy and some plastic cups out of the kitchen. After peeling off his jacket, he took a seat. Both of them tapped the bottle before Flee opened it.

"Wassup, though, Flee? When you come home?" Hitta asked while breaking open a Backwood.

"I touched down three days ago," he responded.

"You on parole?"

"Yeah, I got a year left. I had a one-to-three and did twenty-four months."

"Don't sweat that. Time's gonna fly. What's ya plan, though?"

"I'm just tryin' get in where I fit in," Flee replied honestly.

Ke-Ke walked into the living room just as Hitta lit the blunt. She was Hitta's childhood friend who he had known since grade school. The two were more like brother and sister. Ke-Ke was a classic redbone hunny, with a pretty face and long hair. She was a slim joint, so she didn't have too much ass and titties.

"Wassup, bro?" She playfully slapped Hitta's neck.

"Don't make me fuck you up." He chuckled.

"Them niggas out there scared of you, but I'm not. Anyway, wassup, Flee?" she said, turning her attention to him. "Ain't seen you in forever."

"Ain't shit. How you been?"

"I been chilling," Ke-Ke replied, taking the blunt from Hitta.

After throwing back a shot of Henny, Hitta got down to business.

"Yo, Ke, go grab that Footlocker bag out ya closet and bring down that bread that Zee dropped off."

Ke-Ke passed the blunt back before running up to her bedroom.

"Yo, Flee, you're like my lil' brother. I love you to death," Hitta expressed.

"I love you, too, big bro," Flee replied with the same amount of sincerity.

"I know you just came home and shit is a lil' rough at the moment, but that shit is a wrap. I'm about to get you right. This area back here is ya shit, Flee. It's ya time! Everything back here goes through you from now on. You run shit how you wanna run shit, but feed ya niggas and never turn ya back on them," Hitta stated assertively.

When Ke-Ke returned, she handed Hitta two Footlocker bags.

"Thanks, sis. Now roll another blunt," Hitta told, then turned his attention back to Flee. "Like I was saying, bro, you and ya niggas are the up and coming. Y'all are the future, Flee. Niggas never put me and my niggas in position; we made our own way. You got a headstart, bro. You got me and Peso. Anything you ever need, we got you. Take advantage of this opportunity, because I'm about to put you in position. Only you can fuck this up, baby bro, but I know that won't happen."

Hitta pulled two shoeboxes out of the Footlocker bags.

"Yo, this is four birds right here. I'ma give you two of them. I don't want nothing back. All you gotta do is re-up off of me. Once I see you can handle this lil' bit of shit, the floodgates will be open for you. I'ma be smashing you with bricks on top of bricks. You ready to level up?"

"You know that shit, bro," Flee replied, grinning.

Hitta opened the other box and pulled out two stacks of money.

"That's twenty bands, and here, take this, too." Hitta removed his chain and Rolex watch, handing it over to Flee. "Welcome home, lil' bro."

"Good looking out, big bro."

"That shit ain't about nothing. Welcome to the U.G.F."

***

"Fatimah, just call that nigga Murda so we can let you go," Shoota damn near begged.

"That's not gonna happen," Timah responded, steadfast on her position.

"You know the second I walk out of here, those two niggas out there, ain't gonna cut you no slack. You really ready to die for your husband, huh?"

"Yes, I am," she answered without any hesitation.

Becoming frustrated, Shoota walked out of the room. He went in the living room where Heat and Caine sat smoking a blunt and sipping lean.

"Wassup, bro? She gonna call him?" Caine asked.

"Nah, she not budging. But check this out. Drown that bitch in the tub until she gives you the password to her phone or makes that call. I gotta go meet Hitta real quick. I'll be right back," Shoota said and left the apartment.

When he walked out of the building, he saw Hitta's Ferrari. He walked to the car and got in. Hitta was on the phone. Picking up a blunt from out of the ashtray, Shoota sparked it up and took a puff. After ending the call, Hitta pulled off.

"What's the word, lil' bro?" Hitta asked.

"Same shit, bro. I got some shit to tell you. I don't know how you gonna feel about it, though."

"Nigga, what yo' crazy ass done did?"

"We snatched Timah up."

Hitta didn't respond right away. Not because he was upset, but he really didn't know what to say.

"I'ma be all the way a hunnit with you, bro. Timah will die before she turns on Murda. However, him knowing that we have her will get that nigga to come out and get busy," Hitta finally said.

"I know it would, but shawdy so one hunnit, she won't even call the nigga or unlock her phone. I told them niggas to drown her ass in the tub until she breaks."

"Shoota, Timah is willing to die for that nigga. Trust me. But I got ol' boy's number. We gonna call him and let him know we got his lil' lady."

***

Matt Murda paced the floor of his condo. He was seconds away from losing his mind. For the past three hours, he had been calling and texting Timah, but he kept getting her voicemail and no replies to his texts. When she told him that she was going to see her mother, he wanted to send someone with her, but she wasn't having it.

"Fuck!" he shouted.

His gut was telling him something wasn't right. The sound of his phone ringing snapped him out of his thoughts. He looked at the screen and saw it was an unknown caller. He instantly picked up.

"Yo, who this?" he answered.

"The nigga who got ya bitch."

"Hitta, if you hurt her, I swear on Rico's grave I will bury ya whole family. No one will be exempt."

"You know I love Timah like a sister, bro, but when you had Peso shot, all that fair game shit was over. Me and you got a personal beef, nigga. Stop ducking smoke and pop out. 'Cause somebody gonna die tonight—either you or her. Pick ya poison, nigga."

"Hitta, you sure you wanna do this?" Murda asked through narrowed eyes.

"Nigga, it's already done. I'm done talking! You got two hours to meet me in front of Timah's mom's building. If you ain't there, bro, I'm slumping her."

Click!

The line went dead. Murda threw his phone down on the couch. He was furious. *Think Murda, Think*, he said to himself. These niggas had hit at the heart of him. Timah was his heart. Without her in his life, nothing mattered. Timah had warned him that something like this could happen, but clearly, he underestimated Hitta. He loved his wife with every part of him, but he was not ready to die. Time was ticking, and his options were few to none. He walked to his bedroom and strapped up.

***

After taking a quick ride with Hitta, Shoota headed back to the trap spot. When he walked inside, he didn't see Heat or Caine. He went to the bathroom where Heat and Caine were taking turns dunking Timah's head in a tub full of water. Shoota watched the whole scene play out. Timah still didn't break. She didn't even give them the satisfaction of letting them see her cry. Shoota respected her gangster, thinking he wished he could find a ride-or-die chick like Timah.

"Yo, that's enough," Shoota told Heat and Caine, but they continued to push her head under the water.

"I said that's enough!" Shoota shouted, getting the attention of his comrades. "Y'all niggas take a walk. Murda is on his way. I'll take care of her."

Shoota waited for them to walk out, then closed the door behind them. Timah was completely out of it. She looked like a drowned rat. Her eyes were bloodshot red, and mucus was running from her nose. Shoota reached for a towel to wipe her face.

"You okay, Timah?" he asked, full of concern.

Timah didn't answer him. She took the opportunity to catch her breath.

"Soon as Murda gets here, I'ma let you go," Shoota promised.

"Ty, Matt had nothing to do with Tyler getting shot. He was with me. We went out to dinner at Peter Luger's."

"Timah, he put the hit out. He had the car dealer put a tracking device on Peso's car, and a nigga almost killed him. On some real shit, I hate to have you in the middle of this. I've had a crush on you since I was a baby, but I knew grabbing you would bring Murda out," he said, being honest.

"How did you contact Matt if I didn't unlock my phone?" Timah asked, looking at him as he continued wiping the water off her face.

"Chill, baby girl. I have my ways. You're a real standup chick. Please don't hate me, though. Please understand that this was only business. It wasn't personal."

Ironcially, Timah understood that it was only business. She had been around the game long enough to know that.

"Get ya'self together. Murda will be here in an hour or so," he said, turning to leave the bathroom.

"Tymel!" she called out to him.

"Yes, luv?"

"If y'all kill my husband, y'all might as well kill me, too, 'cause I can't live without him," she told him as a tear rolled slowly down her cheek.

Shoota left out the door without so much as a response.

***

Matt Murda was parked a block away from his destination. He still had about twenty minutes to burn, so he lit a blunt and reclined his seat. So many thoughts were running through his head, he felt like his head was about to explode. In the passenger seat sat his cousin, Mario. The two looked more like twin brothers than cousins. Mario had just come home from prison a few months back and started working for Murda. Truth be told, he cost Murda more money than he made him. Time after time, Murda put him on, and all he did was fuck the money up. Right now, he owed Murda over three hundred thousand dollars. If it had been anybody else, Murda would have rocked him by now.

"Yo, Mario, it's about that time. You ready?" Murda asked, looking over at him.

"Yeah, I'm ready. Let's get this shit over wit'. Once we get wifey back, we even, right? My tab is clear?" Mario double-checked.

"Yeah, nigga. I told you that already. Listen, this nigga is gonna call me any minute. So, call my phone now so when he does, I can make it a conference call. Put ya phone on mute and follow his instructions. Soon as they send Timah out of the building, I'm running down, guns blazing."

"Say no more, cuzzo."

***

Hitta, Shoota, Heat, and Caine stood in the lobby holding Timah as they waited for Matt Murda to show up. Shoota quietly eyed Timah, admiring her strength. Even under pressure, she didn't fold.

"Fuck is this nigga at?" Heat asked, annoyed.

Hitta called Murda, who answered on the first ring.

"I'm here," Murda said.

"I don't see you, nigga. Stop playing games with me," Hitta replied, stepping out of the building.

"I'm across the street. I got on a black hoodie."

"I see you, boy. Now follow my instructions. First, I need you to take that gun off ya waist and slowly place it on the ground."

"I'm not strapped, Hitta. My gun is in the car."

"C'mon, Murda, I know you, kid," Hitta responded, amused.

"Hitta, you have my wife in ya possession. I'm in a lose-lose situation, homie. I ain't come here to shoot it out with you. My strap is in the car. Just let her go, please. She's innocent. Timah has nothing to do with our beef."

"Walk to the middle of the street and lay on your stomach," Hitta ordered.

Matt Murda followed Hitta's instruction. Hitta moved in his direction, but Shoota grabbed his arm.

"Let me do this, nigga. Please, bro. He almost had my brother killed. I'm thirsty for this nigga's blood," Shoota said, looking at Hitta.

As bad as Hitta wanted to do Murda, he gave Shoota a nod, letting him know the shot was his to take.

Shoota quickly removed his P89 from his waist, putting a round in the chamber, and walked to the middle of the street where Matt Murda was lying face down. Shoota stood over him, and without a word, he fired two shots in the back of his head. As soon as the second shot went off, a series of bullets flew in Shoota's direction. Heat, Hitta, and Caine ran out of the building lighting the street up with gunfire. Shoota quickly dived behind a car, taking cover and firing in the direction of the unknown shooter. In the middle of the shootout, Timah slid out the back of the building.

Chapter 25

Matt Murda entered his condo with Rah-Rah right behind him. Both men were surprised to see that Timah was there and packing her things. She acted like she didn't see them walk in as she continued to put her things in the suitcase.

"Babe, what the hell you doing?" Murda asked, confused.

"What does it look like, Matthew? I'm leaving. We're done. It's over!"

Murda reached for her arm, but she snatched away from him.

"Don't touch me. Please don't touch me."

She broke down in tears. This was the hardest decision she ever had to make. Murda felt her pain. He hated to see his wife hurting.

"Fatimah, can we talk? Please?"

"Talk? Talk about what? Talk about how I was kidnapped and nearly killed because of ya stupid pride? I've been begging you to end this shit with Amir, but you didn't wanna listen. Tyler got shot. How many innocent people have to suffer before you swallow ya fucking pride!"

"Fatimah, don't do this. I'm sorry that happened, but you know I never meant for anything to happen to you. I just sacrificed my own fucking cousin to save you. You're my heart, Timah. You know I can't live without you."

Timah looked at Murda in disgust.

"Sacrificed your cousin? Nigga, miss me with that bullshit. Your crazy ass would've killed him anyway over all that money he owed you. All you did was save yourself the trouble. Fuck you, Matt! I'm leaving."

Murda stepped in front of her, blocking her path.

"Matt, my mind is made up. I'ma leave here one way or another, so just let me go." She was now the one pleading.

"So you really leaving me? What I gotta do for you to stay?"

"Call Amir and y'all dead this shit."

When those words left her mouth, Murda lowered his head.

"When you're ready to grow up, give me a call. I'm not gonna continue to risk my life by loving you."

She kissed his cheek and dragged her suitcases out the door.

"Fuck!" Murda yelled, punching the wall.

Rah-Rah just shook his head as he watched the scene play out.

***

Hitta, Shoota, Heat, and Caine sat in the trap smoking back to back blunts and sipping Hennessy. Well, everyone except Caine, who was in a deep nod from the codeine syrup he had been drinking.

"That nigga Murda is slick as fuck. He won't slip through the cracks next time," Hitta promised.

"I don't get it. So who the fuck was the dude I slumped?" Shoota asked, confused.

"Murda has a cousin who looks just like him—like they can pass for twins. But to my knowledge, that nigga is up north doing time. That's the only nigga I know who looks exactly like Murda, so maybe he came home."

"But why would Murda line his cuzzin' to get slumped?" Shoota was even more confused than he was a minute earlier.

"Murda will do anything to save Timah. That girl is his weakness, but his cousin may have crossed him. So, he used us to take care of a problem that he didn't wanna handle himself. Don't stress that, though. Shit happens. We win some and lose some. Y'all be safe, though, I gotta slide. Peso got a show in Miami two days from now. Y'all mobbing out there?"

"Yeah, you know I'll be there," Shoota replied.

"Bet, lil' bro, I'll see you out there. Y'all niggas hold it down."

Hitta gave them dap before leaving the apartment.

As soon as Hitta reached his car, he got a phone call from Melly telling him to come pick up the money he owed him. During the phone call, Hitta could sense something was off in Melly's tone. When he questioned it, Melly told him they would talk in person.

Hitta quickly jumped in his Ferrari and hit the highway. Not long after, he was pulling up in front of Sumner Projects. He walked into the building, taking the steps to the second floor, and knocked on the door. Seconds later, Melly opened the door shirtless and with a big chain hanging from his neck.

"Wassup, bro?" Melly greeted him while letting Hitta in the apartment.

"Ain't shit, nigga. Fuck you doing cooped up in this tiny-ass apartment?" Hitta asked as he walked into the living room of the one-bedroom apartment.

"Nigga, don't walk in my spot being rude!" a pretty redbone retorted, sitting on the living room sofa smoking a blunt.

"My bad, love. I meant no disrespect. Just poppin' shit to my comrade," Hitta replied.

"Yeah, right," she responded, rolling her eyes.

"Shelly, give us a few minutes to chop it up real quick. When I call you, bring that book bag out with you," Melly told her.

When she was out of earshot, Melly got down to business.

"Bro, shit got nasty last night."

"Nasty like how?" Hitta asked, moving to sit on the edge of the couch.

"I had to pack one of them lil' niggas on my side. But before you speak ya peace, hear me out, beloved. I took your advice and didn't come home on no bullshit. Just built me a nice lil' team and fed niggas. Everybody's eating, so everybody's happy except for the niggas who ain't on the team. There's a group of young niggas running around robbing everything. They hit one of my lil' spots, so I caught the ring leader of their lil' clique and stretched him out," Melly explained.

"That'll let niggas know you're not fucking around. I bet niggas will think twice about robbing one of ya spots now," Hitta responded, knowing Melly's reaction was justified. "But my question is, did anybody see you? Who was around when you parked him?"

"Nobody to my knowledge. I caught him at a red light. I went to parole this morning, and they ain't lock me up. So, I'm good for now. I'm just laying low until shit cools down on the block. I got that bread for you, though. Ayo, Shelly, bring me that book bag!" Melly yelled out.

Seconds later, she entered the living room holding the book bag.

"Here, bae. I held the blunt. You want me to light it?" Shelly asked while handing Melly the book bag.

"You could've been lit it, but since you waited, we might as well burn that now. Here, bro." Melly handed Hitta the book bag. "That's two hundred, bro."

"A'ight, say that. You could have waited until everything was done, though."

Hitta's phone rang. It was Mariah. He picked up on the first ring.

"Wassup, sis?"

"Bro, Ashley got arrested," Mariah informed him.

"Arrested for what? What precinct is she in?"

Hitta was on his feet immediately.

"She was driving your Porsche and got pulled over. That's all I know 'cause she didn't wanna say too much over the phone. You may know more than I know. But she's not in the precinct anymore. She's at central booking," Mariah explained.

"Don't worry. I'ma get a lawyer for her right now. I'll meet you at the courthouse in about twenty minutes."

"Bro, I'm in Miami already. You know Peso has a show in two days," she reminded him.

"Oh yeah, I keep forgetting you're his manager," Hitta said, shaking the cobwebs from his head. "But good looking out. I'm heading downtown now. I'll keep you posted."

After hanging up, Hitta turned to Melly.

"Yo, Ashley got locked up, bro. I'm about to head downtown."

"I'ma ride with you."

"Say dat."

When they made it to Hitta's Ferrari, Hitta called his attorney, Mitchell Kattz, and informed him of Ashley's situation. As always, Mr. Kattz promised to handle everything.

***

After being processed into the Metropolitan Detention Center, Breeze was sent to G-41, the facility's intake unit. The officer gave him a bedroll, toothpaste, toothbrush, a bar of soap, a razor, and a brown cup. He walked to his assigned cell, putting his things on the top bunk. Seconds later, a slim light-skinned dude entered the cell.

"Wassup, bull? My name is Eighty. We gonna be bunked together for a few days," the dude said, extending his hand.

Breeze shook it.

"My name is Breeze, homie. What day we go to commissary?"

"Man, this jawn nutty as shit, bull. We don't go to the store until we get to our unit. We don't get shit while in intake," Eighty explained.

Breeze rolled over in laughter, which caused Eighty to look at him like he was crazy.

"Why you laughing, bull?"

"Ya lingo, homie. You must be from Philly."

"Yeah. I'm from North Philly to be exact."

"Ayo, if you from Philly, what the hell you doing all the way out here?" Breeze asked.

"I was making a drop in Brooklyn and ended up catching a case. Where you from?"

"Brooklyn, homie. Born and raised. You smoke?"

"Hell yeah!" Eighty answered, all hype.

"Cool. Say less. Let me shit these loons out."

There was a knock at the cell door. Eighty looked out the cell window.

"It's the orderly," Eighty informed him

"Open the door," Breeze told him.

Eighty opened the cell door, and the orderly stepped in with two net bags full of commissary items.

"Ya name Breeze?" the orderly asked.

"Yeah, why? What's up?"

"Rolex Rich is next door. He wanted me to bring you this."

The orderly set the bags down, then reached in his pocket and handed Breeze a kite before exiting the cell.

Breeze opened the kite, which read:

Peace Brother,

I know you don't really know me, but I'm a friend of Hitta and Peso. They told me that you're family, so I'm gonna treat you as such. I sent you a bunch of food, toiletries, some sweatsuits, and sneakers. I'm letting you know just in case that orderly nigga try some fuck shit. I'ma get you pulled to my unit. Just give me a few days. Anything you need, just holla at me.

   Respectfully,
   Rolex Rich

***

Peso had just finished shutting the stage down with an amazing performance. The crowd was so hype, they were still chanting his name after he walked off the stage. He even had Swagger B pop up as a special guest, which took it to the next level. His security rushed him quickly out of the arena and into the back of a limo. Once the limo pulled away, Peso FaceTimed Princess.

"Hey, daddy. I miss you," Princess answered.

"I miss you, too, my love. What you and my baby girl doing?"

"I'm on my laptop doing some research on this app I'm trying to create, and Mya is asleep. How was the show? I know you killed it."

"Yeah, it was lit! Shoota, Heat, and Caine flew out here. They were on stage buggin' with me. Hitta couldn't fly out because of the shit that happened with Ashley."

"I heard they didn't even given her a bail. That's fucked up. They treating her like she killed somebody."

"Ashley is a rider. She's gonna be alright. The lawyer will get her home soon. I got an interview at the radio station tomorrow. After that's done, I'm heading home to you. I'ma let you get back to what you were doing. I just wanted to check on you and baby girl. I'll call you when I get back to the room."

"Okay, bae. Later," she replied, blowing him a kiss.

"Princess…"

"Yes, bae?"

"I love you."

"I love you more, Tyler."

After hanging up with Princess, Peso saw that he had a few messages from Roxy. The two of them talked every day through text and FaceTime phone calls. Roxy tried daily to get Peso to club with her or go on a date, but he didn't want to be seen with her in public because he knew a story like that would be the headline of every newspaper and magazine. It would also be a slap in the face to Princess. As much as he liked Roxy, he refused to disrespect his lady by being caught in public with another chick. Roxy claimed she understood, but that didn't stop her from wanting to spend time with him.

When Peso entered his penthouse suite, he was surprised to see Roxy laid across the bed in some sexy lingerie. Her body was oiled up, and she looked extremely sexy. He admired her for a few seconds before speaking.

"How did you get in my room, shawdy?"

"There's nothing that a fan wouldn't do for me," she responded with a sly grin.

Peso just shook his head and chuckled.

"You gonna stand there, or are you gonna come over here?" she asked seductively.

"Roxy, I'm about to get in the shower. You can let ya'self out."

His statement caused her to burst out in laughter.

"Boy, quit! We've been talking for months. You refuse to be seen with me in public, and I respect that. Right now, we're behind closed doors, and I haven't had sex in a long time. Tonight, you're giving me some dick."

She climbed off of the bed and walked over to Peso. Like mother, like daughter. He stared at Roxy—her body truly a piece of art that God had created. Peso was fronting like he didn't want to do a bunch of nasty things to her, but the reality was she was his dream girl. Tonight, he was reconsidering his decision and giving in to temptation.

"I want you so bad."

She kissed him. He pulled her into his arms, kissing her back.

"Bae, let me hop in the shower," he said, breaking their embrace.

"Hurry up. Don't take too long," she replied.

Peso headed to the shower. Fifteen minutes later, he came out of the bathroom and found Roxy laid across the bed with her legs open, playing with her pussy.

"Come here, daddy," Roxy instructed.

Peso walked to the bed and let his towel drop to the floor.

Roxy reached for his dick and stroked it a few times before putting it in her mouth. She wrapped her sexy lips around his shaft while still playing in her pussy. The feeling forced him to grab a handful of her hair and thrust in and out of her mouth slowly. Roxy stroked his dick some more. She looked up into his eyes before spitting on his dick and letting the saliva drip off, catching every drop of it.

"Mmmm…" she moaned, before jamming it back in her mouth.

The loud noises of her slurping was turning Peso on even more.

"Do that shit," Peso groaned, still holding a handful of her hair.

She sucked harder. Suddenly, his knees buckled.

"Ahhhhhh," Peso grunted before filling her mouth with his seed.

Roxy licked and swallowed every drop.

Not to be outdone, Peso turned Roxy on her back, diving face first between her legs and planting kisses on the inside of her thighs.

"Don't tease me, daddy. Please don't tease me," she begged with her mouth open and her eyes closed.

Peso locked on to her clit. Roxy's lovebox was wet as fuck. She wrapped her legs around his neck as he spit, licked, and sucked on her pussy. Her body shivered as he jabbed his tongue in and out of her pretty pink box. The more he licked, the wetter she got. The sensation was driving her insane. Her body began to shake as she reached the pinnacle of their lovemaking. Her orgasm came hard and fast.

Peso didn't stop there. He pushed her legs to her shoulders and stuck his tongue in her ass, which sent her into a frenzy.

"Oh my God!" she screamed as he fucked her ass with his tongue.

Her body shook, bringing her to a second orgasm. Peso moved up her body, entering her wet box. When he was done, she would know she had been fucked.

He took it slow, giving her time to recover before he went to work. He continued to stroke her body with his, picking up the pace. Her legs were over his shoulders.

"Yes…right there, daddy. Don't stop," she moaned in his ear.

Peso pulled out and flipped her over. Roxy arched her back as he hit it from the back. Peso was fucking her like a porn star.

"Harder, daddy! Harder!" she shouted.

Roxy's dirty talking put Peso in a trance. He was pounding her, slapping her ass every few seconds.

"That's right. Fuck this pussy. Give me that big-ass dick," she moaned with her head back and eyes closed.

"Whose pussy is this, you pretty muthafucker?" he growled, leaning over in her ear.

"It's ya pussy, daddy!" she shouted, and he pounded even harder.

"That's it! Get it, daddy! Get it! Oh shiiit, I'm cumming!" She screamed. "Oh, Jesus! Fuck me just like that!"

Peso followed her commands, fucking her like she wanted. He squeezed her ass while thrusting in and out of her. Roxy shook uncontrollably. Peso couldn't hold on any longer. Roxy used the walls of her womanhood to milk Peso, bringing him ultimate pleasure.

"Aghhhhh…shit!" he grunted, thumping against her vagina walls repeatedly until he released himself inside her.

Chapter 26

Hitta sat patiently in the visiting room of Rose M. Singer on Rikers Island. He looked around with disgust, mainly because the visiting room was damn near empty. It was sad how in a men's prison, the visiting floor was packed with females, but the female inmates only had visits from their mothers.

"I know all these chicks weren't single in the streets," Hitta mumbled to himself.

Ashley caught his attention when she entered the visiting room. Seeing him, she walked toward him. Even in a prison jumpsuit, she was still beautiful as ever.

"What's up, baby girl?" He stood to give her a hug and kiss.

"Hey, bae," she replied with a weak smile.

Hitta could tell she was fighting back tears.

"How are they treating you in here?"

"Okay, I guess. I pretty much just stay to myself," she responded, looking at him.

"I'ma get you outta here. That's on my word. I just don't understand how the fuck they deny you bail over some fucking money in the trunk."

"Bae, the feds are investigating you. They're only holding me hoping I will flip on you, but we both know that will never happen. I will do a hundred years for you, Amir."

Hitta smiled at his lady and kissed her hand.

"That's why I love you, but you won't be doing no time. You're a queen and shouldn't be here. It was my car. I'ma write an affidavit to the courts and tell them the money was mine."

"Amir, no. Don't do that. I'm strong. I'll get through this. They went in the trunk without a warrant, which is an illegal search and seizure. So, sooner or later, I will be home. They just have a hard-on for you."

"I got you something, ma."

Hitta looked around to see if the C.O.'s were watching him. Since the coast was clear, he dug in his boxer briefs, pulling out a stuffed balloon.

"Listen, ma. In there is some bud, bamboo papers, matchsticks, and two scalpels. If a bitch try your ass, you better cut her."

He quickly handed her the balloon, and she put it inside her jumper.

"Thank you, bae, but you didn't have to. I'm a'ight."

"Cut it out, shawdy. You would have done it for me. I put five thousand on your books. I also brought you a package with some books, pictures, and clothes. If you need anything else, just let me know. I also want you to get me the info for every chick in your dorm."

"What? Nigga, don't play with me," Ashley snapped at him.

"I'm dead ass. Look around. This shit is empty, while the male visiting floor is packed. I feel for these females behind bars. I understand their struggle. I just wanna do a good deed, ma. So, get that info so I can send them some money," Hitta explained.

Ashley could only smile because she knew how good a heart Hitta had. Not everybody got to see that side of him, but this was the reason she fell in love with him.

***

Peso was back from Miami and spending time with Princess and Mya. The three were sitting in his condo watching movies and eating ice cream. Peso's phone vibrated. He checked his text message; it was a message from Katrina. She had texted him to let him know he had been nominated for five Grammys. He looked at the message as if he hadn't read it correctly. Then he scrolled down his contacts list and tapped Katrina's name to call her. She answered on the third ring.

"Congrats, Peso! I'm so happy for you!" Katrina exclaimed.

He could feel her bright smile through the phone.

"Hold up. Wait. You're dead ass?"

"I'm so dead ass! I see you haven't been on your social media today."

"I actually haven't. Since getting back from Miami, I've been spending time with my daughter and my lady. I'm so hype right now, Kat. I've been dreaming of this day all my life."

"We have to celebrate," she told him.

"Yes, we do, but I ain't gonna hold you. I just wanted to see if I read your message correctly. Let me get back to my family time, and I'll hit you tomorrow," Peso said before hanging up.

When Peso put his phone down, he was grinning from ear to ear. He really couldn't believe the news he received. Peso suddenly became emotional, thinking of his long road to achieve this type of success. He covered his face with both his hands. He knew his mother was smiling down on him from heaven.

Princess and Mya had stopped watching TV and were now watching Peso.

"What's the matter, bae?" Princess asked, concerned.

"I've been nominated for five Grammys!"

"Oh my God, bae! I'm so happy for you!"

Princess jumped on him, planting kisses all over his face. Mya didn't know what was going on, but she jumped up and smothered her dad with kisses, too.

When Hitta and Mariah entered the condo a few moments later, they were both all smiles.

"Baby daddy, I'm so proud of you." Mariah hugged Peso.

"I'm happy for you, bro. You deserve this shit. Why y'all sitting around? We got some celebrating to do." Hitta embraced Peso, then headed to the minibar. "What y'all drinking?" he asked.

"I got Ace in there," Peso replied, referring to Ace of Spade champagne.

"So, Ace it is, and apple juice for my baby girl?" Hitta asked, turning to Mya.

"Yes, Uncle Mir, apple juice for me."

After having a few drinks and sharing a few laughs, Mariah and Princess took Mya to her room so she could get ready for bed. Peso and Hitta sat passing blunts back and forth.

"Wassup with Ashley?" Peso asked.

"She's holding up well. I just hate that she's in there. These crackers keep denying her bail. She said something about them investigating me."

"Maybe it's time you fall back for a lil' while—at least until shit cools down."

"Yeah, I was thinking the same shit," Hitta replied.

The vibration from Peso's phone got both of their attention. The vibration wasn't from a text message, though. It was a direct message from Instagram. The message was from the famous actress Nautica Taylor.

Nautica_Taylor: I see your brother isn't on social media.
Peso: Which brother are you talking about?
Nauitca_Taylor: Hitta :->
Peso: Nah, social media ain't really his thing.

Nautica_Taylor: He's too cool for the gram, huh? LOL! Well, does he have a phone number I can reach him at?"

Peso laughed out loud while handing Hitta his phone.

"What are you passing me ya phone for?" Hitta asked, confused.

"You got a message, nigga. Just read it."

Hitta took the phone, seeing the messages were from Nautica. He smiled after reading them. Another time, he probably would have jumped at the chance to get with Nautica, but right now, he didn't need those type of problems. That didn't stop him from texting her his phone number, though.

Peso walked into Mya's bedroom. She was sound asleep. He kissed her on the forehead, then turned to leave the room. He went to his room to find Princess and Mariah lying across the bed listening to music. The R&B sounds coming from the speakers was foreign to Peso's ears, but he knew good music when he heard it.

"Who's that? Shawdy sound a'ight." Peso bopped his head to the music.

"Oh, this is my new artist, Kiyanne Quick," Mariah told him.

"So you doing big things now, huh, Ms. Manager?"

"Thanks to you giving me a shot, a bunch of artists are hitting me up looking for management. Do you like her, though?"

"That song is dope. Lemme hear some more of her shit," Peso said, taking a seat on the bed.

***

Matt Murda cruised up Mermaid Avenue in his cherry red Maserati. He had no set destination. He was just driving around trying to clear his head. Ever since Timah left, Murda had not been himself. She hadn't answered a call or text message, which was driving Murda crazy. He was lost without her.

His phone rang, snapping him out of his thoughts.

"Yo, what's poppin'?" Murda answered.

It was a Blood homie who went by the name Stick Mac.

"That five is poppin' fool. You around?" Stick Mac asked.

"I'm close by. Why? Wassup?"

"'Cause I need to see you."

"Say dat. I'll be to you in twenty minutes."

***

Matt Murda pulled up to a small building in the Crown Heights section of Brooklyn. Entering the building, he went to the third floor. After one knock, the door flew open, and there stood Stick Mac dressed in all black like always.

Stick Mac was a homie that Murda met years back while doing time. He was a few years older than Murda, but he worshiped the ground his big homie walked on. After getting shot, Stick Mac fell back from the streets and went back to school. He was now a private investigator.

"East coast G'z," Stick Mac saluted.

"Ain't no G'z like these," Matt Murda replied, walking in the apartment.

"Listen, Blood, I have five hunnit grand cold cash right now, but I need you to drop the number for me. Fifty a key is way too high for the amount of cash I'm spending," Stick Mac said.

Not only was Stick Mac a private investigator, but he was also one of the biggest heroin dealers in the state of New York.

"Stick, you're my comrade, but this is grade A dope that has never been stepped on. My price stays as it is. Lemme ask you a question, though, Blood. How the hell do you move this shit so fast?"

"I'm a private eye, skrap. I get paid to watch people. I scope out some of the biggest hustlers in the game and get them on my team," Stick Mac responded honestly.

"Check this out. I'm not gonna drop the price, but I'll double ya order. Just bring back the bread on the next flip."

"That'll work," Stick Mac replied.

"Cool. I'ma have Rah-Rah drop the work off to you, but did you ever look into that situation for me?"

"Yes, but this guy moves around so much that it's hard to get a set address. Gimme two days, and I will have all the info you need. Ayo, did you hear about B-Gunnz?"

"Nah. What about him?"

"He got fucked up real bad up top, but he pulled through."

"When the fuck did this happen?" Matt Murda asked, confused since he had spoken to B-Gunnz not too long ago.

It was evident Timah had Murda's mind fucked up, because he was slipping.

***

Hitta entered the Royal Estate, but to his surprise, he didn't see anyone. Katrina had buzzed him in after he rang the doorbell.

"Kat!" Hitta called out to her.

"I'm coming down," she yelled from the top of the stairs.

Within a few minutes, Katrina came down the stairs wearing a sheer robe with sexy lingerie under it. Her body was oiled, making her skin glow, and she held a bottle of champagne in her hand. Hitta watched as she descended the staircase. She was captivating. He felt his dick jump in his pants.

What the hell is she up to? Hitta thought.

Whatever it was, he would fight his craving tonight, even though he had been fantasizing about how her pussy would feel.

"Hey, handsome." Katrina kissed him on the cheek.

"Sup, Kat? Why you call me over here?"

"I called you to celebrate! Have a drink with me."

"First, put some clothes on. And what the fuck are we celebrating?" he asked, confused.

He was trying to establish some boundaries with her, but he already knew it was too late.

"Thanks to you bringing Peso to the label, we are the number one major label in the industry. Now, come sit down and have a drink."

"Hold on. I gotta piss," he said, then made his way to the bathroom.

Several minutes later, he walked back into the living room to see Katrina pouring some type of substance in his glass.

"What the fuck you doing?!" Hitta exclaimed.

She jumped from the sound of his voice. Hitta rushed over to Katrina and started choking her. He gripped her neck so tight he cut off her airflow.

"Bitch, you tryna kill me?" he asked furiously.

Katrina tried to speak but couldn't. So, he loosened his grip.

"Answer me, bitch! Are tryna kill me?"

"No, I'm not trying to kill you. I'm trying to fuck you, Hitta! It's only Molly."

"So you tryna date rape a nigga? What the fuck is wrong with you, Kat?"

"I'm married to a nigga who got fifty years in prison. I have needs. I was married when you let me suck your dick," she reminded him with a smirk.

"Kat, I told you that was never gonna happen again," he responded, although he was finding it hard not to look at her titties through the material she wore.

"I don't think you're as sure as you think you are," Katrina said, her voice dripping with seduction.

Like the men before Hitta who thought they could say no, it was just a matter of time before he succumbed to her. She was about to have the dick she was willing to beg for.

"Yeah, I'm sure. Rich is a good friend of mine. I betrayed him once, and I promise you I'll never do that again."

The whole time they were having this conversation, he still had his hand around her throat.

"Do you know how wet my pussy is right now?" Katrina asked, ignoring his little speech. "Food for thought I will lie and say you tried me Hitta. Don't make me lie on you just fuck me!" she adds.

"Kat…" Hitta knew he was being backed into a corner. *Leave, leave, leave*, he repeated over and over in his head.

While he was talking to himself, Katrina reached for his other hand, placing it between her legs.

"It's ready for you, baby. All you have to do is want it," she whispered.

Hitta felt the wetness between her lips. While fingering her slowly, he pulled her closer and kissed her.

"You tryna get me killed," Hitta said between kisses.

Katrina wrapped her arms around his hard body, moving her body slowly against his hand, wanting to feel everything.

"Nah, baby, I just want you to fuck my brains out," she responded, opening her mouth to let his tongue inside.

Hitta couldn't stop now if he wanted to; he was looking forward to fucking a seasoned woman.

Breaking the kiss, Katrina took his hand and led him to her bedroom. Entering the room, it was everything Hitta thought it would be. It was beautifully decorated, and the doors to the terrace were open and overlooking the huge swimming pool.

"Here, baby, have a drink," Katrina said, snapping him out of his haze as she handed him a glass of Hennessy.

Being in her bedroom was surreal. He could still escape if he wanted to, but he wanted to find out if she was worth it. There was always some "untouchable" pussy, and Katrina was it.

"You didn't put anything in this?" he asked, looking down at the glass.

"No, baby. It's not necessary now," she said, smiling at him.

Katrina downed her shot, wanting to get down to business. Hitta followed her, downing his drink, as well. She set her glass on the nightstand, and taking the one from Hitta, she placed it next to hers.

She then undid the stash to her robe, letting it fall to the floor, exposing her taunt breasts, flat stomach, and shapely ass. For a moment, Hitta wondered if her ass had been surgically enhanced, but he quickly decided it was all her. He was mesmerised.

"You're beautiful."

"Thank you, handsome," Katrina responded, blushing. "You gonna show me that big dick of yours?" she asked, fighting the urge to rip off his clothes.

Hitta quickly began removing his clothes and toeing off his shoes. Katrina marveled over his body as he stood naked in front of her. She then reached for his hand, leading him to the bed.

"I want you to do wicked things to me," she said, wrapping her hand around his dick.

In minutes, Katrina had Hitta on his back and was destroying his dick. Hitta reaffirmed to himself that she gave the best head in the world. After his release, it was time to show her that all the fantasies she had about him were true.

Hitta grabbed Katrina, pulling her to him after he sat up in bed.

"You sure you wanna fuck wit' me like this?" Hitta asked, hoping she would give him the out he needed.

He had her on her back, with her hands pinned above her head.

"Fuck me."

Hitta did what he was told. He placed himself at her opening, pushing into her. His mouth fell open at the sensation of feeling her pussy wrap around his dick.

Katrina's hands gripped his ass, pushing him deeper before he started to stroke her.

This is some good pussy. Gotdamn!

"You better beat this pussy up, nigga," she hissed.

Hitta looked into Katrina's eyes as she continued to talk dirty to him, telling him how good his dick felt inside of her. Hitta flipped over, positioning her on top. She proceeded to ride him like a rodeo star, with Hitta raising his hips to meet her body.

"I want you to shoot that shit in my mouth!" Kat exclaimed before climaxing.

Hitta pushed her off him and quickly moved around the bed, holding his dick in his hand until he was on his knees and leaning over her mouth. He came hard, making him throw his head back in pleasure. Katrina sucked, licked, and swallowed all that he unloaded in her mouth. Once he finished releasing, Hitta leaned over to kiss and suck her lips.

"You can *fuck,*" she whispered, trying to catch her breath.

Smiling, he let his body fall next to hers.

"That pussy is *fire.*" Hitta couldn't lie about that if he wanted to.

Katrina turned her head to look at him.

"Thank you," she replied.

As vulgar as the statement may have been, she appreciated it nonetheless. Hitta had made her feel beautiful and desirable. They went two more rounds before they fell into a sated sleep.

***

Hitta woke up to find Katrina asleep with her head on his chest. He looked around the room, momentarily not remembering where he was. Then the night came flooding back to him. He remembered the best night of fucking he'd had in long time. With those memories came images of Rolex Rich and what he would do if he ever found out. No, it wouldn't be as simple as a bullet to the head. Rich would kill him slowly and painfully. The pictures in his head moved him to get up from the bed. As he searched the room for his clothes, Katrina began to stir, waking up.

"Where you going?" she asked, pushing her tousled hair back from her face.

"I gotta go," Hitta said, pulling his pants on.

"I was hoping you would stay until morning," she replied, sitting up in the bed.

"I can't," he responded, giving her the shortest answers possible.

The realization of what he had done and the possible consequences were becoming even clearer.

"When will I see you again?"

"You won't."

"What the fuck does that mean?"

"This was a one-time thing, Kat. I would call it a mistake, but I was in it just like you. This can't and won't happen again."

'Motherfucker, who do you think you're playing with?"

For some reason, Katrina had it in her head that Hitta was about to become her boy toy. How wrong she was to assume that. Nobody told Hitta what to do, not even a horny, middle-aged bitch.

"I'm out," Hitta said, carrying the rest of his clothes under his arm as he left out the room.

"You just fucked with the wrong one!" she shouted after him.

Hitta heard bellowing high power threats as he walked down the staircase and out the door. Once he got to his car, he threw his clothes in the passenger seat. Then he sat behind the steering wheel for a minute thinking through the poor decision he had made and Katrina's threat.

I hope I don't have to kill that bitch, Hitta thought as he started the car and left the Royal Estate.

***

Peso had just finished shooting a video for his new single, "Count it Up". He was in Gravesend Houses, the heart of Coney Island, a place where most people weren't allowed. It was freezing cold out, but by the amount of people outside, you would think it was a warm summer day. Peso was signing autographs when Flee walked up to him and Princess.

"What's the word, big homie?" Flee greeted Peso with a one-armed hug.

"Same ol' shit, lil' bro. Welcome home. I see you out here gettin' ya shine on," Peso said, eyeing Flee's jewelry.

"I learned from two of the best." Flee smiled, giving respect.

"Flee, this is my lady, Princess. Princess, this is my lil' bro, Flee," Peso said, introducing them. "Take a ride with me, Flee. I wanna holla at you, but let's get out this freezing cold."

Peso led the way to his brand-new snow white 600 Benz.

Thirty minutes later, Peso and Flee were sitting in the studio passing blunts back and forth while listening to Peso's new mixtape. Peso gave Princess his black card and told her to go shopping so he and Flee could talk in private. Peso turned the music down.

"Flee, you're my brother, and I wanna see you win by any means. You're a solid young nigga. Don't ever change who you are for nobody. When I make it, the whole team makes it. This label belongs to all of us, not just me and Hitta," Peso explained. "We lost so many of our brothers to the streets, and I ain't tryna lose no more. You're ya own man, so you gonna choose ya own path. But I wouldn't be a true friend if I didn't at least try to change ya circumstances."

"Talk to me, big bro. What's on ya mind?"

"You already know, I'm on the road a lot traveling state to state, and I have no bodyguard or security team. Mainly because I don't trust many people with my life. Why pay some random strangers to watch my back, when I can give that bread to the nigga I came up in the trenches with? I know you got a good thing going in the streets. You the man now and all the way plugged in, but we both know this street shit don't last forever. Nowadays, the plug can be working for the feds. I'm giving you the same offer I just gave my blood brother. You can take it or leave it."

"I'm all ears, big bro," Flee told him.

"You can leave the hood, come with me, and get paid six figures a year to do what you're already doing. You strapped right now?" Peso asked, although he already knew the answer.

"I'm always strapped. You know that shit," Flee answered, smiling.

"Exactly. So, like I was saying, you can make six figures doing what you're already doing. Only difference is you don't gotta worry about going to jail for it. On top of the six figures, I'ma give you a two-hundred-thousand-dollar bonus, a car, and I'll even help you start ya own business. Flee, you gonna get to travel all over the world and fuck models, R&B divas, and all types of other freak hoes," Peso added to make the opportunity sound even more appealing. "It's time to level up. You with it?"

"This is a hard offer to turn down, but let me think about it," Flee replied.

"Bro, ain't really much to think about. We ran the streets at a young age. We did shit the older niggas before us never did. We're all legends in the hood. It's time we take our legacy to a whole nother level, my nigga."

"I know, bro, but the moment I've been waiting on has finally come. The rap dream is yours, big bro, not mine. My dream was always to be the plug. Now I got my chance. I'm not turning down ya offer, bro. Just give me a lil' bit of time to think on it."

"Damn, you sound just like Hitta." Peso shook his head, still not understanding what there was to think about.

Chapter 27

Hitta sat at a cozy table in Ruth Chris. Sitting across from him was Nautica Taylor, one of the most beautiful women he had ever seen. This was Hitta's first real date in a long time. He usually grabbed a bottle of liquor, some weed, and hit the telly, but tonight, things were different. Hitta stared at Nautica, admiring her beauty. Not only was she drop-dead gorgeous, but she was the highest paid actress in the industry.

Hitta was dressed in a black and gold Givenchy sweater, a pair of black Balmain jeans, and a pair of high-top Givenchy sneakers. As always, his jewelry complemented his outfit. Nautica was dressed in a black Alexander Wang mini dress that hugged her body perfectly and a pair of six-inch Giuseppe Zanotti heels. Her hair was pulled up in a high bun, leaving her beautiful face on full display. The smell of her Chanel No.5 perfume flirted with his nose. Hitta couldn't help but smile.

"What are you smiling about?" Nautica asked, snapping Hitta out of his musing.

"I ain't gonna lie, Nautica. You fire," Hitta replied.

"I'm fire?" she asked, confused.

"You're bad...pretty...gorgeous. It all means the same thing," he explained.

"You New York guys have some funny slang," she commented with a chuckle.

"Maybe that's why all outta town ladies love us. Where you from?"

"I'm originally from North Philly, but I moved to L.A. with my dad when I was thirteen. What about you? Where in New York are you from?" Nautica asked.

"I'm from Brooklyn. Coney Island to be exact."

"I have a question, but it's a little bit off topic."

"Talk to me, love."

"What made you get involved when Roy was hitting me?"

Hitta paused for a moment before answering.

"Honestly Nauti, I don't even know. I just hate to see a woman getting beat by a man. Something about that shit causes me to snap. A woman is supposed to be cherished, not abused."

Nautica was the one smiling now.

"Why you cheesing so hard, shawdy?" he asked.

"'Cause you just gave me a nickname, and I think it's kinda cute. On top of that, I like the way you answered my question. Now tell me your real name, because I'm not gonna be calling you Hitta. Like what type of name is that?"

"My name is Amir Moore. Hitta is a name an old head gave me when I was a lil' boy, and it just stuck wit' me," Hitta informed her.

"How old are you? And when is your birthday?"

"I'm twenty-three, and my birthday is January twenty-third. What about you?"

"Damn, you're young! But I'm twenty-six, and my birthday is January third. You have a lady, or are you a bachelor?"

"I would never lie to you. Yes, I have a special someone."

Hitta's honesty caused Nautica's facial expression to change.

"Why the long face all of a sudden?"

"The good ones are always taken. If you have a lady, why are you here with me and not with her?" she asked with a slight attitude.

Nautica didn't want someone else's man. She wanted her own man.

"The same reason you're here with me and not wit' Ray. Besides, this dinner is innocent. We're two friends tryna get to know each other. Is there something wrong with that?"

The tension was cut by Hitta's phone vibrating.

"I gottta take this, love. This is a business message. You mind if I check it?" Hitta asked, looking down at his screen.

"Do ya thing," she replied, then sipped her champagne.

Hitta opened the message and began reading.

Rolex Rich: *You snake ass nigga! I bring you around my family, help you get rich, and this is how you repay me? What happened to loyalty being ya way of life and not just a slogan? Ya loyalty ain't mean shit when you date raped my wife. Hitta, you're a dead man. I may be locked up, but my power is limitless.*

Hitta's heart raced in his chest. *What the fuck?! What did Kat tell him? She wouldn't have told him about us, would she?*

He had been naïve enough to believe that Katrina wouldn't carry out her threat, telling a lie that was sure to get him killed. How could he defend himself? Tell Rolex Rich that he hadn't raped her but fucked her the way she begged him to?

Stupid motherfucker, he chided himself.

After reading the message, he had no other choice but to try and lie his way out of this until he could talk to Katrina.

Hitta: *Big bro, I would never do no shit like that. You know me better than that.*

Rolex Rich: *Nah, nigga, I thought I knew you. We have nothing to talk about. You violated, kid. Ya days are numbered.*

Hitta knew Rich was dead ass. He tried to call Rolex Rich but got his voicemail.

"Fuck," he mumbled to himself.

"You okay, bae?" Nautica asked.

"Yeah, I'm cool," he lied.

The two sat for another two hours eating and getting to know each other, which was a struggle for Hitta since he could only think of Rolex Rich. After dinner, Hitta dropped Nautica off at her hotel, with promises of seeing her again.

***

Breeze stood in front of his cell talking to Eighty. True to his word, Rolex Rich got Breeze pulled to his housing unit. Eighty just got lucky and happened to get moved with Breeze. Rolex Rich only dealt with Breeze. He never really said anything to Eighty, but he kept it respectful.

"Aye, Breeze, I ain't feeling ya man's vibe. The bull been drawn lately," Eighty said.

"Who's that?"

"The bull Rich. His vibes been a lil' off lately. Watch the bull," Eighty warned.

"That nigga prolly trippin' over one of his hoes. You know jail makes a nigga emotional," Breeze joked. "Speaking of hoes, lemma go call one of mine."

After walking to the phones, Breeze picked up the receiver, dialed his inmate pac#, and waited for the call to process.

***

Rolex Rich sat in the back of the common area. He was staring at the chess board, debating his next move. The man sitting on the opposite side of the board happened to be one of the most dangerous men in the entire jail. Jermaine Sanders a.k.a Priest was a retired Blood member who got convicted two years ago for multiple murder charges.

Subsequently, he was sentenced to three life sentences plus five hundred and forty months.

Priest was respected by everyone, but he was a man of few words. Not many people could get next to him, but he loved a good chess match. So, he and Rolex Rich got along just fine. He moved through the unit like a ghost, his demeanor calm but threatening.

"Checkmate!" Rich exclaimed, placing his queen directly in front of Priest's king.

"That was some bullshit. I should've seen that coming," Priest said, frustrated with himself.

"You never see it coming, good brother. But, yo, right now is the best time to strike. That nigga is on the phone with his back turned."

"Say no more. I'm on it," Priest said, then got up from the table.

Rich had paid him twenty thousand dollars to send a message.

***

Breeze was in a deep conversation with Amina when he felt a sharp object enter his rib cage. He turned around to see Priest holding a bloody shank. Breeze dropped the phone, rushing toward Priest, but the old head sidestepped him, swinging the blade again. This time, the shank hit Breeze in the chest.

Eighty saw what was going on and ran up behind Priest, throwing a swift haymaker that caught Priest on the chin and sent his body to the concrete floor. Eighty then picked up the shank and rushed toward Rolex Rich.

Chapter 28

A few weeks passed, and Matt Murda still hadn't heard from Timah. He had been moping around ever since she left him. *I can't believe this bitch really left me after all we been through*, Murda thought to himself.

He pulled his phone from his pocket to call her. To his surprise, she picked up.

"What do you want, Matthew?" she answered, exhausted.

"I want you to come back home, Timah. I'm incomplete without you, babe," he slurred.

Murda was pissy drunk. He had been drinking heavily ever since Timah left, and if she didn't come back soon, there was no telling what the lasting effects of it would have on him.

"Matt, are you drunk?"

"A lil' bit, but that don't matter. Come home, babe. Where you at? I'm coming to get you."

"Matt, I'm not coming home until you swallow ya foolish pride and end this beef with Amir and Tyler. I don't know how many times I have to tell you that! Bye, Matthew!" she exclaimed before the line went dead.

"Fuck!" Murda yelled, rolling off of the bed and heading to the bathroom.

After splashing water on his face, he stumbled back to his room and lay back down on the bed. The water hadn't helped his situation like he had hoped. Timah had him stuck between a rock and a hard place. Realizing that nothing in this world was worth losing her, he swallowed his pride and sent Hitta a text.

Matt Murda: *I know we haven't been seeing eye to eye, but I wouldn't feel right keeping this info from you and Peso. I got the drop on the pig that killed Relo.*

Hitta: *Beloved, you don't gotta use Relo's name to get the drop on me. I ain't hiding. Whenever you ready to get busy, just pick the time and the place.*

Matt Murda: *Hitta, I ain't tryin' to line you, and that's on Rico's grave. I know you and Peso want this nigga as bad as I do. The addy is 549 F.D.R. Drive. He leaves the building every morning at 5 A.M. I'm gonna strike in two days. Y'all niggas can stand beside me as I off that nigga or y'all can miss the opportunity to avenge our comrade's death. Don't matter to me. With or without y'all that nigga is a body.*

This time, Hitta didn't respond to the message.

***

Hitta exited the corner store on 36th and Neptune Avenue where he bought a pack of Backwoods. He was headed to check on Flee when his phone vibrated in his pocket. He pulled it out and saw he had a new message from Rolex Rich.

Rolex Rick: *I just told ya man Breeze you said wassup.*
Hitta shook his head as he texted his reply.
Hitta: *These ain't the games you wanna play, Rich. You have family out here. If you touch one of mine, I'll touch all of yours. You KNOW how I roll, homie!*
Rolex Rich: *You won't get a chance. You'll be dead in the next five minutes, fuck boy.*

Hitta was so caught up in texting that he didn't notice the car slowly creeping in his direction. The screeching tires of the Audi A8 quickly caught Hitta's attention. When he turned around, he saw a handgun being pointed at him from the passenger's window.

POP! POP! POP! POP! POP!

Five shots sounded off. Hitta dove behind the closest car to him.

POP! POP!

Shots kept ringing out as the car attempted to get closer to Hitta. He ran in a full sprint in the direction of the parking lot, running up the ramp that led him to the front strip of the building complex. The dude in the passenger seat hopped out of the Audi and began chasing Hitta on foot.

Pop! Pop!

A bullet flew past Hitta's head. Hitta quickly spun around, firing his Desert Eagle .45 back at his would-be assassin.

Boom! Boom!

The sound of the huge cannon had the dude to take cover behind a wall. Hitta used that to his advantage, dashing towards the entrance to one of the many buildings. When Hitta reached the fifth floor, he crossed through the smaller section of the building, which people in his hood called "the old folks" section. He stood on the balcony catching his breath when his phone rang. He looked at his phone and saw it was Flee.

"Yo!"

"You good, big homie? I just heard shots, and I know you were on your way over here."

"Yeah, I'm Gucci. Where you at?"

"I just walked in ya mom's old building."

"Say dat. Meet me on five," Hitta replied, hanging up.

Before he put his phone away, it started ringing again. This time, it was Ashley's lawyer calling.

"Kattz, wassup, my guy?"

"I got some good news, that's wassup," Mr. Kattz replied.

"Fill me in."

"Turns out that Detective Brown is as dirty as they come. In one of his cases, a defendant turned over a recording from a time he was pulled over that has Brown and his partner basically admitting to unlawful activities."

"That's wassup. So when will Ashley be released?"

"Her court date is on Tuesday. The case will be dismissed then."

"Cool. Good looking, Kattz. I'll see you then."

Chapter 29

The time was 4AM, and Peso sat in the driver's seat of a tinted black-on-black Dodge Challenger, while Hitta laid back in the passenger's seat. Both men were strapped. They had been parked in the same spot for the last hour waiting on their prey.

"Yo, you think Murda tryna line us?" Peso asked, passing Hitta the blunt.

"He swore on Rico that the info was valid, but ain't no tellin' when it comes to Murda. That's one crafty muthafucka," Hitta replied while inhaling the potent weed smoke.

"Well, if the info is valid, where the fuck is Murda?"

"He's somewhere around here. That sneaky-ass nigga prolly watching us." Hitta passed the blunt back to Peso.

"Well, after we bump this pig, I'ma off Murda, too."

"Bro, you just read my mind."

As the words left Hitta's mouth, a cherry red Dodge Charger pulled up and parked directly in front of them.

"Nobody is getting out of the Charger. I can bet my bottom dollar that's Murda," Peso said.

Hitta didn't reply. He just stared at the car in front of him with an itchy trigger finger.

"Ayo, here come Brown walking out of the building now," Peso pointed out.

"It's now or never, bro," Hitta replied, looking at Peso.

Matt Murda got out of the car with a hood pulled over his head. Detective Brown was walking down the block to his car. Murda followed behind him but kept a safe distance so he wouldn't be spotted. When Detective Brown reached his Benz truck, Murda was right on his heels with his gun drawn, but to his surprise, Hitta and Peso popped up in front of the detective.

BOC!

Peso fired the first shot, hitting the detective under his left eye. His body dropped to the pavement. Hitta fired two more shots in the detective's face after he fell. Matt Murda aimed his gun on the detective, but before he had a chance to pull the trigger, Peso raised his gun and shot Matt Murda in his face.

BOC!

To Be Continued…

Lock Down Publications and Ca$h Presents
Assisted Publishing Packages

BASIC PACKAGE $499 Editing Cover Design Formatting	**UPGRADED PACKAGE** $800 Typing Editing Cover Design Formatting
ADVANCE PACKAGE $1,200 Typing Editing Cover Design Formatting Copyright registration Proofreading Upload book to Amazon	**LDP SUPREME PACKAGE** $1,500 Typing Editing Cover Design Formatting Copyright registration Proofreading Set up Amazon account Upload book to Amazon Advertise on LDP, Amazon and Facebook Page

***Other services available upon request.
Additional charges may apply

Lock Down Publications
P.O. Box 944
Stockbridge, GA 30281-9998
Phone: 470 303-9761

Submission Guideline

Submit the first three chapters of your completed manuscript to ldpsubmissions@gmail.com. In the subject line add **Your Book's Title**. The manuscript must be in a Word Doc file and sent as an attachment. Document should be in Times New Roman, double spaced, and in size 12 font. Also, provide your synopsis and full contact information. If sending multiple submissions, they must each be in a separate email.

Have a story but no way to send it electronically? You can still submit to LDP/Ca$h Presents. Send in the first three chapters, written or typed, of your completed manuscript to:

LDP: Submissions Dept
P.O. Box 944
Stockbridge, GA 30281-9998

DO NOT send original manuscript. Must be a duplicate. Provide your synopsis and a cover letter containing your full contact information.

Thanks for considering LDP and Ca$h Presents.

NEW RELEASES

BLOODLINE OF A SAVAGE 1&2
THESE VICIOUS STREETS 1&2
RELENTLESS GOON
RELENTLESS GOON 2
BY PRINCE A. TAUHID

THE BUTTERFLY MAFIA 1-3
BY FUMIYA PAYNE

A THUG'S STREET PRINCESS 1&2
BY MEESHA

CITY OF SMOKE 2
BY MOLOTTI

STEPPERS 1,2&3
THE REAL BADDIES OF CHI-RAQ
BY KING RIO

THE LANE 1&2
BY KEN-KEN SPENCE

THUG OF SPADES 1&2
LOVE IN THE TRENCHES 2
CORNER BOYS
BY COREY ROBINSON

TIL DEATH 3
BY ARYANNA

THE BIRTH OF A GANGSTER 4
BY DELMONT PLAYER

PRODUCT OF THE STREETS 1&2
BY DEMOND "MONEY" ANDERSON

NO TIME FOR ERROR
BY KEESE

MONEY HUNGRY DEMONS
BY TRANAY ADAMS

Coming Soon from Lock Down Publications/Ca$h Presents

IF YOU CROSS ME ONCE 6
ANGEL V
By Anthony Fields

IMMA DIE BOUT MINE 5
By Aryanna

A THUGS STREET PRINCESS 3
By Meesha

PRODUCT OF THE STREETS 3
By Demond Money Anderson

CORNER BOYS 2
By Corey Robinson

THE MURDER QUEENS 6&7
By Michael Gallon

CITY OF SMOKE 3
By Molotti

CONFESSIONS OF A DOPE BOY
By Nicholas Lock

THA TAKEOVER
By Keith Chandler

BETRAYAL OF A G 2
By Ray Vinci

CRIME BOSS
By Playa Ray

Available Now

RESTRAINING ORDER 1 & 2
By **CA$H & Coffee**

LOVE KNOWS NO BOUNDARIES 1-3
By **Coffee**

RAISED AS A GOON I, II, III & IV
BRED BY THE SLUMS I, II, III
BLAST FOR ME I & II
ROTTEN TO THE CORE I II III
A BRONX TALE I, II, III
DUFFLE BAG CARTEL I II III IV V VI
HEARTLESS GOON I II III IV V
A SAVAGE DOPEBOY I II
DRUG LORDS I II III
CUTTHROAT MAFIA I II
KING OF THE TRENCHES
By **Ghost**

LAY IT DOWN I & II
LAST OF A DYING BREED I II
BLOOD STAINS OF A SHOTTA I & II III
By **Jamaica**

LOYAL TO THE GAME I II III
LIFE OF SIN I, II III
By **TJ & Jelissa**

IF LOVING HIM IS WRONG…I & II
LOVE ME EVEN WHEN IT HURTS I II III
By **Jelissa**

PUSH IT TO THE LIMIT
By **Bre' Hayes**

BLOODY COMMAS I & II
SKI MASK CARTEL I, II & III
KING OF NEW YORK I II, III IV V
RISE TO POWER I II III
COKE KINGS I II III IV V
BORN HEARTLESS I II III IV
KING OF THE TRAP I II
By **T.J. Edwards**

WHEN THE STREETS CLAP BACK I & II III
THE HEART OF A SAVAGE I II III IV
MONEY MAFIA I II
LOYAL TO THE SOIL I II III
By **Jibril Williams**

A DISTINGUISHED THUG STOLE MY HEART I II & III
LOVE SHOULDN'T HURT I II III IV
RENEGADE BOYS 1-4
PAID IN KARMA 1-3
SAVAGE STORMS 1-3
AN UNFORESEEN LOVE 1-3
BABY, I'M WINTERTIME COLD 1-3
A THUG'S STREET PRINCESS 1&2
By **Meesha**

A GANGSTER'S CODE 1-3
A GANGSTER'S SYN 1-3
THE SAVAGE LIFE 1-3
CHAINED TO THE STREETS 1-3
BLOOD ON THE MONEY 1-3
A GANGSTA'S PAIN 1-3
BEAUTIFUL LIES AND UGLY TRUTHS
CHURCH IN THESE STREETS
By **J-Blunt**

CUM FOR ME 1-8
An LDP Erotica Collaboration

BLOOD OF A BOSS 1-5
SHADOWS OF THE GAME
TRAP BASTARD
By **Askari**

THE STREETS BLEED MURDER 1-3
THE HEART OF A GANGSTA 1-3
By **Jerry Jackson**

WHEN A GOOD GIRL GOES BAD
By **Adrienne**

THE COST OF LOYALTY 1-3
By **Kweli**

BRIDE OF A HUSTLA 1-3
THE FETTI GIRLS 1-3
CORRUPTED BY A GANGSTA 1-4
BLINDED BY HIS LOVE
THE PRICE YOU PAY FOR LOVE 1-3
DOPE GIRL MAGIC 1-3
By **Destiny Skai**

A KINGPIN'S AMBITION
A KINGPIN'S AMBITION II
I MURDER FOR THE DOUGH
By **Ambitious**

TRUE SAVAGE 1-7
DOPE BOY MAGIC 1-3
MIDNIGHT CARTEL 1-3
CITY OF KINGZ 1&2
NIGHTMARE ON SILENT AVE
THE PLUG OF LIL MEXICO 1&2
CLASSIC CITY
By **Chris Green**

A GANGSTER'S REVENGE 1-4
THE BOSS MAN'S DAUGHTERS 1-5
A SAVAGE LOVE 1&2
BAE BELONGS TO ME 1&2
A HUSTLER'S DECEIT 1-3
WHAT BAD BITCHES DO 1-3
SOUL OF A MONSTER 1-3
KILL ZONE
A DOPE BOY'S QUEEN 1-3
TIL DEATH 1-3
IMMA DIE BOUT MINE 1-4
By **Aryanna**

A DOPEBOY'S PRAYER
By **Eddie "Wolf" Lee**

THE KING CARTEL 1-3
By **Frank Gresham**

THESE NIGGAS AIN'T LOYAL 1-3
By **Nikki Tee**

GANGSTA SHYT 1-3
By **CATO**

THE ULTIMATE BETRAYAL
By **Phoenix**

BOSS'N UP 1-3
By **Royal Nicole**

I LOVE YOU TO DEATH
By **Destiny J**

I RIDE FOR MY HITTA
I STILL RIDE FOR MY HITTA
By **Misty Holt**

THE LEVEL UP | LUXURY KING

LOVE & CHASIN' PAPER
By **Qay Crockett**

TO DIE IN VAIN
SINS OF A HUSTLA
By **ASAD**

BROOKLYN HUSTLAZ
By **Boogsy Morina**

BROOKLYN ON LOCK 1 & 2
By **Sonovia**

GANGSTA CITY
By **Teddy Duke**

A DRUG KING AND HIS DIAMOND 1-3
A DOPEMAN'S RICHES
HER MAN, MINE'S TOO 1&2
CASH MONEY HO'S
THE WIFEY I USED TO BE 1&2
PRETTY GIRLS DO NASTY THINGS
By **Nicole Goosby**

LIPSTICK KILLAH 1-3
CRIME OF PASSION 1-3
FRIEND OR FOE 1-3
By **Mimi**

TRAPHOUSE KING 1-3
KINGPIN KILLAZ 1-3
STREET KINGS 1&2
PAID IN BLOOD 1&2
CARTEL KILLAZ 1-3
DOPE GODS 1&2
By **Hood Rich**

THE STREETS ARE CALLING
By **Duquie Wilson**

STEADY MOBBN' 1-3
THE STREETS STAINED MY SOUL 1-3
By **Marcellus Allen**

WHO SHOT YA 1-3
SON OF A DOPE FIEND 1-4
HEAVEN GOT A GHETTO 1&2
SKI MASK MONEY 1&2
By **Renta**

GORILLAZ IN THE BAY 1-4
TEARS OF A GANGSTA 1/&2
3X KRAZY 1&2
STRAIGHT BEAST MODE 1&2
By **DE'KARI**

TRIGGADALE 1-3
MURDA WAS THE CASE 1-3
By **Elijah R. Freeman**

SLAUGHTER GANG 1-3
RUTHLESS HEART 1-3
By **Willie Slaughter**

GOD BLESS THE TRAPPERS 1-3
THESE SCANDALOUS STREETS 1-3
FEAR MY GANGSTA 1-5
THESE STREETS DON'T LOVE NOBODY 1-2
BURY ME A G 1-5
A GANGSTA'S EMPIRE 1-4
THE DOPEMAN'S BODYGAURD 1&2
THE REALEST KILLAZ 1-3
THE LAST OF THE OGS 1-3
By **Tranay Adams**

MARRIED TO A BOSS 1-3
By **Destiny Skai & Chris Green**

KINGZ OF THE GAME 1-7
CRIME BOSS 1-3
By **Playa Ray**

FUK SHYT
By **Blakk Diamond**

DON'T F#CK WITH MY HEART 1&2
By **Linnea**

ADDICTED TO THE DRAMA 1-3
IN THE ARM OF HIS BOSS
By **Jamila**

LOYALTY AIN'T PROMISED 1&2
By **Keith Williams**

YAYO 1-4
A SHOOTER'S AMBITION 1&2
BRED IN THE GAME
By **S. Allen**

TRAP GOD 1-3
RICH $AVAGE 1-3
MONEY IN THE GRAVE 1-3
CARTEL MONEY
By **Martell Troublesome Bolden**

FOREVER GANGSTA 1&2
GLOCKS ON SATIN SHEETS 1&2
By **Adrian Dulan**

TOE TAGZ 1-4
LEVELS TO THIS SHYT 1&2
IT'S JUST ME AND YOU
By **Ah'Million**

THE LEVEL UP | LUXURY KING

KINGPIN DREAMS 1-3
RAN OFF ON DA PLUG
By **Paper Boi Rari**

THE STREETS MADE ME 1-3
By **Larry D. Wright**

CONFESSIONS OF A GANGSTA 1-4
CONFESSIONS OF A JACKBOY 1-3
CONFESSIONS OF A HITMAN
By **Nicholas Lock**

I'M NOTHING WITHOUT HIS LOVE
SINS OF A THUG
TO THE THUG I LOVED BEFORE
A GANGSTA SAVED XMAS
IN A HUSTLER I TRUST
By **Monet Dragun**

QUIET MONEY 1-3
THUG LIFE 1-3
EXTENDED CLIP 1&2
A GANGSTA'S PARADISE
By **Trai'Quan**

CAUGHT UP IN THE LIFE 1-3
THE STREETS NEVER LET GO 1-3
By **Robert Baptiste**

NEW TO THE GAME 1-3
MONEY, MURDER & MEMORIES 1-3
By **Malik D. Rice**

CREAM 2-3
THE STREETS WILL TALK
By **Yolanda Moore**

THE STREETS WILL NEVER CLOSE 1-3
By **K'ajji**

LIFE OF A SAVAGE 1-4
A GANGSTA'S QUR'AN 1-4
MURDA SEASON 1-3
GANGLAND CARTEL 1-3
CHI'RAQ GANGSTAS 1-4
KILLERS ON ELM STREET 1-3
JACK BOYZ N DA BRONX 1-3
A DOPEBOY'S DREAM 1-3
JACK BOYS VS DOPE BOYS 1-3
COKE GIRLZ
COKE BOYS
SOSA GANG 1&2
BRONX SAVAGES
BODYMORE KINGPINS
BLOOD OF A GOON
By **Romell Tukes**

CONCRETE KILLA 1-3
VICIOUS LOYALTY 1-3
By **Kingpen**

THE ULTIMATE SACRIFICE 1-6
KHADIFI
IF YOU CROSS ME ONCE 1-3
ANGEL 1-4
IN THE BLINK OF AN EYE
By **Anthony Fields**

THE LIFE OF A HOOD STAR
By **Ca$h & Rashia Wilson**

NIGHTMARES OF A HUSTLA 1-3
BLOOD AND GAMES 1&2
By **King Dream**

GHOST MOB
By **Stilloan Robinson**

THE LEVEL UP | LUXURY KING

HARD AND RUTHLESS 1&2
MOB TOWN 251
THE BILLIONAIRE BENTLEYS 1-3
REAL G'S MOVE IN SILENCE
By **Von Diesel**

MOB TIES 1-7
SOUL OF A HUSTLER, HEART OF A KILLER 1-3
GORILLAZ IN THE TRENCHES
By **SayNoMore**

BODYMORE MURDERLAND 1-3
THE BIRTH OF A GANGSTER 1-4
By **Delmont Player**

FOR THE LOVE OF A BOSS 1&2
By **C. D. Blue**

KILLA KOUNTY 1-5
By **Khufu**

MOBBED UP 1-4
THE BRICK MAN 1-5
THE COCAINE PRINCESS 1-10
STEPPERS 1-3
SUPER GREMLIN 1-4
By **King Rio**

MONEY GAME 1&2
By **Smoove Dolla**

A GANGSTA'S KARMA 1-4
By **FLAME**

KING OF THE TRENCHES 1-3
By **GHOST & TRANAY ADAMS**

THE LEVEL UP | LUXURY KING

QUEEN OF THE ZOO 1&2
By **Black Migo**

GRIMEY WAYS 1-3
BETRAYAL OF A G
By **Ray Vinci**

XMAS WITH AN ATL SHOOTER
By **Ca$h & Destiny Skai**

KING KILLA 1&2
By **Vincent "Vitto" Holloway**

BETRAYAL OF A THUG 1&2
By **Fre$h**

THE MURDER QUEENS 1-5
By **Michael Gallon**

FOR THE LOVE OF BLOOD 1-4
By **Jamel Mitchell**

HOOD CONSIGLIERE 1&2
NO TIME FOR ERROR
By **Keese**

PROTÉGÉ OF A LEGEND 1&2
LOVE IN THE TRENCHES 1&2
By **Corey Robinson**

THE PLUG'S RUTHLESS DAUGHTER
By **Tony Daniels**

BORN IN THE GRAVE 1-3
CRIME PAYS
By **Self Made Tay**

MOAN IN MY MOUTH
By **XTASY**

TORN BETWEEN A GANGSTER AND A GENTLEMAN
By **J-BLUNT & Miss Kim**

LOYALTY IS EVERYTHING 1-3
CITY OF SMOKE 1&2
By **Molotti**

HERE TODAY GONE TOMORROW 1&2
By **Fly Rock**

WOMEN LIE MEN LIE 1-4
FIFTY SHADES OF SNOW 1-3
STACK BEFORE YOU SPLURGE
GIRLS FALL LIKE DOMINOES
NAÏVE TO THE STREETS
By **ROY MILLIGAN**

PILLOW PRINCESS
By **S. Hawkins**

THE BUTTERFLY MAFIA 1-3
SALUTE MY SAVAGERY 1&2
By **Fumiya Payne**

THE LANE 1&2
By Ken-Ken Spence

THE PUSSY TRAP 1-5
By **Nene Capri**

DIRTY DNA
By **Blaque**

SANCTIFIED AND HORNY
by **XTASY**

BOOKS BY LDP'S CEO, CA$H

TRUST IN NO MAN
TRUST IN NO MAN 2
TRUST IN NO MAN 3
BONDED BY BLOOD
SHORTY GOT A THUG
THUGS CRY
THUGS CRY 2
THUGS CRY 3
TRUST NO BITCH
TRUST NO BITCH 2
TRUST NO BITCH 3
TIL MY CASKET DROPS
RESTRAINING ORDER
RESTRAINING ORDER 2
IN LOVE WITH A CONVICT
LIFE OF A HOOD STAR
XMAS WITH AN ATL SHOOTER